A Man of Middle Age

& Twelve Stories

PATRICIA ZELVER

A Man of Middle Age

& Twelve Stories

HOLT, RINEHART AND WINSTON
NEW YORK

Library of Congress Cataloging in Publication Data
Zelver, Patricia.
A man of middle age & twelve stories.
I. Title.
PZ4.Z52Man [PS3576.E45] 813'.5'4 79-1929
ISBN 0-03-048986-5

First Edition

Designer: Amy Hill
Printed in the United States of America
1 3 5 7 9 10 8 6 4 2

"It's Not the Picture Tube, He Said" and "Landmarks"
first appeared in *The Ohio Review* as "Two Stories."
"On the Desert" and "The Little Pub" first appeared in
The Atlantic Monthly; "The Flood" in *The Virginia
Quarterly*; "Norwegians" in *Esquire*; "My Father's
Jokes" in *Shenandoah*; and "Señor Muerte" and "A
Special Occasion" in *Ascent*.

For Alvin, Nicholas and Michael

Contents

A MAN OF MIDDLE AGE

The Winkles could not plant out the Schultzes. Sam Winkle had discussed the problem with his landscape architect, but there was no way. The Schultz house loomed up from every direction, was the focus of every important Winkle vista. The only possibility was a hedge that would, at least, protect the sanctity of the Winkles' garden. But any hedge high enough to hide Chez Schultz, as Sam had dubbed it (an irony that made his fury only slightly more palatable), would also shade the Winkles' swimming pool.

The pool was important to Sam. Every morning—rain or shine—before he took the train to the City, he swam forty laps in the buff, wearing a rubber cap to keep his hair dry, earplugs and a noseclip to protect his sensitive membranes from the chlorine, and a pair of black floppy rubber flippers on his small, almost-dainty feet. He was a short plump rosy-cheeked man; his skin was soft, of a spongelike texture. "A dear little man," his wife's aunt once called him. Emerging from the pool, he resembled a Moon Man in a cartoon.

On weekends, after his swim, he dressed in khaki shorts and a faded blue sweat shirt—the very picture of a modern country gentleman. For the City, where he was an account

3

executive for Laiken, Baxter and Brown (a venerable San Francisco advertising agency), he wore suits with natural shoulders and not-too-wide lapels; in deference to the more flamboyant times he had added a silver Zuñi belt buckle—a gift to him from his only child, Cindy, on his fiftieth birthday. He had allowed what was left of his pale hair to grow cautiously longer and had had it shaped and blown dry by an English hair stylist. A Napa Valley winery account had introduced him to vintage wines, and he had assembled a small cellar. Food had been an interest since childhood; he presided over the patio barbecue at his home in Vista Verde, an upper-income suburb on the San Francisco Peninsula; lately, when the mood struck him, he took over the kitchen from Alice (a loving wife but unimaginative cook), and prepared one of his specialties—a roasted duckling with orange sauce; linguini with clams; or cassoulet, whose ingredients required long and happy hunting hours at various delicatessens and fancy-food groceries. He was a member of the San Francisco Advertising Club, the World Trade Club, the Commonwealth Club, the Sierra Club, the Peninsula Chapter of the ACLU, and the Vista Verde Swimming and Tennis Club.

He also belonged to the Bohemian Club. Once a week he had lunch there, and, after lunch, a game of dominoes with Harvey Perkins, a courtly white-haired gentleman from an old San Francisco family, the President of his family's shipping firm. (Laiken, Baxter and Brown's long-term clients were banks, insurance companies, import and export firms—San Francisco institutions as established as they.) Each summer, Sam spent two weeks at the Bohemian Grove on the Russian River, where, for the annual Hi Jinks, he played the jazz songs of his era on an old barroom piano. It was an all-male club, and Alice was vocal in her disapproval of it. In principle, Sam agreed. But the Agency paid for his membership—it was good for client relationships—and his first responsibility, after all, was to support his family. That he enjoyed the ambience and camaraderie at the Grove, he neglected to mention to Alice.

When Cindy was in high school, he and Alice had both been active in the PTA; twice he had been Chairman of the Vista Verde Neighborhood Association. "Country living with all the amenities of the City," read the Real Estate ads for this attractive wooded neighborhood with its view of the hills and the Bay; during Sam's term of office he had worked to keep it that way.

He enjoyed the latest films, theater, the symphony, sporting events (live and televised); the Sunday *New York Times*, the daily *San Francisco Chronicle*; the biographies of the great figures of history and an occasional novel. Once he had joined the Great Books Club but had been too busy to attend its seminars; the books were still on his bookshelf waiting for the day, ten years from now, when he would retire.

He was good-humored, gregarious—content with his life, whose focal points were his family, his business, and his friends (in that order). His family consisted of Alice and Cindy, now eighteen, and four older sisters who lived in nearby suburbs and who worshiped him, trusting his advice on financial and domestic matters more than their husbands'—a fact that irritated Alice, but there was no help for it. Until Schultz entered the picture, Sam had considered himself one of the most fortunate of men.

Why should he have thought otherwise? His paternal grandparents, who died when he was still very young, had come to this country as Jewish emigrants from Middle Europe, settled in San Francisco's Fillmore district. Somewhere along the line (Ellis Island, perhaps), they had Americanized their name. Winklestein to Winkle. Sam, who would have been ashamed to do this for fear it might be thought he was trying to hide his Jewish origins, was grateful that his grandparents had done it for him—not because Winkle hid anything; it was simply less clumsy and awkward a name than Winklestein.

His grandfather had died first, and his grandmother—urged on by his parents (both high-school teachers in the suburbs)—had sold her flat and bought a small bungalow in the same block as her children's home. Sam had once come across the contract of sale.

"Emma Winkle conveys to Wesley Jingles," it read. These six words, he thought, told all there was to be told about the American Dream. The Upper Mobility of minority groups. The Fillmore (represented by W. Jingles), though now a Black Ghetto, had to be better than a slave's shack; his grandmother had left this world in a Catholic Hospital in San Mateo, nursed by nuns who politely overlooked the fact that the crucifix that hung in her room had been covered with a towel by her only grandson, a request she had made of him and with which Sam had complied after apologizing to the Sister Superior.

Sam, himself—a graduate of U.C. Berkeley, married to a gentile, at home in the gentile community, fully "assimilated"—was the very epitome of the American Dream. He knew little of Jewish customs or religion; his parents had been Free Thinkers, and, though he made no secret of his Jewishness, it was, simply, that in the life he led (other than contributing to the Jewish Welfare Fund), it played little part.

Alice, a former sociology major and a social worker, was an avowed atheist who took an intellectual interest in all religions except the Christian faith, in which she had been raised. Sam called himself an Agnostic. This seemed to him to be the more sensible and cautious and even more scientific approach. After all, how could one be sure? The facts, perhaps, were not all in.

Once, when Cindy was small, Alice had suggested celebrating Chanukah—not for religious reasons, but so that Cindy would not grow up unacquainted with this part of her "cultural tradition." She could get no help from Sam; he had only a dim memory of the ritual practiced by his grandparents. Undaunted, Alice had bought a Menorah and checked out a book from the library, entitled *The Meaning of Chanukah.*

"We'll light a candle every night," she said, handing Sam a match. It was their practice session; Cindy was not present.

"I don't know how; my parents never did it. My grandparents did, but that was so long ago—"

"You can read the prayer from the book."

"It seems . . . contrived, somehow."

"Then I'll do it!" She snatched the match back.

He watched her solemnly going through the hocus-pocus; then—he couldn't help it—he burst into paroxysms of laughter.

"Is something wrong?" Alice's tone was icy.

"No! Yes! I don't know how to say it . . ." He wiped away tears. "I suppose it's accurate, if the book says so, but—"

"But *what?*"

"It doesn't matter what the book says; you could never do it right," he cried, the laughter rising in him again, so that he had to bend double in a hopeless attempt to suppress it.

She had flung the Menorah at him. He ducked and it sailed through their picture window, making a great splintering crash. This enraged her further. She screamed at him that he was a bad father, mean-spirited and arrogant, to boot. Then she had rushed into their bedroom, slammed the door, and wept. The window was repaired the next day while he was at work, and nothing more about Chanukah was ever said. From then on, it was Christmas all the way.

Sam's ebullient nature was consistent with the Christmas spirit. He shopped for presents, helped Alice with the UNESCO cards and to decorate the Tree; presided cheerfully over the festive board, paid the bills cheerfully. And, yet, something she had said during the Chanukah fiasco remained in his consciousness. "Arrogant," she had called him. Perhaps he was—a bit. For, though to all outward appearances he was the very spirit of the Yuletide, it was this time of year that provoked in him the proud knowledge that he was, indeed, of a different and more ancient lineage. Despite his outward participation in the celebration, he remained, inwardly, a bit aloof.

It had never occurred to Sam that anyone who bought the neighboring lot would choose to site their house on top of the treeless knoll (some peculiarity of the soil or the lack of soil had made it barren), instead of tucking it into the hill-side among the oaks. All of the homes in Vista Verde, like the Winkles' redwood, exposed-beam house (designed by a well-known architect in the City and featured in a shelter magazine), fitted their sites; all were handsome, tasteful. But the Schultz house not only sat solidly on the highest and most-visible portion of their acre, it was—there was just one word for it—an atrocity!

The Schultzes broke ground in April of 1975, while Alice and Sam were away visiting Cindy, a freshman at Smith College. To Sam's disappointment, she would not come home for the summer: she was going to paint sets for a summer theater on the Cape and support herself by working as a cocktail waitress. He didn't like the sound of either job.

Both he and Alice had put a lot of themselves into this only child. Before Alice became pregnant she was studying for her Ph.D. in Social Psychology; Sam was working on a novel, based on his experiences in WW II. Alice dropped out in the middle of a term to take lessons in Natural Child-birth; Sam had put the novel aside to job hunt. The Creative end of Advertising appealed; he was a wordsmith and, it turned out, something of an Image Maker. (Moreover—he would have been the first to admit it—the long hours of solitary work required to write a novel did not suit his temperament.)

When Cindy was born Alice postponed returning to college in order to nurse her for a year; at the end of the year, neither she nor Sam could bring themselves to leave her in the hands of a sitter; she gave up the Ph.D. idea for good. When Cindy was three, they enrolled her in a progressive cooperative nursery school; the mothers took turns helping out and taking notes of their children's behavior; both mothers and fathers met one evening a week to go over the notes and discuss any concern with the supervisor. Later—finding the public school wanting—they sent her to a private progressive elementary school. Alice helped here, too: she drove the school bus and worked in the cafeteria. Sam spent a month of Saturdays with other fathers painting the

Multipurpose Room. They further implemented Cindy's
education with lessons—swimming, dancing, piano, guitar,
tennis. In high school, they bought her a red Fiat, so there
would be no nonsense about hitchhiking.

Additional income was necessary. The Creatives did not
rise in the business; much of their flair, it seemed, vanished
with their youth. The business side of the Agency was more
lucrative; the future, more dependable. He moved into this.
It was the right time. Laiken was dead; Baxter, semiretired,
attended only Board meetings; Brown was fully retired, and
his place was taken by his son who had married an heiress;
when he was not jet-setting about the world, he came into
the office late, having spent the morning at Dean Witter's
watching the fluctuation of his wife's wealth upon the
Board. Baxter and young Brown were both delighted to
have a sensible and responsible man like Sam, who worked
well with people, to relieve them of the business-social client relationships.

Now Sam hired the Creatives, with their more up-to-date
Life-Styles and their current vernacular. His own style had
set sometime in the forties and, in the office, surrounded by
these new Image Makers, he had the quaint old-fashioned
air of the aging urban liberal. This was his Image and he
cultivated it, remaining faithful to the Ivy League suits,
polka-dot bow ties and heavy-rimmed tortoiseshell spectacles. He was pointed out as the man who, in the late forties,
had coined the slogan for a well-known western beer, a slogan that had appeared on tin cocktail trays and illuminated
signs hung in bars; these trays and signs were now sold in
antique shops as collector's items, and Sam had one of each
displayed on the rolltop desk he had inherited from Laiken,
along with layouts of other old favorite accounts in dated
graphics, his collection of paperweights, a photograph of the
University of California's Class of 1940, a photograph of the
minesweeper on which he had served as a Lieutenant (J.G.)
and numerous snapshots of Alice and Cindy. On the wall
was a bulletin board where he pinned *New Yorker* cartoons
depicting advertising-agency life.

So many men, particularly in his line, disliked their jobs;

they were angry with the System, the Establishment, the Media. Their youthful expectations had gone unfulfilled. They spoke of "selling out," being "trapped." Sam was an exception. Everything about his work delighted him. He enjoyed the walk from the station with his fellow commuters, many of whom he knew by name. The complexity of the City, its sordidness and glamour, still fascinated him: the sadness of Skid Row, the garish bustle of Market Street, the sudden shift to the sober decorum of Montgomery, where the façades of the older Beaux Arts buildings were reflected in the new, glass-walled high rises. Good morning to the ancient newsboy in front of the Wells Fargo; a smile and nod at the policeman at the corner of Sutter; an appreciative glance at the legs of the secretaries on the California Street cable car; a chat with the middle-aged woman with rouged cheeks and dyed pink hair who operated the elevator in the Brannan Building (one of the few buildings that did not have push-button elevators); good morning to the young secretaries in the outer office of the Agency, who called him by his first name and brought him coffee, along with little jokes about Women's Lib, and "Only for you, because you're so old and decrepit"—all of this gave him a High, a euphoria. The same was true of going home. A game of cards on the train, then the drive to Vista Verde, past green well-kept lawns, well-kept houses, healthy children at play, to the domestic sanctuary of 7 Manzanita Lane. He was one of those rare birds, he often told people, who had found the right roost.

When Cindy entered public high school, Alice and Sam had suffered some trepidation. It was needless; she was a conscientious worker who made the honor roll each year; she was a member of the Girls' Tennis Team, Vice-President of the Student Body and, at her graduation, gave the valedictory address.

She wasn't all brains, either. Sam often marveled that he and Alice—neither one of them exactly glamorous—had produced this tall, slim girl with long blonde silky hair,

Sam's fair skin, Alice's dark eyes, long, well-shaped athletic legs. Was it something in the climate, some mineral in the water that made her look as if she had come out of an ad for California oranges or a California condominium resort?

She had her share of boyfriends, too, but it was obvious none of them were up to her. She could afford to hold out for Mr. Right.

A professional man. A doctor, a lawyer, perhaps a distinguished scholar. A girl, he felt, did not need a career, but a good education was like a debut: through it she would be introduced to the society in which she would meet this husband-to-be. When she was accepted at Smith, he and Alice postponed their long-planned trip to Europe, in order to meet the high tuition. They had no regrets.

But what about this summer-job business? The morals of theater types were well known. And working in a bar! Waiting on lecherous barflies, collecting their tips, at the mercy of their unsavory advances? His daughter? This lovely, intelligent, talented girl?

Alice patiently explained to him that this was what young people did nowadays; moreover, it was connected with her interest in the drama. When they visited Cindy in April, he brought up the matter, and Cindy laughed at his fuddy-duddy concern. On their return, the foundation of the Schultz home was in, the framing up.

All that summer, as the house rose before them, Sam and Alice looked on in dismay. Friends who stopped by commiserated; some made little jokes.

"I didn't know the Pentagon had purchased that property."

"Is it true that Disney Corp. owns that land?"

"That's an impressive set. Who's playing Henry the Eighth?"

If the witticisms were inconsistent, they told a great deal about the eclectic style of Chez Schultz. A grim fortress? A giant cozy cottage? Ye Olde English Manor? An ostentatious mansion, with cutesy-quaint Mother Goose detailing?

It was immense, two-storied, half-timbered, with mullioned windows and gabled shake roof adorned with a molded plaster chimney, purposely crooked, a bit of gross whimsy, an effect—for the fireplace, itself a baronial stone horror, equipped with false logs and a gas jet, had a separate outlet. It was just a stage set.

The interior plan was conventional. Five bedrooms; three baths; living room, dining room, kitchen, study (for the laird, no doubt); garage (not a carport), and a semidetached workshop in back, which, very early during construction was already in use and protected by a heavy padlock.

What sort of imagination could have conceived it? What warped fantasies had inspired its design? Certainly they belonged to Schultz and Schultz alone, for no architect's sign was put up, and it was Schultz himself who supervised the job.

He arrived early every weekend and holiday morning in a VW Bug or a Datsun pickup. A goblin of a man! A huge head. Tow-colored hair cropped so short that the skin of his scalp glistened through it. A pasty face. Large chestnut eyes. A fat button of a nose. Hardly any mouth, merely a line. A thick trunk. Thick muscular hairless arms. Short muscular legs. A peculiar gait, a kind of scuttle. Thermal undershirts, Big Mac shoes. Meticulously, he would inspect the work, pace off spaces, make notes on a clipboard—then he would bring out a heavy carpenter's toolchest from his workshop and spend the rest of the day hammering, measuring, sawing: he was doing the cabinetwork himself.

Occasionally he brought a child along. A miniature version of Schultz. A boy. Somewhere between six and nine, who, like Schultz, wore his tow-colored hair cropped close to his skull, and who followed his father about, a silent apprentice, handing him nails, fetching tools, sweeping up sawdust, picking up odd ends of lumber and piling them into a bin. (The bin was closed and padlocked at night: no neighbor was going to salvage firewood; no neighbor's child, material for a tree house from the Schultz job!) Schultz and/or Schultz and son left promptly at five.

It was then that Sam and Alice made their inspections.

They toured the premises, searching in vain for some violation of the Vista Verde Neighborhood Association rules. But no one on the Board had ever possessed the imagination to predict a Schultz! All was legally in order; the setbacks were correct; there was the required amount of off-street parking.

This Schultz was taking no chances in any other way, either. He had selected the heaviest shakes; the strongest earthquake could not budge the foundation; the walls were thickly insulated; fire sprinklers had been installed in the plastered ceilings. There was an attic that would provide even more insulation. (No one built attics anymore in the Bay Area.) There was a basement—another anachronism—running the full length of the house. If a natural disaster or a nuclear bomb leveled Vista Verde, Chez Schultz would survive. It would be, thought Sam, the monument that would represent their civilization!

At night, in bed, Sam found himself making calculations. A house like that! In times like these! Even with Schultz doing part of the work, it had to come to an impressive sum. The VW Bug? The pickup? The thermal underwear. The no-nonsense toolchest? Most of all, Schultz, himself! None of it was consistent with such an expenditure! Perhaps he was building on spec? Had some kind of agreement with the contractor. A spec house in Vista Verde? Something was *up*. A gross and tasteless and menacing something! A sinister scheme, thought Sam, tossing fretfully next to the sleeping Alice.

At the end of May Cindy wrote that she would be allowed to spend her Sophomore Year Abroad, in Florence. This would mean more money, another postponement of their own trip. Still, seeing Italy through Cindy's letters would make up for the delay. She would come home for a week in September; Alice began to plan a farewell party for her.

On a Saturday morning in early September, a procession appeared. Sam and Alice watched from their deck. The procession in the VW was led by Schultz. Following Schultz, a

Sears truck. Then the pickup, pulling a U-Haul, piled to the top with Schultz household effects, a large Mrs. Schultz at the wheel. Following this, a Checker sedan. (A Checker sedan! Of course. Naturally. I might have guessed, Sam said to himself. Alice would have accused me of making pat assumptions!) The Checker was driven by a young girl just old enough to have a license. It had jump seats in the back, and the jump seats were occupied by four tow-headed, skinned-skulled little boys. (Mrs. Schultz was obviously the family barber.) They were so similar in appearance, except for a slight variation in size, that it was almost impossible to tell them apart.

Four Schultz sons, then. Four apprentices. The boy they had observed on the job had probably not always been the same boy. This Schultz affair had gotten out of hand. Four was too many. But why should Sam—a man fond of children—find this so annoying? What did it matter to him that the carpet carried into the house from the Sears truck was hideous, the sort favored by motels? In what way was he injured to note that the furniture in the U-Haul was lumpish, solid, the kind you saw on TV ads; that the few odd pieces that had not come from stores—a highly varnished, blond coffee table and a desk of "Danish design," though lacking all the grace and lightness of the originals—could only have come from the Schultz Workshop?

The U-Haul was emptied by all hands, and the girl (a former neighbor perhaps?) drove the pickup with the U-Haul away. The Schultzes vanished indoors. The heavy draperies were closed. Sam was about to leave the deck—he felt the sudden need for a drink—when he saw Schultz appear from the back of his house. He was carrying a large wooden object, which he deftly hammered into a post by the curb. He stood back to examine it with a critical air. Evidently satisfied, he disappeared. As soon as possible, Sam and Alice took a closer look with Sam's bird-watching binoculars. It was a miniature replica of Chez Schultz—gable shake roof, contorted chimney, and all; its front door opened to receive Schultz mail. The Schultzes were officially in residence.

"Perhaps we should invite them for a drink," said Alice, over their before-lunch martinis. "Or, send some food over. I have a casserole in the freezer." She looked at Sam. "We did it for the Jessups and the Hunters," she said. "I don't want to seem unfriendly. There's no point in starting off on the wrong foot."

Sam, always neighborly, told her that he could see no reason to start off at all. "What would we do," he said, "if they invited us back, or started sending us casseroles?"

They stared at each other in silence.

"Yes, well, I suppose you're right," said Alice.

School had not yet begun, and the Schultz boys played quietly in their own fenced yard. Sam could hear the thud of a bouncing ball, but never boyish voices. They kept to themselves; seemed to have met no friends on the Lane; if you passed one of them walking down the Lane, he averted his eyes. There certainly would be no high jinks from this source, thought Sam. The Schultz boys had been taught, as the saying goes, "to mind their *p*'s and *q*'s."

And what about Mrs. Schultz? Naturally, she must have been desperate. She was bigger than Schultz, both sideways and in length. A blonde Viking of a woman. She walked with a glide, as if she were on skates. Her smooth, moon-shaped face was impassive; her fleshiness almost hid her eyes and gave her a Mongoloid look. She wore what Alice called "housedresses"—huge tents of printed material which she probably ran up herself from one standard pattern. Like Schultz, she was extremely active about the house. Alice could see into her kitchen from her front deck. She sewed, baked, scrubbed, waxed, polished, and even though they had just moved, seemed to be putting up jams and jellies. If you happened to see her out in front, picking up the mail, she averted her eyes like her children.

You didn't need a watch, it turned out, if the Schultzes lived next door. Schultz left for work in the VW precisely at 7:00 A.M.; the family had had their dinner by 6:30, when

Sam got home. As he and Alice sipped their before-dinner cocktails on their patio in the sweet, sad, dead air of the Indian summer, they were conscious of the Schultz family, above them, sitting in a row in plastic garden chairs on their porch! Front porches, in Vista Verde, were mere entranceways; no one *sat* upon them; one retreated to the privacy of patio or deck. It was an affront, Sam thought, to the Vista Verde way of life; it was ungracious, déclassé. He would have been ashamed to have had a friend drive up and see them there, lined up, like silent sentinels.

They have things mixed up, he thought. This evening vigil was their public life; in every other way, they were an entity unto themselves. They seemed to have no visitors. On Friday and Saturday, at the time of evening when couples in Vista Verde were getting into their Mercedeses, their BMWs, their station wagons, dressed for dinner at a friend's home or for the theater in the City, or preparing to greet friends at their own door, the Schultzes had already moved indoors and pulled the heavy draperies. They apparently had no social ties, belonged to no church, lodge, or club. Spooks, he thought with a shiver.

He gave up talking about them; there was nothing new to say. They had become part of the atmosphere, a climactic change, like a series of shorter days, barely perceptible, that foretells the coming of an Ice Age.

Alice, who minded her civic duties, collected on the Lane for the Heart Fund.

"I skipped the Schultzes," she told Sam. "I didn't feel I could ask them for money until we had met socially."

He thought he detected an accusing tone in her voice. "Who's stopping you from meeting them socially?" he said.

She did not reply.

A few weeks later, a special school bond election was announced. Sam and Alice had always supported the public schools, even when Cindy was attending a private one. It was, they felt, still their duty. Alice helped to register voters. She looked up the Schultzes on the precinct list. Mrs.

Schultz was not registered at all. Schultz was listed as Independent.

Independent! Nonpartisan! Uncommitted! This explained Schultz, thought Sam. He had created his own kingdom, was lord of it. A man like Schultz did not fit into the democratic system. You mind your business, I'll mind mine. This was his motto, the code he lived by.

"I couldn't offer to register Mrs. Schultz," said Alice. "I've never called on her. I wish you'd let me observe the protocol."

"Call on them! Observe the protocol!" he said in a strained voice. "Only, for pity's sakes, don't blame me. I'm not responsible for what happens."

"Oh why," she cried, "are we always fighting over the Schultzes?"

The Indian summer lasted into late September, and Cindy's party was held on the patio beside the pool. Sam thought it a bit subdued, but both Alice and Cindy assured him it was a success. The problem was, Sam didn't feel comfortable on his patio, anymore. He was conscious, the whole time, of Chez Schultz, looming over it. Not that there was any sign of its occupants. If the rock music that went on into the morning, the comings and goings of cars annoyed them, they made no complaint. Still, he could not forget their presence, up there, on their knoll. Chez Schultz. Fort Schultz. Now, Mouse Manor. This was his new name for it. He thought of them like one of those families of mice in the children's books he used to read to Cindy—safe, content, cozy—the kettle boiling on the stove; a fire (though he knew it was only a gas jet) crackling in the grate; Mother Mouse, in an apron, kneading bread; Father Mouse, in his armchair, slippered feet, pipe in mouth, perusing the evening paper. Smug. Satisfied in their domestic felicity. Their lights, he noted, went off at 9:30. He imagined them tucked away in their beds. Mouse beds, with feather bolsters and patchwork quilts. Sleeping a dreamless sleep. The round moon shining down upon their rooftop. Peasant mice, that's what the Schultzes are, he thought. Rich, comfortable mice peasants.

He went to bed while the rock music still blared. Tomorrow, Alice would drive Cindy to the airport. Probably that's the root of my depression, he said to himself. I'm worrying about her over there. Her natural, outgoing manner (like his) could easily be mistaken for something else. Italian men, he had heard, were especially attracted to blondes.

Alice scoffed at his concern. The main problem with those foreign campuses, she said, is that the kids just stick with their own group and don't meet foreigners.

He supposed she was right; she kept up on that sort of thing. It seemed easier for her, too, to think of Cindy as grown-up. But wasn't it possible, he thought, that she went overboard in that direction? After all, she was only eighteen. Three years ago—three years was not very long—she had been fifteen. Three years, before that ... How fast time went. How quickly things changed. A year ago, for example, if anyone had told him there would be Schultzes on the knoll, overlooking his patio, he would have smiled complacently. That sort, he would have thought, were not attracted to Vista Verde.

In October, shortly after the schools opened, another Schultz surprise. A girl. The same girl who had driven the Checker was also a member of the Schultz ménage. He saw her one morning, as he went out for the newspaper. She emerged from Chez Schultz, walking by herself, school books under her arm, toward the school-bus stop. She could not have been more than sixteen. She was fair, like all Schultzes, but slimmer, more appealing. A pretty, piquant face. Breasts, like small apples, beneath her sweater. A womanly curve to hips and thighs. A grave, sweet, grown-up manner. A girl like that, with parents like that? Ah, but it would not last. In no time at all, the way time passed these days, she'd marry, settle down, have babies, grow fat and ponderous like her mother. His heart went out to her. As she walked by, he spoke.

"Back to school, eh?" he said.

She smiled shyly, nodded. The smile was not just on her lips; it lit up her eyes. She had green eyes. Quite lovely. He watched her until she disappeared around the turn in the Lane.

"Yes, yes, there's a girl," said Alice, when he inquired about her. She spoke in a hurried, weary way, as if she wanted to put an end to the discussion.

"You never told me!"

"It never occurred to me you'd be interested."

"How did I miss her? Where do they keep her? In the attic?"

"She doesn't play. She's a Mother's Helper," said Alice.

On a Saturday morning, a few weeks later, Sam was on his patio, struggling to put up a new trellis for the espaliered, fruitless pear. He was suddenly aware that Schultz was watching him. He was standing on his property, in back of the absurd wall—another symbol of Schultz paranoia—that he had erected to mark the boundaries of his realm. It was only a row of bricks, barely a foot high! Was Schultz afraid we would encroach, Sam had wondered? Was he afraid Winkle rosemary would lunge across the survey line, or the roots of Winkle oak creep craftily beneath it? Then he heard a voice. Schultz was addressing him for the first time.

"Hi, there, neighbor, how's the garden growing?" said Schultz.

"I'm afraid I don't have much of a green thumb," said Sam. "My wife is the gardener." He spoke in as noncommittal a tone as possible. Actually, the Winkle landscaping, planned by one of the best firms in the City, had won a prize from Alice's Garden Club.

Schultz watched for a time in silence, which had the effect of making Sam more awkward. Then, "Let me give you a hand there, neighbor," he said. Before Sam could stop him he bustled into his workshop and returned with the proper instruments. Adroitly, he completed Sam's task.

"There! Presto chango, neighbor! Done!" cried Schultz,

and he danced away, with his odd gait—holding up five stubby spread fingers to ward off any thanks.

The ice had been broken; they now spoke. It irritated Sam to think that Schultz had broken it. Perhaps I ought to be more charitable, he thought. It was obvious poor Schultz had a personality problem. He could not say "Hello"; it was always, "Hi, there, neighbor!" Instead of "yes," he said, "affirmative"; instead of "no," "negative." He didn't walk, he did a dance. He wiggled and grimaced and blinked his big chestnut eyes, as if he was afraid if he stayed still for a moment he would wind down like a mechanical doll.

Yet, despite his tics, his mannerisms, he had an air of fierce self-sufficiency. He lived in a peculiar little tribal world of his own. When he said, "Hi, there, neighbor!" Sam was convinced he was playing some kind of game, trying to show him something—laughing, perhaps, behind his back.

What could charity accomplish? It was hopeless to go out of one's way for such a person. He seemed to desire nothing that he couldn't provide for himself. A simple neighborly friendship was out of the question. The "Hi, there, neighbor," was as much of a wall as the heavy masonry of Chez Schultz. And who would want to pierce it? Whatever lay beyond it was unsavory, distasteful; it was material for a psychoanalyst who had the stomach for such things. Yes, what Schultz needed (though it was probably too late) was a long stretch on the couch. On top of that, a Charm School. Some cultural education, too. Schultz had picked up the technical skills of their civilization; but his instincts were those of a barbarian.

Schultz, Sam discovered, in the course of their brief conversations, was in Electronics, a Research and Development man. The woods were full of them nowadays. Many had been laid off; Schultz had survived. He possessed some kind of patents; obviously had money laid away. (Did he trust banks, or was it in a mattress?) But, except for the ostentatious vulgarity of his house, the Schultzes lived frugally.

"I never make a purchase without consulting my bible,"

Schultz told Sam one Sunday afternoon, gazing archly at Sam's new power mower, which had broken down.

"Your bible?"

"*Consumer Reports*, neighbor."

"I just picked this thing up below at the hardware store," said Sam. He had meant to relay a disinterest in such a material matter; imply that he (if not Schultz) had more important values to consider. But it didn't come out that way. Instead, his tone was apologetic, almost deferential. Well, what did it matter? He was willing to admit that Schultz knew more about power mowers than he. Anyone who excluded so many of the amenities from his life had time to focus on mowers.

"That brand isn't recommended, neighbor. Built-in obsolescence. Not a Best Buy. Let's see what we can do . . ."

Schultz fixed it, of course. But that was his territory. He was constantly oiling, sanding, polishing, varnishing, waxing, clipping, spraying, fertilizing, planting, pruning, repairing, improving. He kept his possessions in excellent order. No rust, dust, or mold was allowed to accumulate; no surface flake or tarnish. Always on the alert for Enemy Forces, whether in the forms of "not acceptable" buys, a snail, or a silverfish, he patrolled his property with a sharp eye.

After he repaired the mower, he invited Sam into his workshop; stood proudly by as Sam admired it. It was immaculate. His hand tools—oiled and shining—hung tidily, each against a painted outline of itself. Rows of Mason jars containing different sizes of nails, screws, bolts, were suspended from their lids and screwed to the bottom of shelves. His power tools looked as if he had bought them that morning.

"He has the engineer mentality," Sam said to Alice. "But he can't communicate with human beings."

It turned out that the Schultzes did have a social life—of a sort. On late Saturday or Sunday afternoons, the Winkles watched as the Schultz ménage, with scrubbed faces and clean clothes, piled into the Checker. Their destination was no longer mysterious. Schultz had tipped Sam off. This family outing was not to a movie or a Chinese restaurant; it was a trip to Sears, with their weekly list of Best Buys. They returned weighted down with packages and paper bags. The little boys might be wearing new sneakers; Schultz, new eyeglass frames. Mrs. Schultz might carry a bundle, which, judging from its shape, was a bolt of cloth. The girl (like all Schultz children she remained nameless) helped out with other household articles—a sack of fertilizer, perhaps, or a new wheelbarrow. Her grace, her delicacy, her graveness stirred him. It seemed, to him, an indignity for her to haul such objects. She's made of finer stuff, he thought. She has quality. But it would all come to nothing. She didn't have a chance in the world. He yearned to rescue her; introduce her to the civilities, the refinements, to "savoir faire" and "bienfaisance"—this last, a term picked up and stored away in his Creative Days, for the right occasion (a perfume ad? a fine liqueur?). There were other things, also, to which she had certainly never been exposed. A glimpse of the majesty, the sublimity of existence. Values. That was what it all came down to. Oh, how he wished that he might be of assistance to her!

"You know, perhaps they have something," said Alice, watching the Schultzes unload Best Buys. "No matter how hard you work, how hard I try to save, we never seem to get ahead. Everyone says Inflation is only going to get worse. We're running out of oil, natural gas, water! We probably pay twice as much for everything, compared to them. There's no point in being foolish nowadays."

"Life is short. You have to decide what's important," said Sam. "Do you want to spend your weekends at Sears? What kind of memories will you have for your old age?" His voice was angry because he knew she had a point. They shopped carelessly; he went wild in fancy-food shops; their house wine was of a higher quality each year. Like a blind man who kept to old familiar paths he chose the well-known name brands of his youth and still bought his suits, shirts, ties—even, when he was in a hurry, his underwear—at Brooks Brothers. They selected the best medical practitioners in the area. His attorney, judging from his bills, was one of the best, too. The same was true of Cindy's education. He was interested in quality, not Best Buys. You got what you paid for had always been his motto. Quality was a value, too. Now, in his middle years, to go the way of Schultz? In certain instances, death was preferable to compromise! This, he declared grandly to Alice, was one.

"Delusions of grandeur, maybe?" said Alice. "Your grandmother spoiled you."

"Shut up about my grandmother; she's not here to defend herself," said Sam.

The first Christmas without Cindy hit hard. If not a religious feast, it was the most important family celebration; Dickensian was how Sam thought of it. Alice had always gone to great lengths to make it festive. Last year, for example, she decorated the Tree with Mexican ornaments—tin angels, fanciful straw animals, strings of hemp, pink, orange, purple. Ordinarily an indifferent cook, at Christmastime Alice entered the kitchen with zest and determination. She spent weeks kneading dough, chopping glazed fruits, shelling nuts, stuffing dates; dipping cherries into chocolate, stringing festoons of popcorn, cutting cookies into trees and stars and Easter bunnies (the bunnies had come with the cooky cut-out set), sprinkling them with raisins and colored sugar. After all, the feast had begun before the invention of packaged foods; the tradition required loving hands. But this year, she faltered. Such a creative effort seemed unwarranted for just the two of them.

Invite Sam's sisters and their families? Sam vetoed this (to Alice's relief). Christmas, *yes*, for Cindy. This was how his sisters would think. This was how things were with Jews these days. But without Cindy? He could sense their polite disapproval of any show of seasonal spirit on his part. They would make him feel self-conscious. Friends? So many of their friends now had married children whom they went to visit; others flew to ski resorts or to Acapulco, Guatemala, the Caribbean. There seemed to be no one available whom both of them really wanted to invite. Call the County Home for the Aged and put in an order for a few of their ambulatory patients? Theoretically, a nice proposition; in practice, awkward, contrived. A check to the Home would be more welcome. How about foreign students from Stanford? Sam could not work up any enthusiasm for this. The strain required to be a good host, to talk to people with foreign accents (an Englishman could be as hard to understand as a Japanese) seemed out of proportion to the pleasure to be derived. At the end of the evening they would be presented with their guests' home addresses, urged to call when they visited their country so that the hospitality could be returned. It would be most unlikely that this would ever occur. After a time the guests' names, perhaps even their nationalities, would be forgotten. It was not his notion of the way to spend the holiday.

For many years now, the Winkles had held, besides the family celebration, an Open House for friends and their children. It had begun when they were younger with a punch bowl of hot mulled wine. At some point, the palates and stomachs of the adults (including Sam's and Alice's) rebelled at such a concoction and they had switched to champagne for the grown-ups, plain eggnog for the kids. Now, most of the kids were grown-ups, too; more champagne was consumed, and most of the eggnog thrown out after the party. The eggnog party had become a champagne party.

"We can't afford the Caribbean or Europe, at the moment, but for the price of all that champagne, we could spend a week in the Islands," said Sam.

Before they left, Sam saw Schultz in his yard and mentioned his plans. It was hard to say why he felt compelled to do so. It was, he decided, like reporting his comings and goings to the Block Captain, and he was angry with himself.

"Off to faraway, exotic places, eh, neighbor?" said Schultz, grimacing and bobbing up and down.

"Yes. I thought you might wonder if you noticed the house was empty."

"I'll keep an eye out. You can't be too careful nowadays. An empty house attracts them. They look for empty houses this time of year."

"Them? They?" Paranoid terms, thought Sam. Just the same, crime had begun to creep into the suburbs. Even Vista Verde, tucked away from the main thoroughfares, had not been spared. The liquor store in the shopping center had been burglarized; friends on Los Robles Lane had come home from the movies and found their stereo and color TV gone. Vandals had thrown rocks through the windows of the elementary school. And only three doors down, on Manzanita, the Mayfields' mailbox had been smeared with red paint. In the old days, the Winkles had not even bothered to lock their front door when they went downtown; now they had grown cautious. They had joined the recently formed Vista Verde Patrol—a private organization—and before they left for Honolulu, Sam bought special bolts for the sliding glass doors. He told Schultz what he had done. Schultz approved.

"You can't be too careful," he said again.

Every year Alice took colored paper plates of her Christmas cookies around to their closest neighbors; this year, she added the Schultzes to her list.

"Do you think that was really necessary?" Sam asked her.

"You asked them to watch our house."

"I didn't *exactly* ask." Sam was embarrassed. "*He* offered."

She took them, anyhow. Mrs. Schultz, she told Sam, met her at the door with a puzzled look; had not even invited her in. It was as if she had never received—possibly never even desired—a gift or a neighborly gesture. "She looked at them as if they might be poisoned," said Alice with an embarrassed laugh.

The Hawaiian week—a package at the Hotel Kamehameha Surf & Sand—was not entirely successful, though it was hard to say why. Perhaps Schultz's remark had made Sam fret about his house. Or perhaps he had lost his old zest for swimming. The ocean seemed chilly. He stood with his feet in the water and watched old codgers floating serenely out beyond the breakers; their bellies, like the bellies of pregnant women, rose and fell with the waves. An elderly woman jogged past him. She wore a sweat suit, and her short gray hair was cut like a man's. At the sea's edge, she slipped out of her costume. Underneath was a black tank suit, which hung loosely on her spare, muscular frame; her feminine fat had vanished. Where, he wondered, does fat go when you lose it? Matter, he had read somewhere, was fundamentally restless; in an eternal state of metamorphosis. Had whatever made up this woman's womanliness transferred itself to the old men's bellies? Probably too simplistic an answer for this phenomenon. He wished he knew more about molecules, atoms, nuclear particles, Black Holes. There was something of importance, here, but it had gotten beyond him. In high school he had had an inquiring mind, open to new concepts; after that, it had been downhill all the way. There were entire new views of the Cosmos of which he was ignorant. When he someday read the Great Books he would have only begun to catch up. All of this took time and energy, perhaps even a ruthlessness of which he was not capable. He was like a man who still believed that a person could fall off the edge of the world long after Columbus had made his voyage. An anachronism. Not just behind the times—behind centuries. This is how he would remain for the rest of his life, and he knew he had no one to blame but himself.

He watched the old woman enter the water without hesitation; he admired her strong, purposeful crawl. She swam far out, past the breakers, past the inflated, floating humps. A breeze came up, and goose pimples popped out on his flesh. He wrapped himself in his towel and returned to the hotel and took a quick dip in its heated pool. In the room he examined his naked body in a long mirror under fluorescent lights and was appalled by its unsightliness.

Alice, who had talked of the importance of doing nothing but lie on the beach, swim, and read, with perhaps a little meditation thrown in, became restless on the second day. She was up before Sam; had had her swim and sunbath and breakfast before he was dressed. During his breakfast, she sat with him, enumerating the abominations of the Hotel Kamehameha Surf & Sand. The list was long. Their fellow guests, in their resort clothes, with their ever-present cameras, loud voices, childlike holiday mirth. The bland and overcooked food. The Muzak (Hawaiian favorites and Christmas carols). The humidity. The air conditioning. The rows of luggage in the lobby, which announced the arrival of a new Tour. The wheelchairs, discreetly stored out of sight in a utility room, which she had glimpsed when a porter opened the room's door. The hundreds of electric golf carts (a regular traffic jam!) zigzagging about on the hotel's golf course. The spectacle of old people taking hula lessons on the Lanai. To come so far! To spend all this money! Just to stay in an ugly high rise, with its ersatz ambience. Why had he fallen for such a rip-off? Was it because he was in the advertising business? Was he so brainwashed as to believe the ads? Yes, she supposed that was it. In order to live with oneself, one had to believe in what one did. If only he had not been so hasty, had consulted her. They should have taken a condominium—like the Jessups, the Mayfields—instead of a resort-hotel package!

On the third day, she rented a car and prowled the Island alone, looking at condominiums with some future visit in mind. She returned with a different notion. All of the condominiums were filled. More were going up. Perhaps they should consider investing in one? Who could tell, they might decide to retire here? She had talked to a nice broker, she had literature on the subject.

"—Please don't comment until you've at least looked at it. Try to keep an open mind, for once. It could be our salvation."

Her excitement turned to fury when Sam mentioned the risks.

"Risks! That's all you've ever thought about. It's no wonder we slip behind every month. You have to take chances in business. You've always put down my ideas just because I'm a woman. You're accustomed to women's worship. Your sisters treat you as if you're a financial wizard—a god! The fact is, it's possible I have a better business head than you. Remember that little row of duplexes I pointed out to you once? Near the campus. Do you know what students pay to rent them today? Oh, if I'd been given half a chance, if you hadn't destroyed my confidence ... No. Your ego is more important to you than our security. Just wait ten years and see what this 'risk' is worth," said Alice, and threw the condominium literature at his feet.

Christmas Eve was the worst. They spent the entire night trying to get Cindy by phone. Just after breakfast they made the connection. A hubbub of Italian voices—frenetic, hysterical. Several operators seemed to be on it, too; all of them trying to outscream the others. After some moments of this, a young boy, who spoke some English, was put on the line, but the chorus of Italian continued in the background, making him even more difficult to understand. Alice, standing beside Sam, added to the confusion by offering to take over, then trying to wrest the phone from his hand. He managed to give his name (the operator had called him Signor Wingle) and to wish the boy a Merry Christmas. Then he asked for Cindy. The agitation on the other end increased.

Cindy was—excuse me—what? Cindy was—where? (He turned to Alice, begging her to shut up.) Cindy had gone to Spain? She was *in* Spain? For the holidays? Alone? Not alone? With whom, excuse me? With her what? Her fiancé? (More background interference; a woman's shriek.)

"Si, signore. Her fiancé," said the boy.

"The Mama! The Mama!" shrieked the woman.

"Her fiancé and the mother of her fiancé," the boy said.

Overwrought himself and feeling foolish, he asked for the fiancé's name, but the connection was abruptly broken off.

He replaced the receiver and wiped sweat from his brow. His knees felt weak, and he sat down on the bed.

"Spain? Her fiancé?"

"That's what he said."

"Why didn't you let me talk? I'm better at that sort of thing. Foreign languages always rattle you. There are ways of communicating—"

"All right, I'm sorry. I did my best, for Christ's sake. But what's this about a 'fiancé'?"

"If he said, 'fiancé.' "

"I'm not deaf. He said it several times."

"In that case, it's very simple." Alice smiled. A smug, superior smile.

"How is it simple?"

"Italian families are old-fashioned. She probably just told them it was her fiancé."

"So she's gone off to Spain with some boy and he's not her fiancé and that's simpler. Am I supposed to feel better about that?"

"She's not a nun. She's made friends there."

"Why couldn't she let us know? She might have guessed we'd call. Has she mentioned any particular boy?"

"You've read the letters. She's mentioned a number of friends. You don't expect her not to have any fun, do you?"

"I don't know what to expect anymore," said Sam.

The Hotel Kamehameha Surf & Sand had gone all out for Christmas dinner. It was held in the Lanai. Guests were presented with leis and immense goblets of lukewarm Polynesian punch, each with an African tulip floating in it. They were encouraged to take off their shoes and sit on straw mats. A banquet table had been set up for those who preferred chairs. Sam's back hurt, and he urged Alice toward the table. It did not make him feel better to see the elderly female swimmer, in a muumuu, squatting cross-legged, her back erect, on the floor.

There was a floor show. Hula dancers from the Electric Company, in grass skirts and elf caps, hula-hulaed to

"Santa Claus Is Coming to Town," played by a ukulele trio. Then Santa Claus appeared in a rickshaw drawn by more half-clad beauties, with silver reindeer horns on their heads. Santa was an immense fat stand-up comedian, in a tapa-cloth skirt, Santa Claus beard, and boots and a top hat. Stepping out of his rickshaw, a girl under each arm, he announced, "*Mele Kalikimaka*," in his Santa voice, "which for the benefit of any malihinis, is how we say Merry Christmas in the Islands. Come on, now, everyone. *Me-le Ka-li-ki-ma-ka!*"

"*Me-le Ka-li-ki-ma-ka!*" the guests roared back.

He told the audience that he was closing his workshop up at the North Pole and moving to beautiful Hawaii, though he might have a little trouble on the distaff side if Mrs. Claus could see him now, with these beautiful wahines. He made the audience promise not to tell. More song and dance, more tasteless jokes. Then Santa led the guests in a Sing Along of Christmas carols, in pidgin English.

Singing was followed by the blowing of conch shells. Then four beach boys trotted in carrying a bamboo litter. On the litter was a shaved, skinned, barbecued pig, which they presented to Santa to carve.

Alice and Sam retired early. It seemed appropriate to make love. Christmas Night. Hawaii. Music drifting up from the ballroom. "Sweet Leilani, Heavenly Flower." The fragrance of the wilted gardenia leis on the dresser; the sound of surf. Their first real holiday in years. Alice had put on a new nightie—a red gossamer garment that was intended to tell him something. He drew her toward him, nestled; stroked her still-firm thighs. But nothing happened. Not even the tiniest stir of lust. A heavy fatigue seemed to have engulfed him, weighing him down. It pressed against his chest, his guts, his limbs. He felt flaccid, limp. His breath came in short gulps, as if he were suffocating. His mind wandered from the business at hand to his imminent death. Yes, he was dying. Only a month ago, he had had a physical examination and been pronounced fit. But his doctor had seemed rushed, preoccupied, had, evidently, overlooked some fatal disorder. It was not uncommon that men left their doctor's office, after passing a physical, and dropped dead on the sidewalk outside. Heart? Lungs? A clotted vein? Something unusual, unique even, that would require a specialist to detect. At his age he probably should have entered a hospital and had one of those thorough, executive-type goings over; his doctor should have suggested it.

Alice gave a little wiggle, made a whimpering noise. "Row, fish, or cut bait," she was telling him.

"I think the humidity's got to me," he said weakly.

He felt her stiffen in his arms. She did not help matters by making a joke about senility. Then she patted his cheek as if he were a child and rolled away from him and fell asleep; her snoring blended with the sound of the surf.

To fall asleep next to a dying man! Even a dying stranger, much less one's husband! It showed a lack of sensitivity and breeding. Tears came to his eyes when he thought that she had borne his child. His child? Oh, God! Those Italians were keeping something from him. They had put on an act, played dumb. Cindy could be seriously—perhaps fatally—injured, and they did not want to be the ones to tell him. The news, he supposed, would arrive officially from the American Consulate in Florence or the head of the Italian Study Program for Smith. If not injured, Roman fever? He supposed one could get Roman fever in Florence. He was not certain what it was, but people, for centuries, had perished of it. Or, if it was true that she was in Spain, with her "fiancé," what did this mean? "Just a boyfriend," Alice had said. More probably a gigolo who preyed on innocent American girls. Alice was too innocent herself; too trusting. This business about the real estate—she could scarcely manage the household budget! These were his thoughts as he lay wide awake, his pulse pounding, waiting to hear his own death rattle.

There was a letter from Cindy when they got back. She had tried to call them from Majorca but could not get through.

Spain was far-out; she and some *friends* had rented a beach
house. The beaches here were better than Italian beaches;
the vibes more mellow. She had a far-out Spanish Riviera
Golden Glow tan. She had decided, if they could spare the
money, to tour around Europe this summer with *friends*. It
seemed really dumb not to see more while she was here, before she got into the Establishment Scene and started worrying about shit like taxes and postponed opportunities until it was too late, like what happened to people when they
got older. (A tactful girl, she mentioned no names.) If she
traveled really cheap and slept on beaches and in parks and
skipped a few meals, she could manage on six hundred dollars. Any surplus would go toward upgrading her Life Style.
But if they were really short, she could get along, somehow.
("Somehow"? thought Sam. What in God's name was
"somehow"?)

"She's absolutely right," said Alice, in a harsh voice. She
was sitting in front of the bedroom mirror, brushing her
hair. She stopped and held out a strand and examined it as
if it were a strange foreign substance, not a part of her.

It's gray, he thought with surprise. Then he recalled that
she had pointed out the grayness to him before. Perhaps,
even, on several occasions.

"My hair's getting gray," she had said. "Do you think I
should have it colored? I don't believe in hiding your age,
but the plain truth is that older women are discriminated
against in the professions."

In the professions? What professions, he had wondered.
She had given up such notions, long ago. She had been
happy with her choice; he was certain she had been happy.
You can't have your cake and eat it, too, he had thought. It
isn't fair of her to have regrets. "I like you just the way you
are," he had told her, hoping to end the subject.

Now, it appeared as though she meant to bring it up
again.

"I should never have taken your advice not to have my
hair colored. It will be more noticeable, now that I'm com-
pletely gray. When you hunt for a job, it's held against
you." She turned, confronted him, laughed, a self-deprecat-

ing laugh. "Can you imagine them hiring *me* in your office?"

She had him there. He could not. The girls at the Agency—secretaries, copy girls, receptionists, even the female Creatives—were chosen, he had to admit, for their decorative appeal. They almost always left, after a few years, to get married, anyway. It was the state of the art, which dealt in illusions, images of perpetual youth and beauty, sexual nubility. This, outside of dogs and children, sold the beer and wine, the hair sprays and deodorants, detergents, automobiles—even, often, the banks, insurance, the import-export trade. What was she saying? That he worked in a whorehouse where they put aging employees out on the street? He had fed and sheltered her and was willing to continue to do so. What was all this about job hunting? She had accomplished her main life's work; why couldn't she sit back and enjoy the results? Gray hair, for a woman of her age, in her line, was appropriate.

"Cindy," said Alice, "should see everything. While she *can.*"

He assured her that he would come up with the money for Cindy's summer. He tried not to think about what they already owed for the Hawaii fiasco.

Schultz had a new surprise in store for them. On the Saturday afternoon, a week after their return, he drove up the street in a gigantic recreational vehicle. A King of the Road. On the back of it was a bumper sticker that read, THE SCHULTZES. 5 MANZANITA LANE. VISTA VERDE, CALIFORNIA.

Ugly. Déclassé. A congester of the highways. A polluter. But what would you expect from a man like Schultz? He watched from his deck with disdain as Schultz parked the monstrous caravan at his curb. The four Schultz boys trotted out. Then Mrs. Schultz, with her impassive face, her glide. Then—the girl. The girl had just washed her hair; she ran lightly down the steps, winding it into a coil, as she ran. She looked like Spring. She wore jeans and was barefoot. He was afraid for her feet. Schultz kept the steps clean, but still there could be a jagged rock, a sliver of glass. He could not bear the thought of this lithe, graceful creature crying out in pain.

Shoes! Put on your shoes, he wanted to call out to her, but, of course, he could not, and while he was thinking this, she had followed the others into the van to inspect the new acquisition. A Best Buy, of course. Schultz would have done his research. He watched as the family filed out again and vanished into the house.

They are not worthy of her, he thought. She should be rescued. He fantasized calling the Authorities. "I can't give you my name, but there's something you should know. You should make an investigation."

Then Schultz looked up and saw him and beckoned. There was no way out of it. He wanted to show off the King of the Road to Sam, too. He received Sam on the retractable steps, beaming and twitching, with both a proud and wistful expression in his eyes.

"This one headed the list for All-Round Family Purposes," he said, as Sam joined him.

He ushered Sam in; led him on a tour with all the expertise of a salesman. He recited statistics. The mileage. The horsepower. The number of people it could hold. Then all the accouterments. The swivel seat for the driver, the sofa that could be made into a double bed; the table that could be let down from a hinge on the wall; the clever storage units, the stove, the refrigerator, the sink that had a cover that doubled for a cutting board; the practical industrial, indoor-outdoor carpet, the oversize alternator, the CB radio. They were going on a Trial Run to the beach this weekend.

"Yes, it's something all right," said Sam. "Your family should get a lot of pleasure out of it."

"It's the only way, neighbor. We're not much for hotels or motels. This way we can have all the conveniences of home without giving our money to strangers."

A peculiar atmosphere had begun to pervade the Agency office, a change of mood, nothing you could quite put your finger on; still, putting two and two together, and this and that, he realized it had existed for several months. Baxter appeared more often and sat in his office with the door closed, making long phone calls. When Brown came up from Dean Witter's, he joined Baxter instead of going to his own office. Linda, who had been at Sam's beck and call, now devoted all of her time to Baxter's correspondence. The Agency's attorneys showed up at frequent intervals and closeted themselves in Baxter's office, which had taken on the aspect of a top-security headquarters. A group of men and a modish woman with frosted hair—Sam was introduced to none of them—appeared and cloistered themselves with the others. The easy-going, relaxed office banter, the kidding and jokes ceased. Nerves were on edge, tempers flared. Linda took trays of coffee into the Secret Command, neglected Sam, and pouted. In late July, Baxter called Sam in for the first time and broke the news. Laiken, Baxter and Brown had been sold to Mitchell-Zeigler, a large New York Agency that handled national and international accounts. The Agency's name was to be changed to Zeigler-Laiken. Both Baxter and Brown were retiring; the office would be moved to Sansome Street. A man from New York, Calderwell, would take charge of the San Francisco division; most of the old employees would be phased out, but it was an explicit part of the contract that Sam would be kept on. He would continue to handle his regular accounts, none of which were, at the moment, especially profitable, with the exception of the Napa winery, which was going national—"the plum," said Baxter wryly, that had attracted them.

"We've told them they couldn't survive without you," said Baxter, patting Sam on the back, as if he were trying to reassure an old family retainer.

"It was bound to happen, someday," said Sam to Alice. "I mean, if I'd thought about it, it would have been obvious. Baxter had a cancer operation two years ago. And, of course, Brown's hopeless."

"They couldn't have run things without you, and Baxter said so," said Alice. "Did he mention anything about a raise? Stock in the company?"

"No, that didn't come up."

"You should have taken this opportunity to bring it up."

"It didn't seem appropriate, somehow. Baxter seemed so relieved the negotiations were over. He didn't look well. He appeared to have his mind on . . . other matters."

"The man from New York? What's-his-name? Calderwell? He'll find out soon enough what your value is. Those New Yorkers think they know everything, but when they get west of the Mississippi they're fish out of water. They're more provincial than small-town people; have to go to the zoo to look at a cow. Wait until he tries to work with some of those old San Francisco firms, the people you've known for years. You know my opinion of the Bohemian Club, but you've played dominoes with old Mr. Perkins there now for years. How do you change a relationship like that?"

You do not change it, thought Sam. Events changed it for you. To some extent, events already had. Why remind her that Harvey Perkins had retired, himself, six months ago and was living up on his ranch in Sonoma? That his son-in-law (who did not play dominoes) ran the shipping firm, which, to tell the truth, had been in the red since the Longshoreman's strike? Perkins' Shipping ran fewer ads in the trade journals, and the son-in-law had told Sam he had inherited a mess.

"This Calderwell will come to you on his hands and knees," said Alice.

Calderwell, when Sam met him a week later, was still upright and confident. He was, it turned out, not a New Yorker, but the former head of Mitchell-Zeigler's Los Angeles division and had gone to New York only for "the transition." Sam had often thought Los Angeles more foreign and exotic than New York, and Calderwell bore out this conviction. A man in his late forties. Tall. Sunburned. A pockmarked face. Long yellow wavy hair. (Dyed? Probably.) He wore an expensive, Italian-cut suit with a nipped-in waist, alligator shoes. A monogrammed shirt. The kind of dark glasses that changed from dark to clear, or vice versa, depending upon the light; the change was not immediate, and Calderwell groped like a blind man for a while after they entered the elegant, red plush "Victorian whorehouse" interior of a Nob Hill tower restaurant, where (without bothering to consult Sam—a native *and* a gourmet!) he had made their reservation for lunch. Already, it seemed, he was on good terms with the head waiter; they were shown to a table with a view of the Bay, which Calderwell had obviously occupied before. He enjoyed friendly relations, too, with several of the young waitresses, costumed like "doxies." He looked them up and down, in a sleepy, lizardlike way, with special attention to their décolletage. "I approve," his eyes seemed to say.

Women aren't supposed to be treated as sex objects anymore; it's old hat, and they don't go for it, thought Sam.

Yet this Calderwell got away with it. Their waitress hovered over him, eager to oblige. Calderwell called her "Sweetheart" in an offhand, yet somehow intimate, way; it contained promises that either were or were not meant to be kept. Whichever, the girl seemed to understand. It was Sam who was puzzled. Not only was Calderwell's manner patronizing ("chauvinistic," Alice would call it), but the man was not even good-looking. Those pockmarks. Acne scars, probably. Or, perhaps, from a burn. His skin fitted too tightly over his face, and his cheeks were sunken. He had a physique like a scraggly rooster. He was not the type you would trust with your daughter (unless she had Cindy's good sense), but, after all, this was not the issue.

We're here to discuss business, he told himself.

Calderwell was enthusiastic about a crab concoction, which was not on the menu, and recommended it to Sam as if he were honoring him with secret classified information; Sam, who preferred his crab in the shell, unadulterated, ordered it to be polite. He let Calderwell order the wine, too, without offering a suggestion. It seemed to mean a great deal to him, for he studied the wine list with an earnest, scholarly air. He ordered a dry martini, first, and Sam, who had long ago given up cocktails at lunch, made an exception and had one with Calderwell.

"God, you people are lucky," said Calderwell, gazing out at the view. "This is the real thing, isn't it?" He took photographs of his family out of his wallet. A pretty, much younger wife, a four-year-old son. It was his third wife and his only child, he said. "My kid's going to be brought up here, not in Fantasyland. That had a lot to do with my decision." He appeared to be talking more to himself than to Sam. Then he adopted a serious, businesslike tone. He wanted Sam's advice.

Sam waited to be asked about the Agency, but the advice Calderwell wanted was of a different sort. He was searching for the right apartment for his family.

"Right here, in town, in the heart of things," he said.

Sam mentioned various family neighborhoods. The Sunset, Twin Peaks, Cow Hollow. Neighborhoods with real houses, and yards where children could play. Twin Peaks had beautiful views; the Sunset, the best weather. There were sections of Pacific Heights, too, that weren't all mansions.

It was soon obvious he had lost Calderwell's attention. Calderwell knew the "right" districts; he had evidently boned up. The decision was really between Telegraph Hill and Russian Hill (both expensive); at the moment, Russian Hill was favored. When Sam brought up school districts, he learned that Calderwell's son was already enrolled in the fashionable, private Town School. Yes, Calderwell knew his way around and had sized things up. He must have money, too. Family money, maybe? A rich wife? At any rate, he hardly needed advice in this department, and had only succeeded in making Sam feel foolish.

At the end of the lunch, almost as an afterthought, Calderwell brought up the Agency. If Sam could get his own things in order, he could take a couple of weeks off; when he re-

turned, the Agency would have moved. He spent the remainder of the time telling about his personal life. He had
married young. His first wife had been much older than he,
a hopeless psychotic. His second wife was a manic-depressive, in and out of institutions. He, himself, had spent years
in therapy. This third marriage was It. What it was all
about. He was now a domesticated animal. His openness
about such matters was disarming. It was hard not to wish
him good luck.

It was the summer of the Impeachment Hearings. During
his two weeks vacation, Sam moved the portable Sony out
on the patio. Alice, who had signed up for a Real Estate
course, joined him when she could. Impeachment? His instinctive dislike for the President as a man did not make
the affair as gleeful for him as it did for Alice; it provoked,
instead, a profound disturbance. The President of the
United States! On trial for being a common crook! Saints,
he knew, did not run for public office, but once such an
honor was bestowed upon a man, was it not customary that
he rise to the occasion—consider his place in history? Even
then, certain things—considering that the U.S. was no
longer a young republic but a Great Power—could be overlooked. A President might, for example, be summoned in
the middle of the night from his bed to answer the Hot Line;
swift and portentous action would have to be made; there
would be no time to consult a Congress or the Electorate.
But Second Story stuff? False testimonies and false mustaches? The use of low and vulgar language, while outwardly maintaining the aspect of a Sunday-school teacher?

The President, as President, was a Father Figure, and as
such, set an example to the people. He represented Justice,
the blessings of Liberty, domestic tranquility—even taste!
Now, who could count on anything? For all he knew, George
Washington and Abraham Lincoln had been knaves and
blackguards. He had been lied to, misled, taken in by parents, teachers, school books, the Media! Even, perhaps—
himself!

The Schultzes were often gone that summer. A week here, a week there. Numerous weekends. During their absence lights that Schultz had rigged up turned on and off automatically in various parts of their house to discourage intruders. Schultz, who did not belong to the Patrol, asked Sam to pick up their mail; glancing at it, it was plain they paid cash for everything. There was no need to collect newspapers; they took none.

Each time they returned, another sticker had been added to the King of the Road. DISNEYLAND. BUFFALO BILL'S GRAVE, THE OREGON CAVES, THE MYSTERY TREES, FRONTIER VILLAGE, KNOTTS BERRY FARM. One sticker said, WE'VE BEEN TO THE JUMPING FROG JUBILEE. HAVE YOU?

What a contrast, he thought, to Cindy's Odyssey. Paris. Rome. Palermo. Syracuse. Dubrovnik. Athens. Now, this was something! The saints and philosophers who had written the Great Books wrote of such places. What would St. Augustine have thought of Disneyland? Dante, of the Oregon Caves? Taste, perhaps, even in a democracy, was something you were born with, which, despite the public school system, separated the aristocrats from the herd. You either had it or you didn't, and he counted his blessings as Cindy's cards arrived.

He pictured Schultz, Mrs. Schultz, the four little Schultzes, on the road. (The Girl did not fit into the picture.) A pale, sluggish, mindless brood, obediently following their energetic mindless Leader. Swarming over America. Infesting the countryside. Returning with their stickers to prove that the Schultzes had been there. Ruining travel before he and Alice had even begun ... No wonder the country was going rapidly downhill!

From one of his expeditions, Schultz returned with a dog. A six-month-old, high-strung Doberman, which quivered and shied as Sam put out his hand to pat its sleek head.

"It's not a family pet, neighbor," said Schultz. "Please don't pet him. I'm training him to be suspicious of strangers. A one-family dog. If we leave the camper, he'll discourage anyone from breaking in."

In a station break, during the Impeachment Hearings, Sam heard Schultz in his yard, giving the dog commands. "Stay." "Heel." "Sit." "Charge!"

He's in his element, thought Sam. The military missed out on a good thing, there. He would have made the perfect sadistic sergeant. Paranoia, that's his problem. People like the Schultzes, who barricaded themselves up in their houses, who kept to themselves and lacked all social impulses and graces, who did not register or vote and called themselves Independents, who averted their eyes when you met them, obviously suffered from this malaise. Such people had imaginary enemies; they were the snipers who shot innocent people down in the streets, the men who dressed in white hoods and burned crosses on the lawns of Black churches, who painted swastikas on the doors of Jewish homes. Anti-Semites! Of course! What else could they be? He had never been able to admit this to himself, before; now, though the effects upon him were highly deleterious, it was not to be avoided. Sam, who had prided himself on never having hated anyone (unless you counted certain people, such as Hitler, whom he had never known personally), was, for the first time in his life, filled with hatred. He hated not merely someone he knew; he hated his neighbor. An ancient and unforgivable sin! It was as if this insignificant little man had touched some deep insecurity he had not imagined he possessed. His open, optimistic nature had been dealt a death blow. It was too shameful a revelation to confess, even to Alice.

Zeigler-Laiken was only a few blocks from Laiken, Baxter and Brown, and yet it was a different world altogether. A neighborhood of architectural offices, import-export firms, elegant antique shops, chic decorators, boutiques. Opening the oversized door that said ZEIGLER-LAIKEN in magnagraphics, Sam felt like Rip Van Winkle, returning to old, but no longer familiar, haunts.

A showplace, no question about it. The walls were sandblasted to reveal the "honesty" of the old brick. The underpinnings of the structure showed, were part of the architectural intent. A ceiling of heavy wooden beams; criss-cross steel eye-beams for support. Exposed heating, plumbing, and electrical ducts primed in orange. Baskets of tropical ferns hung from the beams; tapestries, woven with hemp and beads, and immense canvases—brightly colored acrylic shapes—decorated the walls. The place reeked of flair and style and, despite Calderwell's yearnings to escape his former environment, of Los Angeles.

The immense space was divided, cleverly, into glass cubicles, one of which was Sam's office. The old rolltop desk, along with the other old furnishings from Laiken, Baxter and Brown, was gone, replaced by severe modular pieces. There was no place for bulletin boards, personal mementoes, photographs. The beer sign and the tray had been wrapped in brown paper and stowed away in a drawer out of sight; he assumed this was meant to tell him something.

Calderwell occupied a cubicle not far from his. In the front, in a kind of bullpen, were the secretaries and copy girls. Linda and Sharon were gone. The receptionist was a stylish Black girl; one of the secretaries was Chinese; Calderwell's private secretary was English with an upper-class accent. Sam sat down at the flat expanse of desk and, not knowing precisely what was expected of him, took out a memo pad and wrote a long letter to Cindy. It was several hours before Calderwell appeared in his doorway, greeted him with a friendly air, and introduced him to the staff. Then he vanished again, without offering any direction. Sam called young Perkins, who was on vacation, then one of his insurance accounts to make sure they had received notice of the change. An Iranian in a dark suit came in to confer with Calderwell. At noon, Sam walked several blocks back to the old neighborhood and had lunch, alone, at the counter at Tadich's. He spent the remainder of the day acquainting himself with the computer program for Cost-Benefit analysis for Media Selection. His only interruption was from the bookkeeper, who dropped a sealed envelope on his desk. It was a bill for his Bohemian Club dues. A mistake, no doubt, but he could wait until things had settled down a bit before bringing the matter to Calderwell's attention.

The Isles of Greece! Crete. Mykonos. Delos. Rhodes. From Rhodes, Cindy wrote that, if she had more money, she would go on, during the Fall, to India, Kathmandu, Japan. After all, here she was almost halfway around the world! It would be a cop-out to turn back now. Whole new vistas were opening up to her. If money was a problem, only a small amount would do. She could always hitchhike and sleep in parks. It would be worth it, for such an education.

The word *education* did it. Sam took out a second mortgage on the house and sent her a money order that would cover decent hotels; in places like India, where cows counted more than human beings, it was important not to take chances.

"My daughter's seeing the world before she's trapped by the Establishment," he told the woman at the American Express.

Sam drove to work, now. The new office was just far enough away from the station to make it impractical to walk from the train; cabs were unreliable. He had given Alice the Mercedes; kept the old Ford wagon for himself. But the wagon was not in shape for the long drive to the City, and he was obliged to leave it for her. She was doing her last-minute cramming for her Real Estate exam and often arrived home after he did. Though he had tried to teach her to use the stick shift properly, the grind of the gears always announced her arrival.

She's not dumb: wrecking the transmission is her way of getting back at me, he thought helplessly.

She had other ways, too. She had grown penurious. Wasn't it time to ask for a raise? Driving in was expensive. Had he brought this to What's-his-name's attention?

"Those New Yorkers respect assertiveness. They aren't going to just hand you things on a silver platter."

"You'll have to let me feel my own way, play it by ear. I'll know when the right time comes."

"Judgment Day?" said Alice.

The meals she served were sermons. Lentils and sesame seeds *combined* were a sufficient amount of protein. Americans ate too much meat, anyhow. Frozen orange juice (which he could not stomach) was cheaper and just as nutritious as fresh oranges. Cabbage had *more* vitamins than lettuce. It was silly to buy name brands; you just paid for the advertising. (No offense intended!)

This last crusade he found especially vicious. All of his life, even though his family had not been well-off, he had been served Best Foods mayonnaise. The shape of the bottle, its familiar yellow and blue label, represented, for him, a kind of security, a time-honored and gracious tradition. Morality, too, was involved. The cheap brands she brought home were symbols of eroding values. Like an alcoholic, he contemplated hiding a bottle of Best Foods in the toilet tank.

In the interests of ecology and economy and sadism, she had become a ruthless energy saver. He came home to a house illuminated by one lamp with low wattage bulbs. She tracked him relentlessly from room to room, switching off lights. She wore an old ski sweater indoors and refused to let him turn on the furnace. If he ran the shower over three minutes, she tapped, like a schoolmarm, on the shower door. Hot showers, he told her, eased his aching joints. His joints would ache more when he got the utility bill, she said.

And this was not all. She informed him they could no longer afford to heat the pool all year round. For exercise, he could ride Cindy's bike—once a handsome ten-speed, now a rusted heap of junk. He had it repaired, but his reflexes were programmed to brake with his foot, and the first time he rode it down the Lane he slammed into a parked car and fell off. He lay on the pavement, surrounded by a group of kindly children.

"Are you hurt bad, Mr. Winkle?" one of them said.

"Shall I call my mother?" said another.

He rose, pain-ridden, and pushed the bike home.
"She's trying to kill me, that's evident," he told himself.
Other recreational pursuits were rationed, too. New movies could wait until they became reruns; the theater was out; also dinner in the City. Even a cheap Basque restaurant, which he had enjoyed, involved driving in; gasoline would have to be added to the price of the meal. They not only could not afford it; it was ecologically unsound.

"We'll just have to develop simple pleasures," she said.

She's developed hers—harassing me, thought Sam. We're like a comic-strip couple. Too old for Blondie and Dagwood. Maggie and Jiggs? Did the new comics portray this kind of domestic horror? He had stopped reading the Funnies, and this, too, was undoubtedly a bad sign—a symptom of senility, particularly harmful for someone who worked in the Media.

The pace Calderwell set for himself was extraordinary. Conference calls. "In conference." Dashing out for an appointment. Ushering in clients—a representative of an Eastern textile firm, a motel chain, a national travel agency, a dog-food manufacturer, a Houston oil company, the head of the Moroccan Travel Bureau (who, according to Agatha, the English secretary, was a member of the Moroccan Royal Family). Meeting with media people from television, radio, newspapers, and magazines; a marketing-analysis consultant; the woman with frosted hair from New York. Catching planes to Houston, Los Angeles, New York, Casablanca, Tokyo (with a stopover in Tehran), Algeria (with a stopover in Kuwait). In between, he sent Agatha out to pick up his cuff links at the jewelers or buy flowers for his wife or a five-foot Stieff giraffe for his son's birthday. One Wednesday he hurried off to deliver a speech at the San Francisco Ad Club, a duty that Baxter and Brown had been happy to turn over to Sam and that he had, heretofore, happily performed.

They'll ask about me; he'll find out from them I'm an Old Hand over there. Everyone shows up for my talks and enjoys them, too. Still, he needs the exposure at the moment. For the time being, it's the right thing for him to do.

Calderwell's only recreation, it seemed, took place in the bullpen on his way in and out of the office. Here, he would adopt his lazy, lizard manner; dally, for brief moments, massaging a girl's neck, talking to her in a whispery way. With them, he assumed the role of Lay Analyst or Father Confessor. He was greedy to learn their most intimate problems, devouring them, like a hungry man over a quick lunch.

Passing Sam, he'd say, "Wanda's having love problems. Her old man's split." Or, "I told Suki to take the afternoon off. Her new IUD is giving her cramps." Or, "Candy thinks she's frigid. I gave her a book of exercises to help women reach climax. *Orgasm and You.* If I had a teenage daughter, I'd make her memorize it. Did you catch that steam-beer spot on Channel 2 last night? Would you write me a memo? I'd appreciate your opinion about it. Well, I'm off to Fantasyland. There's a foxy stewardess on the plane who can't decide about having an abortion. She confides in me. It's a responsibility, but what can you do?"

He needs some recreation, thought Sam. And the girls like it. It's a mystery, but they do. If I didn't know how devoted he was to his wife . . . But, it's all in fun, I suppose. He'll slow down one of these days, when he feels more confident, and delegate more authority to me.

Sam parked his car in the garage under Portsmouth Square, a few blocks from the Agency. The dimly lit series of floors reminded him of illustrations he had seen when he had once tried to help Cindy write a book report on *The Inferno* for her Senior English class. The gray cement walls were scrawled with graffiti, and gasoline fumes mingled with the smell of urine. On an early Monday morning, he parked on the lowest level, got out, squeezed between the car in the next stall, and, suddenly, felt a hard metal object thrust into his back. A male voice ordered him to stay where he was, drop his wallet on the floor, and not move for ten minutes if he valued his life. He complied.

When he reached the office he called the police. It took four transfers and long waits before he reached the correct department. The officer in charge took Sam's name, address, age; the name of the garage, description of the wallet; its contents (his credit cards, fifty dollars, snapshots of Alice ar.d Cindy).

"How old did you say you were?" he asked again.

"Fifty-seven."

"Oh, yeah, that one."

"Which one?"

"We call him the Senior Citizen bandit. He preys on Senior Citizens. I doubt if there's much we can do, but we're always happy to have people call. Don't hesitate to ring us again if there are any more problems."

The policeman's response had been disappointing. Adrenaline still pulsed through his body, and he toured the office telling people of his adventure. Everyone took a polite interest. He was advised to try another garage, not to carry so much cash. Twenty dollars would do. They got mad if you didn't have anything. One of the copy girls asked if the robber were a Black. Sam recalled that he had had a Southern accent.

"That figures," she said.

"Put yourself in their position," he told her, in an excited voice. "We brought them over here in the holds of slave ships. They didn't ask to come. It doesn't mean they're natural thieves. They've never had a chance."

The girl gave him a patronizing smile. "My boyfriend works in a Welfare office," she said, and resumed her work.

The next morning there was a small item on the back page of the *Chronicle*.

SENIOR CITIZEN BANDIT
STRIKES AGAIN

The story gave Sam's name and age and was followed by a warning from the Chief of Police to all Senior Citizens concerning precautions they should take. He cursed himself for having reported the incident.

That's what you get for performing your civic duty, these days, he said to himself.

On August 8, Sam and Alice sat on the patio and listened to the President's resignation speech. Alice had wanted to invite friends in, make a party out of it, but Sam had refused. The fact was he found her delight distasteful; it was as if she were dancing on Democracy's grave. After the speech he went into the kitchen and mixed himself a Scotch. His hand trembled. He had just witnessed not only the disgrace of one man but the disgrace of his beloved country. Alice's pointing out that this very resignation proved that the System still worked did nothing at all to alleviate his sorrow. Bad Times are ahead, he thought gloomily.

A second bill for the Bohemian Club dues was put on his desk, and this time someone had underlined the *overdue*.

"I don't need the membership anymore," he decided. "I'll miss it, in a way, but it will make up for the expense of driving in. Besides, it goes against my principles."

This last was the reason he gave to Alice.

"Oh, thank God," she cried. "I've been humiliated about that for years. I tell people you hate it but are forced to belong, but, after a while, you get tired of apologizing. I hope you told them *why* you're resigning?"

"I think they'll get the idea."

"Maybe you should write a letter to the *Chronicle*, so it's on public record. I'll be glad to dictate it for you. I'll even write it and you can sign it," she said.

Fortunately, the mail arrived with a card from Cindy from Afghanistan. Afghanistan was outrageously far-out, but she could hardly wait for India. In India they were going to visit Baba Somebody, unless he was in Kathmandu. If he was in Kathmandu, they would go to Kathmandu to sit at his feet.

Sit at his feet? Some fakir in a filthy turban? Why should Cindy sit at anyone's feet? How relieved he was that she was about to wind up this Travel business and would soon be back on home soil.

Alice had passed her Real Estate exam and been hired by an established Palo Alto Real Estate firm. She would begin work in January. Many of their friends were beginning to move from Vista Verde, giving up their old family homes and buying condominiums or smaller houses; more would follow. She would get these listings, she said with enthusiasm.

Women need to feel they're not just homemakers, these days. It's probably just a passing fancy, but if it makes her happy, that's the important thing, Sam thought.

She was keeping an eye out for the right condominium for them, too, she told him. Their own house was ridiculously large, expensive and difficult to keep up; the taxes were staggering.

But to this, he shut his ears. Vista Verde was not only their home, it was Cindy's, too. Even when she married, she would want to come back to her old room. Wasn't this, after all, what a home was for?

In November, Alice began to pore over cookbooks. Cindy would fly back from Tokyo, be with them for Christmas Eve. She was considering a goose instead of the traditional turkey.

"Why not traditional?" said Sam. Cindy had been out of the country, now, for two years. She was probably dreaming of hamburgers, barbecued chicken, fresh vegetables, milk. For Christmas she would want turkey, mashed potatoes, creamed onions, Brussels sprouts. A mince pie and a pumpkin pie and a plum pudding. Maybe an apple pie, later on. He would make the pies; Alice, the pudding. This was how it should be.

He began to think about Cindy's Christmas present. The occasion, he thought, called for something special. Cindy's old Fiat was still in their carport. It had been easy to persuade her not to drive it East the first time, but she was older now. What if she took it into her head to drive this year? In the winter, too. Even here, during the holidays, he would worry. She had not driven for a long time. Moreover—though he took the car out regularly to keep it in running order—it was slow to start. It could stall on a freeway or at an intersection. If anything happened, she had more of a chance in a newer machine. He broached the matter to Alice, who, despite this new miserly kick, had never stinted when it came to Cindy's welfare. He had, he said, a BMW 2002 in mind. The snappy little Fiat could hardly be replaced with a conservative Chevy or Ford. Cindy would want something with a bit of flair. The BMW met this qualification and was reliable, as well. Didn't she agree that they had no choice when it came to their daughter's *safety?*

Unexpectedly, she did not. He was stunned—not only by the fact that she disagreed, but even more by her reasons, which he regarded as flimsy excuses to hide a hardened heart.

It was not "in" to drive fancy cars anymore, she informed him. Moreover, Cindy had just visited impoverished countries, seen, with her own eyes, the grossly unfair division of wealth. She would not come back the same girl. Already, Alice had caught hints in her correspondence of a new outlook, a feeling of the evils of the American Success Ethic.

"I've sometimes felt she dropped out of college because we pushed her into becoming an Overachiever," she said.

"What do you mean, 'dropped out.' She's going back to school!"

"She hasn't mentioned a word about it, lately. It's just a feeling I have . . ."

To hell with Alice's "feelings," he thought. Her new career had made her *unfeeling.* She had grown cold and calloused, her human and maternal instincts had atrophied.

I'll follow my own instincts. I'll go whole hog, he decided.

He pictured Cindy's starry eyes. "Oh, Daddy!" she would say.

The dealer did not have the color Sam wanted in stock (pumpkin orange—foxy *and* safe). He could get it, however, from another lot and have it for him on the twenty-fourth, the day Cindy would arrive from Tokyo. Sam could pick it up in the morning, keep it in the Jessups' garage, and, on

Christmas day, when Cindy had slept off her jet lag (if he could wait that long!), present it to her.

One more Schultz surprise. A bad one. On an evening two weeks before Christmas, Sam drove home from the City. On Manzanita Lane, he slowed down to take in the outdoor decorations. A single star on the top of a stately pine on the Mayfields' lawn. Rows of candles in paper bags, like fairy lanterns, lined the path to the Jessups' house. The Hanlys' boxwood hedge was sprinkled with miniature lights, like fireflies. Last weekend Sam had strung clear bulbs on their pomegranate tree, outlining its bare branches, producing the effect of an abstract painting. There were no street lamps in Vista Verde; the Association had voted them down to keep the country ambience. The darkness of the Lane made the discreet holiday illuminations even more magical.

The Lane turned just before his house. Alice would have turned on the pomegranate by now. He looked forward to a second look, inspecting his creation from the perspective of a passerby. But a passerby would not have noticed; he, like Sam, would have been overpowered by Schultz's production.

Perched on the top of Schultz's roof was a giant red-and-white Santa, his bag of goodies slung over one shoulder, ready to pop down the crooked stage chimney to distribute gifts to the good Schultz kids. The Santa was illuminated by a rosy light, so triggered that it went on and off in brief nervous intervals like a neon cocktail sign. Cardboard? Plastic? What was the thing made of? Driving closer, Sam saw that it was a balloon, puffed up by helium, held by a guy wire attached to its feet and extending across the roof, down to the Schultz lawn, where it was fastened to a stake. He pictured Schultz in his workshop setting the thing up; then on his roof, scuttling about; Mrs. Schultz and the five Schultzes standing below, watching in admiration. Schultz, thought Sam, had outdone himself!

But even this new horror could not disturb his euphoria. Cindy was coming home.

He did not go into the City on Christmas Eve. Calderwell's style of office party would not be his cup of tea, anyhow. He stopped at the car dealer's and picked up the BMW. It had a purr; the black leather seats smelled of luxury; the stereo had a good clear tone. He was edgy with excitement, and there was no hurry; Alice would be on her way to the airport. He drove the long way home, tried it on the freeway fast; cornered it on country roads, then drove leisurely into Vista Verde, listening to the news.

A Christmas Truce in Lebanon. The Pope's Message to the World. The President's message to the nation. An American couple named Mary and Joseph had just arrived in Bethlehem to give birth to their baby, there. A medley of Christmas carols.

> *Peace on Earth, and mercy mild*
> *God and sinners reconciled!*

He hummed this tune as he stopped at the shopping center for champagne.

"Merry Christmas, Mr. Winkle," said the clerk, as he handed Sam his package.

"Yes, it's going to be a merry one," said Sam. "Mrs. Winkle may have told you. Cindy's coming home after two years abroad. We've gone all out and bought her a new BMW . . ."

"Lucky girl," said the clerk.

"Lucky parents," said Sam.

He parked the car in the Jessups' garage, as prearranged, and removed the keys, which he would wrap in a box and put under the Tree. Just the keys? On white cotton? Maybe a note, too? Or why not a funny, cryptic verse?

> *Try out this little key*
> *The lock it opens is for thee.*

Something like that.

He walked up the Lane to his house. The lights of the

neon Santa flickered over the cul-de-sac, danced on his face, hands, shoes. He felt no animosity. He was full of good tidings, merciful even to Schultz. The pomegranate tree had not been turned on; Alice must have left in a hurry. She had not turned on the Tree in the living room, either. He plugged it in; lit the candles around the Danish crèche.

> *Hark! the Herald Angels sing*
> *This key unlocks a special thing?*

The kitchen door opened, giving him a start. Alice stood in the doorway. She was dressed for the airport in a suit. She held a drink in her hand. It was not like her to drink alone, nor was it like her to drink before driving. His heart gave a leap. Was Cindy here already? But she said nothing. Then he noticed that her face was red and puffy, clumsily coated with powder.

"Cindy?"

"What about her?"

"Where is she? Why aren't you at the airport?" A pulse in his throat pounded, and his knees felt oddly weak. "Is any thing wrong?" he said.

"Wrong? What could be wrong?" Her voice was different, almost flippant, her composure sinister. A horrid little smile played on her lips. "She just called, as a matter of fact. To wish us a Merry Christmas."

"She *called!* From where?"

"Maui. Or was it the other one? I have the number written down."

"Did she miss her plane?" He felt a dreadful letdown.

She shook her head, no.

"Then, why—?"

"I told you. She wanted to wish us a Merry Christmas." She came into the room, sat down on one of the Barcelona chairs, sipped at her drink. She looked at Sam. "Oh, sorry," she said. "May I fix you one?"

There had been times, during their marriage, particularly in the last few years, when Sam had thought she bore him ill will; he had dismissed the thought as unseemly. He could, no longer; it was apparent that she did not want him to dismiss it. Otherwise, why would she be toying with him so cruelly, relishing his torment? He stared at his feet, held his breath, and prayed that she would be merciful and administer the coup de grace.

But it was not to be. The way she settled down in the chair, the false bright smile. The calculated calmness.

"Why don't you put that drink down and tell me."

"Nobody's going to tell me to put my drink down." There was venom in her voice now. Then she burst into tears. "She's not coming for Christmas; she's going to have a baby!" She stood up, spilling some of the drink. Her face turned white, and he thought she might faint. He rose to catch her, but, though she swayed, she did not fall. "The turkey!" she cried. "Oh, Christ, I forgot to baste the turkey!"

An hour or so later—still reeling from shock—he tried to make sense out of it. It seemed that Cindy had met this boy. An American boy. In Italy. Not a college student. No. This fellow didn't believe in colleges, in acquiring knowledge in the Western Conceptual Intellectualized tradition. He relied, instead, on the right, the instinctive, side of the brain.

"On the *what* side? No, no, never mind. Go on."

Just a boy. Some Drop Out who had sailed into Florence on his Vespa, filled with a flimsy idealism, of ways to set the world right, who, in his arrogant self-righteousness, had toppled the foundations of Sam's world. A really "Beautiful Individual." This was how Cindy had described him. She and this Beautiful Individual had been living together since last Christmas, had been traveling together ever since. They were pilgrims on pilgrimage, seeking the Truth. The Path.

"The What?"

"You know, the Meaning!"

On his money? Supported by a second mortgage on his house? He didn't get it.

"What is there to get?"

Cindy and this Beautiful Individual were above gross material matters, such as second mortgages.

"Ah!"

In India, Revelation had come to them from the Baba. Now, they could never face another American commercial Christmas, again.

"Ah—!"

They were going to celebrate, but it would be a different sort of celebration. A spiritual one. Jesus was one of many Avatars.

"One of what? No, please, continue."

It was to be a Feast of Love, not an exchange of store-bought gifts.

A Feast of Love? He could think of a different word for it.

"You see, it's a different Life-Style," said his Social Psychologist–Sadist wife.

Cindy and the Beautiful Individual were going to celebrate the birth of Jesus and the approaching birth of their child.

"Approaching? When approaching?"

"It's due in three months. Everything's going nicely. She's been to a holistic health center and is taking natural childbirth lessons. There was a little bleeding in Japan, but that's all over. They're thinking of the birth as a celebration. They've been given a special Mantra to recite," said Midwife Alice.

Was she *married* to this person?

Yes. And no. They had performed some ceremony of their own. They did not believe the government had the right to sanction sacramental unions. They were entitled to their own beliefs. They were, after all, grown-up.

"I grew up. You grew up. We didn't drop bombs. We didn't break ourselves off with a phone call."

"Who said anything about her breaking off? She didn't want to come home without our knowing, that's all. She wanted to give us time to adjust to the news."

"How very thoughtful!"

"Yes, she's terribly excited."

"Please forgive me for bringing up anything so crass, but how do she and this—Beautiful Individual—plan to support this child?"

Well, naturally, she would not go to college. She had come to that decision, anyhow. After Baby was born, she would get a job of some kind.

Maybe a cocktail hostess?

"We didn't go into details. The important thing is—babies have to eat."

"You mean, that's occurred to her?"

"We might send her to business college."

"*Business* college!"

"You're in business. I'm in business."

"I'm in business to support my family."

"You like the Media. It suits you to a T. Anyhow, life must go on. Besides, I saw the Handwriting on the Wall last Christmas."

"You saw—what?"

"I tried to tell you, but you shut me off. Please stop that ridiculous groaning. You know what I thought when I heard the news this evening? I thought, Sam will be more of a problem than the problem. I was right, too. You're just upset about the car. The car is a symbol of what she's rejecting."

"Please don't give me any shit about symbols, if you don't mind. If you saw signs, portents, it was your duty to tell me. We might have done something—"

"Like what?" said Alice.

She had, despite all this, served Christmas dinner. It didn't matter that he could not bear the thought of food—in particular, a Christmas feast. She had prepared one; he would eat it if he choked. The turkey (dry), the mashed potatoes (raw), the Brussels sprouts (overdone), the creamed onions (lukewarm) stuck in his craw.

A nice case of indigestion would result from this. How much tougher she was than he! He marveled at her resiliency. Of course, people who did not have deep feelings had an advantage here. If Women's Lib succeeded, it would not be because women were equal; it was because they were survivors.

Then adjustment! (Already, she was probably thinking of baby clothes!) A little cry. Then life, as she had said, must go on. He wondered why. His world crumbled, and she asked, in her hostess voice, for his opinion of the Julia Child stuffing? Even her animosity toward him had evaporated. Shallow—even in this department!

The only sign that she was not wholly herself was that she served dessert without clearing the table. Plum pudding on a polished silver tray. Decorated with sprigs of holly.

"It's not a plum pudding, actually. It's a carrot pudding."

"Shit pudding, for all I care."

"Pardon?"

"Nothing."

She poured a good half-bottle of brandy over it, lit a match, and dropped it into the liquid. Flames leaped up, enveloping her face; there was an odor of singed hair. Sam grabbed the platter from her. Tongues of fire darted toward him, and he dropped it on the floor.

"The pudding! Oh, the pudding!" she cried, staring at the mess. She began to weep. Large sorrowful tears poured from her eyes. "You've ruined the pudding. Darling, you'll have to excuse me. I think I've had a bit too much of Christmas cheer." She bent over him, kissed his forehead. "Merry Christmas, darling," she said, then staggered off to bed.

In a moment, she was back. She held a package, which she handed to him. It was a gold paper plate covered in Saran Wrap, tied with a red ribbon. He stared at it with dulled eyes. It seemed to contain Christmas cookies.

"It's for the Schultzes, darling. I meant to take it over before I left for the airport. You take it, please." She giggled. "I wouldn't want the Schultzes to see me in this shape." She staggered away again; popped back.

"You mustn't worry, darling," she said, "everything's going to be all right." Once more she tottered off; this time he heard the bedroom door close, the plop of a body falling on the bed.

The Schultzes! He held the package gingerly, as if it might be a bomb. She had made cookies for the Schultzes? Cindy was coming home—*had* been coming home—and she had thought of Schultzes! Now, Cindy was not coming home—anyhow, not the same Cindy. Yet she had thought of them. Of Schultzes. Cindy. Schultzes. Puddings. Her lack of taste was a source of both wonder and revulsion.

He put the package down upon the sideboard, stepped over the pudding, picked up the brandy bottle and a glass, and went into the living room. He pulled the plug from the Tree, blew out the candles, sat down in the Boston rocker, and poured brandy into the glass. His eyes roamed the room wildly. The walls, on which he had once lavished so much thought—the right grade, the right grain, the right finish— closed in on him; he felt stifled, as if the lid had just been slammed down upon his coffin. The snuffed candles gave off an aromatic, funereal odor. The Tree, already beginning to dry out, reminded him of a withered floral offering on a grave. His mouth tasted of ashes, death. In the old days, he thought, a man might have gnashed his teeth, torn his hair, wailed, rent his garments, beat up his wife. None of this was now acceptable. There was only despair and booze.

He sat there until he had finished the bottle, then went back to the sideboard for more. There were the gaily wrapped cookies. The Schultzes had not only destroyed his view, dominated the cul-de-sac, invaded his patio and his dreams—now they intruded upon his most private agony. The little package pointed up the vanity of all that he had once held so dear.

Life must go on? Well, either it did or it didn't! He glanced at the carving knife, which lay beside the ravished bird. In less fundamental matters, she was often right; she had erred in this. There was nothing to stop him from picking up the knife and slitting his throat. He saw himself on the floor, the knife through his heart. (The heart, not the throat, would be the appropriate target.) He saw his life's blood merging with the congealed pudding. He saw Alice on hands and knees, soaking up blood and pudding into one sponge. Life must go on, she was saying.

Since it made no difference, one way or the other; since such a grand gesture would not be grand at all, but only call for a sponge, what could he do? He could try it her way. Suppress his finer feelings (unnecessary, in her case), arm himself with cynicism, play the charade. Cindy. Puddings. Schultzes. In the long run, all of equal importance, which was to say, of no importance at all. What a pity he had taken the easy out and studied Spanish instead of Greek or Latin—languages better equipped to deal with the present crisis.

Cindy-um. Pudding-um. Schultz-ium. Omnium-um?

What a cruel trick of fortune that he had no coat of arms on which to emblazon such a motto. The circumstances cried out for some outward form or expression. If not a coat of arms—a ritual, a dramatization. They did something in the Catholic Church with ashes, he recalled. Sprinkled them on their foreheads, a reminder of the vanity of all earthly desires. Ashes to ashes. Dust to dust. Omnium Unum. Cindy. Puddings. Schultzes.

Why not take the cookies to the Schultzes? An empty gesture of this sort was meaningful in its lack of meaning. It was symbolic, ceremonial—not unsimilar to the ashes business. The idea dazzled him.

He peered out of the window. It was only 9:45, but the Schultzes retired early. Their lights were still on; Christmas Eve was evidently an exception. He snatched up the plate of cookies and went out the front door.

The atrocity on Schultz's roof illuminated his way. He climbed the street, walked up the flagstone path, and rang their bell. The bell played a mawkish welcoming tune. Sam had watched Schultz rig it up one day. Whom was it meant to welcome, he had wondered? Certainly, it was not ringing now to welcome him. This fact gave him bitter satisfaction.

Inside the house, the Doberman snarled. He heard Schultz's voice: "Down. Stay."

Schultz answered the door, the one-man beast in back of him, crouched, ready at his Master's command to spring at his throat. Sam felt almost apologetic to disappoint him. Schultz's big eyes blinked warily, as if he, too, suspected he might be opening his door to an assassin. He was wearing a clumsily hand-knit blue coat sweater and new bright-blue fuzzy slippers. He stared at Sam with a puzzled expression.

"Merry Christmas," said Sam, heartily.

"Yes, yes, Merry Christmas to you."

"I've come bearing gifts." He held out the plate.

Schultz reached for it, but Sam pulled it back. Schultz had only opened the door a crack, barely wide enough for a man to slip through, but Sam was adroit; he stepped in sideways and entered their living room for the first time since the Schultzes had been in residence.

The room was hot, oppressive. The gas-lit logs glowed in the fireplace. The mantel was decorated with knick-knacks—coy ceramic skunks and wide-eyed does, color photographs of the children in stiff poses, dressed in their Sunday Best. Hung from the mantel were five red-felt stockings, each with a name embroidered upon it. Above the fireplace, a red-and-white sampler—another of Mrs. Schultz's creations, no doubt—which read, GOD BLESS OUR HAPPY HOME. Overstuffed Best Buys, swathed in Mrs. Schultz's chintz slipcovers, crowded the room; their massive, formless shapes reminded Sam of Mrs. Schultz herself. A maple whatnot, in one corner, held a collection of china cups, dainty, pastel colored—Mrs. Schultz's one indulgence? A Christmas Tree—another Best Buy, judging from its shape—sat on a coffee table, which was a copy of an Early American cobbler's bench, made, obviously, by Schultz.

The doors to the dining room were open, and the rest of the Schultzes were still seated at the table, which was covered with a white lace cloth. The four moon-faced, cropped-haired little boys, who had begun to put on flesh like their mother, and the girl! The girl smiled at him. Surrounded by her gross and sluggish family, she seemed more fragile, more ethereal than ever. In his dreams, he had ravished her (or tried), but his conscience no longer troubled him. Despite her delicacy, she was, he now knew, made of no rarer stuff than the rest. His heart had hardened toward her.

He walked boldly past Schultz into the dining room. "My wife baked these for you," he said coldly, and handed the plate of cookies to Mrs. Schultz, trying at the same time to force her, by strength of ill will, to meet his eyes. But she was skilled at avoiding such a violation; she inclined her head without looking up; nodded at the girl. The girl rose and took the plate from him, smiling again at Sam. Green eyes. Flecked with gold. Agate eyes. It didn't matter.

"Oh, please thank Mrs. Winkle for us," she said. Her voice was a virginal whisper. Ha ha! A woman's tongue dripped honey, but her hindparts were as bitter as wormwood. He had read that somewhere. How it fitted this occasion. A shy and girlish voice, concealing a callow, and sluttish heart! Like *all* of them!

"Yes," he said. "Of course."

Schultz, wriggling and dancing, was edging toward the front door. As if to emphasize his intention, the miniature door of the cuckoo clock over the sideboard burst open, and the bird emerged; it uttered ten piercing cuckoos. This was followed by an uneasy silence. It was plain that all parties were waiting for him to leave.

And yet he stood there, as if rooted, staring at this dining-room scene. It was as if he were suddenly gazing, not at Schultz, not at real people at all, but at a kind of diorama, like one of those historical tableaux one saw in wax museums. This one was labeled:

TYPICAL AMERICAN CHRISTMAS,
TWENTIETH CENTURY

There was a timelessness, and—despite his new philosophy—a poignancy to the scene. All over America, similar ones were being enacted tonight. A similar one would have been enacted in his own home—if circumstances had not intervened. Ah, but circumstances had. He knew what the Schultzes, in their ruthless self-sufficiency, hid from themselves. Like the wax museum, their domestic felicity was Make-Believe.

How vulnerable they are, he thought. He longed to address them rhetorically.

You feel so safe, so insular, but a few words (a phone call, for example), and the whole structure is gone.

Schultz, however, was halfway to the door; the little boys and Mrs. Schultz were intent upon their pie. Only the girl watched him—the false, innocent smile still on her lips. No, he could not make his speech; it would not be well received. He was helpless to warn them. Let them find out for themselves!

He turned and walked back through the living room; Schultz, dancing ahead of him, opened the door.

"Merry Christmas," said Sam, in a tone used commonly to express condolences.

"Yes, yes. Same to you, neighbor. Same to you."

He walked down the lighted path into the street. Suddenly, the night turned dark. He was briefly puzzled. Then he realized that Schultz—waiting for him to reach the bottom step—had turned off the Santa. Was he afraid he might appear with another gift and further disturb their tranquility?

They don't need me to disturb it, he thought. There are other forces—far more malignant than I.

But something else had happened when Schultz had turned off the Santa; at the same time, he had turned on the stars. Hundreds. Thousands. Billions—even scientists had never counted all of them—sparkled above him in the inky heavens.

Stars! The Universe! A vast void, empty and hostile. How could anyone ever have thought it anything else? Yet people had ... This particular human frailty had existed since man walked the earth. Savages had put on makeup and frolicked, hoping for favors. People and animals were sacrificed; heretics burned; inquisitions carried out in the name of one True Faith or another. On a night such as this, wise men—philosophers, kings—had followed one of these stars to worship a baby. Folklore, Alice called it. How right she was! So much for what people called religion!

The same was true for domestic felicity. One "fell in love"—that was what one called it—sired a child, propagated the species; pinned one's hopes and dreams on this progeny, and this, too, was as phony a proposition as the other.

He crossed the street, still gaping up at the gaseous immensity. The stars glittered back, malicious, mocking. They have my number. Schultz's, too, poor fellow. Both of us have made unwarranted assumptions, entertained false expectations; isolated ourselves in our Mouse Houses. Oh, yes, I have been just as wrong-headed, as smug, as Schultz. The difference was that Schultz still labored under an illusion and he did not.

I was remiss. I should have spoken. It was my duty to warn him, and I backed away. I am chicken-hearted and contemptible. Lacking in mettle and courage. There is no gallantry in me.

He could feel the effects of the brandy now. It seemed to clear his brain, provide inspiration.

If I fail in this last obligation to a poor fellow creature, I am not even worthy of being called a man.

But what to do? How to discharge this duty? He suddenly knew. Crouching low, in a criminal attitude, he ran furtively back across the street and up the steps to Schultz's lawn. There, on his knees, in the starlight, he felt for and found the stake that held the Santa's wire. With all his strength he pulled on it; it popped up, and he fell backward, still clutching it in both hands. He felt a tug, looked up, and saw that the Santa had toppled sideways. He scrambled to his feet, and hanging on as one hung on to a straining kite, he staggered backward again; feeling his way with one foot, then the other. Down the steps, into the Lane, into the middle of the cul-de-sac. He wound the wire around the stake and pulled the Santa toward him. On the edge of the

Schultzes' roof, the Santa paused, hesitated, then took off, floating majestically away into the air.

When it was almost above him, safe from any obstacles, Sam dropped the stake. Slowly, solemnly, the old saint ascended. The stake dangled from the wire. Up, up, he went, poised for a moment in a cross current of breezes, then up and away, sailing over the roofs and treetops of Vista Verde, until, at last, he was only a small dot, difficult to distinguish among the brighter constellations.

Sam watched from a squatting position in the Lane until the Santa dot had vanished over the horizon. The phone lines were no doubt busy, he thought dreamily. People calling the newspapers, the police, the National Guard, the United States Army. Reporting an Unidentified Flying Object in the night sky. An airline pilot radioing a report of it to his control tower. A bearded guru, perhaps, on some mountaintop had sighted it and was now prophesying a New Millennium. Shepherds in the field—were there still shepherds in the field at night?—huddled together in wonder at the strange and marvelous apparition. He recalled his ancestors—those clever, noble men, with their globes and charts and telescopes, who had also observed mysterious celestial bodies. How fitting it all was! Poor Schultz. A peasant. His eyes, as well as his feet, firmly on the ground. He wondered if Schultz had ever looked at stars.

Alice was sitting in bed, bolt upright. She had combed her hair; the puffiness in her face had subsided. She looked alert, ready for steps, measures.

"Where have you been?" she said. She did not wait for a reply. "I've been thinking, we should call Cindy back. Tonight. *You* should talk to her, assure her. She knows you're stuffy, but she dotes on you. The poor girl is probably on pins and needles. She called because she was afraid to come home. Call and wish her a Merry Christmas. After all, it's a very special one. We're about to become grandparents—you and I!"

So! That's what it's all about, even though it's not about

anything, he thought. Christmas Eve. The birth of a baby. A
new Life. An awesome thing. As awesome in its way as
stars. So certain dreams were shattered—who had asked
him to dream them? On the whole, babies were more satisfactory than dreams. You could cuddle babies. Poke them.
Get them to coo, make gurgling noises. You could give them
rattles and teddy bears; later on, bicycles. You could make a
fuss over babies—in particular, your own grandchild.

"Then it's all right?"

"Yes, yes. Call."

She had the number on a piece of paper in her hand. She
picked up the phone and dialed. "You were gone so long,"
she said, as she waited. "I worried about you. You haven't
seemed yourself lately. I was thinking, maybe you should
consult somebody who . . ." She spoke cautiously, "who is an
authority on the emotional problems of well . . . the aging
syndrome. It's a very common problem at your time of life.
It happens to everyone."

"Yes, yes. Well, I've had a few things on my mind." He
tried to think what they were. His work. He would leave the
Agency. The idea had occurred to him, but now it was no
longer just an idea; it was a decision. He would open up a
small office of his own. In Palo Alto. Buy a rolltop desk and
put up the beer sign and beer tray and photographs of his
grandchild. He would choose his own clients, run things his
own way. A Peninsula ice-cream chain and an Organic Food
manufacturer from Santa Cruz had approached him recently, but the accounts were too small for Zeigler-Laiken.
He would not have Zeigler-Laiken's overhead. There were
political candidates, too, who needed their campaigns managed. Local supervisors, legislative representatives, council-
men. He would handle the campaigns of those he would
vote for, anyhow; have the pleasure of turning down the
ones he would not. Philanthropic organizations could use
public relations; he could offer them his services at a re-
duced rate. Small potatoes, maybe. But the Corporate Life
was not for him. Alice was right about the house, too. They
could sell, buy a condominium. This would provide money

to help Cindy and the baby. Business college would cost something. And he could walk to work. Perhaps he would even have the opportunity to read the Great Books, though a baby, he knew, had a way of monopolizing one's time.

"Well?"

"Well, what?"

"That's what I mean, dear. You're off in some little world of your own. You aren't listening. Where *have* you been all this time?"

He looked at her. He tucked in his belly, threw back his shoulders, held his head high, assumed the posture he imagined a man of ancient pedigree would assume. His voice was slurred from drink, but he spoke proudly, with just the right touch of arrogance in his tone.

"I was launching a new constellation," he said.

TWELVE
STORIES

My Father's Jokes

The Horrible Hairy Spider was dangling over Cissy's head. "Jello, again, this is Jack Benny," said Jack Benny.

Cissy was sitting on the rug—the Peck hooked rug, made by our New England great-grandmother on my mother's side; her golden corkscrew curls spilled down her back. Father sat in his faded sprung armchair. A Ryan armchair. Grand Rapids, Mother called it, which meant that it was not an antique, which meant that it was common. I sat on the Peck Boston rocker; I sat very straight, as if I were hanging my head from a string in order not to grow up to be a hunchback. I was eleven; Cissy, six.

Mother? Mother was down with one of her Spells. She often had these Spells, which had something to do with a New England conscience.

"Thank God I don't have a New England conscience," Father used to say.

Was it a disease, I often wondered? If so, would I inherit it?

The Horrible Hairy Spider (*revolting, nearly five inches across; fat rubber body with long hairy legs; 15 cents*) dropped lower; it hung menacingly near Cissy's forehead, just above her large, long-lashed baby-blue eyes, Ryan eyes, like Father's. Father's eyes were choirboy blue. They were uplifted, now, toward Heaven. Father was one, once—a choirboy. There was a photograph of him in a lacy robe, holding a candle snuffer—that same sweet sly expression in his choirboy eyes. That was before he stopped being Catholic.

"It's the only church if you go to church," he sometimes said. "They know how to do things up right," he said, with a touch of vanity in his voice, which aggravated Mother. There was no one, really, less vain than Father. Why, then, I wondered, was he vain about having once been Catholic, when decent people, according to Mother, would be ashamed?

> He only does it to annoy,
> Because he knows it teases—

Father loved Mother. On her last birthday he had given her a peekaboo blouse and a transparent purple nightie, which hung in her closet, unworn, except when Cissy played Dress-Up. Father was also concerned about Mother's Spells. Mother wore her long chestnut hair in a tight bun at the back of her neck. Could it be that she was exerting too much strain upon her scalp, Father asked her? Perhaps, he said, if she let her hair down, let it fall more loosely, it would ease her suffering? His suggestion had no effect. Every year, it seemed, Mother drew her hair tighter; no loose wave or tendril was permitted to escape. Still, he continued to urge her. Such lovely hair, he said. Hair like yours should be displayed for people to admire.

"Beauty," said Mother, "is as Beauty does."

Father loved Mother, whatever love was. I was not sure. But the absolute token of his affection was that he liked to tease her. Father always teased the people he loved.

He liked to tease Cissy most of all. Now, he seldom teased me. Did this mean that he loved Cissy more, or did it mean that I had grown too old for most of his jokes? Or, possibly, too dignified? Was love undignified? No. Mother had great dignity, and Mother loved Father.

"We are One," she used to say. "When two people marry, they become One."

Why then did she suffer so? Why did she grieve? Why did she feel that our home, at 43 North Elm, in Norton, was not truly her home, that her marriage had forced her into some sort of awful exile? Why did she never laugh at Father's jokes? It was her pride, her terrible Peck pride. Those were my thoughts, as I watched, with an ill-disguised scorn, the descent of the Horrible Hairy Spider.

"Oh, yes, they do things up right," Mother said, when Father talked about having been Catholic. "All that Mumbo Jumbo! It's for people who have nothing else, who want to crawl on their knees in front of the Pope and kiss his feet. Crawl!" she added, with a shudder.

Father's hands were folded, *innocently*, in his lap, in a kind of prayerful attitude. But I knew what was in them. The Secret Control Ring! I tensed my body for what was about to occur.

Another jerk! The Spider dropped, swayed to and fro in front of Cissy's eyes. Cissy shrieked. Oh, that shriek! Even though I had prepared myself, it went through me like an electric shock.

Father? Father was looking at Cissy with a deep concern. What dreadful thing can have happened to this little girl? What had caused her to cry out in such an anguished manner? Was she in some sort of awful peril? Oh, me! Oh, my! Poor Cissy!

Then Cissy caught on. She got it. If she were in the Funny Papers a shimmering lightbulb would have appeared over her head.

"Oh, Dad-dee!" cried Cissy. She plucked the Horrible Hairy Spider out of the air and examined it; she giggled; she stared at Father with unabashed admiration. "Oh, Dad-dee," she said again.

Father's eyes lost their innocent look; they twinkled. The little laugh wrinkles around his eyes and mouth erupted. His chest beneath his old coat sweater heaved, and chuckles exploded out of his mouth—little "heh, heh, heh"s, like the "heh, heh, heh"s in the balloons over Funny Paper people.

Father and Cissy were Funny Paper people. "Did you see
Father and *Cissy* today? Wasn't the Spider *funny?*"

"She's the perfect Fall Guy, isn't she?" said Father, wink-
ing at me, as if I were a co-conspirator.

I refused to be implicated; I did not acknowledge the
wink. I was not a Funny Paper person, could not have been,
even if I tried. I was Emily Peck Ryan, more Peck than
Ryan, everyone said.

If Justice ruled the World, which I had, by then, learned
it did not, my name would have been Charity Peck Ryan, instead.

CHARITY PECK IS MY NAME; IN PEACEFUL WARREN BORN
IN SORROW'S SCHOOL MY INFANT MIND WAS PIERCED
WITH A THORN,
IN WISDOM'S WAYS, I'LL SPEND MY DAYS, HUMILITY BE
WITH ME
SHOULD FORTUNE FROWN OR FRIENDS DISOWN, DIVINE
SUPPORT CAN'T LEAVE ME.

This was the verse Great-Great-Grandmother Charity
had embroidered on the Sampler at the age of nine, following the death of her father. Above the verse she had
stitched three rows of the alphabet and numbers up to ten
in different calligraphic design in order to demonstrate her
skill at needlework. Below the verse, a tombstone presided
over by a Grieving Angel, such as the one in the Peck Plot
in the old 100F cemetery in Metropolis, which the Reverend
Gideon Freeland Peck, owner and publisher of *The Democratic Christian Evangelist* (SOUTHERN OREGON'S FIRST
NEWSPAPER, it said on the historical plaque), had copied
from the one he remembered in the Warren cemetery. Below the tombstone were embroidered these lines:

PHINEAS PECK DEPARTED THIS LIFE AT A
MEETING OF THE CITIZENS OF WARREN ON
JULY THE FOURTH, 1820, FOLLOWING THE
DISCHARGE OF A CANNON.

"Why would a man step in front of a cannon at a Fourth
of July celebration?" asked Father one Sunday afternoon as
he stood in the parlor of my grandmother's house in
Metropolis, five miles from Norton, the house where
Mother had grown up and which was known by all the right
people and even some of the wrong ones as "the Old Peck
Place." Father was examining the Sampler on the parlor
wall. He gazed innocently at Granny, at Aunt Dee, at Uncle
Gideon, at Mother. "Unless," he said, "he was perhaps not
quite sober?"

Uncle Gideon, who was mixing Granny's before-dinner
martini—the most important thing, perhaps the only thing,
he learned at Harvard, Father sometimes said—stirred the
pale liquid in the frosted pitcher somewhat more vigorously
than usual; Aunt Dee bustled out of the room to see to dinner; Granny, an Abbot, not a Peck, whose reaction, therefore, did not matter, smiled; Cissy giggled; Mother was silent. A silence fraught with meaning, I thought. I had just
learned *fraught*. A fraught-with-meaning silence. A silence,
meaningfully fraught. This was how so many of Mother's
silences were.

"It was only an idle question, to satisfy a point concerning
which I have often been curious," said Father.

When I was born there was already a Charity Peck Ryan, a
year older than I, who was now known as Poor Charity; she
died of scarlet fever when I was three and now lay under
the left wing of the Angel in Metropolis. Mother's sorrow
impaired her delicate Nervous System. Dr. Conroy pre-
scribed warm baths, brisk walks, and no more babies. Both
Mother and Father were deeply concerned over Mother's
Nervous System; neither would have wilfully disobeyed Dr.
Conroy's orders. What had happened? I should never know.

> Where did you come from Baby dear?
> Out of the Nowhere into the Here.
> Where did you get those eyes so blue?
> God gave them to me, as He did you.

This was how Mother responded when Cissy asked Where She Came From, at an age when she was too little to comprehend. I knew, of course, that babies were the result of the most intimate physical expression of the deepest spiritual love between one man and one woman. Cissy had been told this now, too, but Heaven only knew if Cissy "got" it. Heaven only knew what went on in Cissy's head. "Out of the Nowhere into the Here," though hardly a scientific explanation, seemed to me, on the whole, the best explanation for Cissy's existence.

Cissy, by being born in mysterious violation of the Doctor's Orders, had stolen my Rights of Primogeniture, in more ways than one. Being named Charity, she would inherit the Peck Sampler. Would she spend her days wisely and humbly? Should Fortune frown or Friends disown, would she be able to count on Divine Support? Knowing Cissy, it seemed to me unlikely.

Father and Cissy were a Team. Like Jack Benny and Rochester. Like Edgar Bergen and Charlie. Like George Burns and Gracie Allen. John C. Ryan and His Little Daughter Cissy. John C. Ryan and His Bag of Magical Tricks and Practical Jokes. Little Cissy, the Perfect Fall Guy! Watch her "Fall" for all the Tricks, no matter how many times performed.

FATHER: Adam and Eve and Pinch Me
 Went down to the Water to swim
 Adam and Eve were drowned-ed
 And who do you think was saved?
CISSY: Pinch Me.
 (*Father pinches Cissy.*)
CISSY: (*squealing*) Oh, Dad-dee!

◆

FATHER: I can row a boat, canoe?
MOTHER: Oh, John, not again.

EMILY: It's a pun, stupid. A pun on *words.*
            (*One of the lowest forms of humor, despite
            Shakespeare's use of it, Miss Wilson, her sev-
            enth-grade teacher, had said*)
            One of the lowest forms of humor.
CISSY: Boat! Can-you? I get it! (*giggles*)

◆

MOTHER: Old Mr. Henry died last night in his sleep.
FATHER: Mr. Henry is with Barnum and Bailey.
CISSY: What's Barnum and Bailey?
EMILY: (*who knows her History*) It was a famous cir-
            cus, with Buffalo Bill.
CISSY: Why is Mr. Henry with them?
EMILY: Barnum and Bailey are dead, stupid.
CISSY: (*silence, giggles*) Oh!

◆

Watch Cissy perform, too. A Chip Off the Old Block. Enjoy her impersonation of Shirley Temple, singing "On the
Good Ship Lollipop." A Mimic. A Great Little Trouper. Can
really strut her stuff.

MOTHER: Now, now, Cissy. Judge and Mrs. Blair want to
            talk.
JUDGE BLAIR: It isn't every day that an old man is enter-
            tained by a pretty little girl. Let's hear your
            song, Sweetheart.

Jack Benny was over. They were playing the Theme Song.
Father turned off the Zenith. "I better go look in on poor
Mama," he said.

Cissy's response to this was to stand on her head; her
dress fell over her shoulders, revealing her pink panties;
then she dropped, plop, in a giggling, quivering heap upon
the rug.

"When I was a little girl, I always went to bed the moment Jack Benny was over," said Father.

Cissy looked up at Father, blue eyes big. Silence. Then, "Oh, Dad-dee, you were never a little girl!"

Father picked up Cissy and threw her over his shoulder, marched out of the room with a shrieking Cissy, dimpled legs kicking at the air.

I rose and went into the dining room and sat down at the round oak table (Grand Rapids, Ryan) and prepared to begin my seventh-grade Original Research paper.

"Why don't you write about Old Metropolis?" said Miss Emmeline Trowbridge, my friend and Head Librarian of the Norton Public Library, when I had consulted her about the theme. "After all," she said, "you are a Peck. Your grandmother and your Uncle Gideon are filled with information. You must pick a particular subject. The journey of your great-grandfather from Massachusetts to Metropolis. The Gold Rush. Your great-grandfather's Temperance Crusade, the visit of Rutherford B. Hayes . . ."

I had decided to write about the Railroad. If it had not been for the Railroad, all Pecks would have been rich today. Not that Pecks cared about material wealth in itself. It was the respect that went with it.

If it had not been for a man named Norton, who bought up one thousand acres of land in the fertile valley below Metropolis, who bribed the Southern Pacific—

"It was flatter land, it was easier to lay track," said Father.

"He *bribed* them," said Mother, said Uncle Gideon, said Aunt Dee.

History, I sometimes thought, consisted as much, if not more, of what did not happen as of what did.

Father was a lawyer in a small Oregon town. *John C. Ryan, Atty-at-Law*, it said in curly gold-leaf letters on the window of the Union Building, where he had his office. He had never finished law school; he had gone to World War I, instead. After the war, they made a law that veterans who had left college to enlist could get their degree by passing a formal examination. Father traveled to Salem and was interviewed by the Chief Justice. This is the story he liked to tell concerning the interview:

"The Chief Justice asked me a question, which I wasn't able to answer. Then he asked me another question, which I wasn't able to answer. Then he said, 'You are now admitted to the practice of law in the State of Oregon.' "

Father enjoyed being a lawyer in a small town. He was not ambitious, either for money or fame. You don't have to be, if you have the rare privilege of enjoying your work. He was a popular man among people of every social and economic level. He was unassuming, courtly, gentle, genial, honest. He spent little time in court. By temperament, he was a "settler," not a litigator.

Outside of his work and his family, to whom he was devoted, he fished, gardened, and, after age fifty, played gin rummy every Saturday afternoon at the University Club in town. Outside of the Bar Association, this was his only affiliation; he was not a joiner. Once, someone talked him into the Kiwanis Club, because it would be "good for business." He went to one meeting and found it too serious.

He enjoyed his liquor but drank like a gentleman. He smoked too much; his rumpled clothes were covered with cigarette ash. His other vice—if you can call it that—was his addiction to practical jokes. He kept *The Catalogue of Magical Tricks and Practical Jokes* on top of the toilet tank. The jokes, which he sent away for, were the only things he ever bought for himself, outside of necessities. This story is about my father's jokes.

THE RUBBER-POINTED PENCIL

Looks like lead—Fools and annoys 'em.

MOTHER: This pencil doesn't work, John. This pencil—
Is this one of your *jokes*, John? Will you be so
kind as to find me a proper pencil, please?

◆

THE FAKE FLY

Sticks to almost any surface.
Put it on your lapel, on the butter dish.
On Mrs. Social Register's lace tablecloth.
Watch 'em try to brush it off.
Confound your hostess.

MISS SINGER: (*County Recorder at the Courthouse, to Cissy
and Emily, who are waiting for Father in her
office*) Well, if there's anything I can't tolerate,
it's a nasty, filthy fly. I tried to brush it off,
and it wouldn't move. It just—stuck. I should
have guessed! He was going all over the courthouse last week with his squirting flower in
his buttonhole. Well, we all know your dad! He
makes life just a bit brighter for everyone. No,
things are never dull when your dad's around.

◆

THE JUMPING SPOON

Greatest Laugh Producer ever invented.
A startling after-dinner trick. The performer
places one of the teaspoons to be found on the
dinner table into an ordinary drinking glass.
In a few seconds, the spoon jumps out of the
glass! This is really surprising and funny.

MRS. BLAIR: *(Wife of Judge Blair)* It was really surprising and funny. I couldn't believe my eyes, it just *jumped* out of the glass!

♦

—————— THE LIVE MYSTERY MOUSE ——————

MISS JOST: *(Elevator operator in Union Building, to Cissy and Emily)* Going to see your dad?

(The elevator is like an iron cage; through the bars of the cage one sees the cables move past as the elevator rises. Miss Jost had fixed up the interior of the cage like a miniature living room. She sits in an old chintz slipper chair; her knees are covered with a multicolored afghan; her knitting is on her lap. Taped to one of the bars is a photograph of her nephew, Carl, who lost an arm in the service of his country; taped to another bar is a postcard—a pretty rural scene of Denmark, where Miss Jost's parents grew up. Above this, a calendar with a photograph of the Norton Valley with the pear blossoms in bloom, courtesy of the Norton Groceteria.)

"Fifth floor, Miss Jost," he says. *(Creaking and grinding of chains, as she pulls the wheel)*

Every morning, every noon—"Fifth floor, please." *(The Union Building only has three floors.)* He fooled me with that mouse of his last week. "Could that be a *mouse* in your elevator, Miss Jost?" he says. I looked down and let out a frightful scream. "Don't worry, Miss Jost, I'll get the rascal," he says, and he leans down and picks it up and puts it in his pocket. Very solemnlike. Very calm. You would think

he was accustomed to picking up mice everyday! "Oh, Mr. Ryan, you almost gave me a
heart attack!" I said. "You really shouldn't,
Mr. Ryan!" But you know your dad. There's no
stopping him. Heaven only knows what he'll
think up next!

◆

THE MECHANICAL HAND VIBRATOR

Startle your friends with a "friendly" handshake.

MISS PORTER: (*Father's stenographer to Cissy and Emily*) My
hand was still tingling in bed that night.

Miss Porter is Mother's age. An old maid. They knew
each other, *slightly*, at Norton High. Miss Porter lives very
quietly in the Kingscote Arms with her widowed mother.
She is the only person Emily and Cissy know who lives
"downtown." Miss Porter wears too much rouge. She has
her dyed hair done once a week at the Fountain of Beauty;
every six months she gets a permanent. She plucks her eyebrows to a fine line and dresses in frilly frocks and sheer
silk hose. "It's a pity someone can't tell her how to dress
suitably for an office," says Mother. "I'm sure it must give a
bad impression when she meets the Public." Miss Porter is
short and plump. Her freckled flesh is so soft it looks as if it
would dent if you touched her. She has a soft voice and a
slight stammer and is extremely meticulous. Since Mother
doesn't drive—"I don't care to run around like other
women," Mother says—she often asks Emily to phone the
office and give Miss Porter a shopping list for Father. If
Emily says, "one dozen oranges," Miss Porter will say,
"What sort of oranges, dear? Does your mother prefer juice
oranges or eating oranges?"

This is the part of her meticulousness, which, though appropriate for legal stenography, irritates Mother. (Emily is not sure *why*.)

"Miss Porter wants to know if you want juice or eating oranges?" Emily says. "Oh, isn't that just like her! Tell her either kind will do!" Mother's cavalier attitude toward oranges, or, perhaps her cavalier attitude toward Miss Porter, imposes a burden on Emily. "You better say *which*," she tells Mother. "Juice, then! Tell her *juice!*—or, *eating*. Tell her eating! Tell her anything you like." "Juice, please," Emily says. Then Miss Porter inquires after Mother's health. "How is your mother feeling today?" she says. Or, "Is your mother feeling better today?" "Yes, better, thank you," says Emily, no matter how Mother is feeling. She senses that it is not proper to go into more personal details; that neither Miss Porter nor Mother would care for that. Mother, in fact, would prefer that Miss Porter not inquire after her health at all.

Mother never phones, herself, if she can avoid it. Having known Miss Porter, *slightly*, in high school, where they called each other by their first names, it is awkward to phone and say, "This is Mrs. Ryan." On the other hand, it will not do to say, "This is Jean." When it is necessary, for one reason or another to call, herself, Mother says, "Is this Vera?" Then she waits for Miss Porter to recognize her voice, which Miss Porter always does. Miss Porter, recognizing Mother's voice, says, "Oh, how are you?" "Very well, thank you. And you?" says Mother. "I can't complain," says Miss Porter, or, "Chipper, I'm always chipper," she says. Then she says, "I bet you'd like to talk to the Boss." "Yes, please, if he's not occupied," says Mother. "I think I can arrange for you to speak to him," says Miss Porter. "I'll just put a little flea in his ear."

Mother does not care for Miss Porter calling Father "the Boss," nor does she care for the expression, "a little flea in his ear." But this carefully worked-out telephone ritual (carefully worked out by Mother *and* Miss Porter) solves the awkward social problem for both of them. In all the ten years in which Miss Porter has worked for Father, she has, somehow, managed never to call Mother either Mrs. Ryan or Jean.

MISS PORTER: That dreadful vibrator! It sent funny little shivers all through me. (*She gives Cissy a box of paper clips to make into a chain; she gives Emily a stack of magazines*—The Elks Magazine, Field & Stream, *an old copy of* The Saturday Evening Post—*to entertain them while they wait for Father to drive them home from the dentist's. She opens the drawer of her desk and takes out a small tin box and opens it and offers them hard little white mints called "pastilles."*)

(*Cissy, listening to the story of the vibrator, giggles.*)

(*Emily finds story embarrassing. Why would Father shake Miss Porter's hand? she wonders. That soft plump freckled hand. Sending little shivers through her soft plump body. Making Miss Porter tingle. She does not want to think of Miss Porter in bed. Tingling. She does not want to think of Miss Porter as having any existence at all, outside of her duties as Father's stenographer. She looks up from the* Post *and scowls at Cissy for giggling. Cissy, she thinks, lacks the Pecks' innate good taste and proud reserve.*)

"Isn't Miss Porter beautiful?" Cissy said one night, when we were in our beds in the upstairs bedroom we shared at 43 North Elm.

"Beautiful?" I said scornfully. "What could possibly make you think she's beautiful?"

But Cissy was already asleep.

FATHER: *(driving our Buick on the way to the Peck House in Metropolis)*
As I was driving to Salt Lake
I met a little rattlesnake
I fed it some jelly cake,
It got a little bellyache.

MOTHER: *(in front seat, holding Father's jacket and tie on her lap; at her feet flowers, in a Mason jar, for the Peck Plot.)*
Tummy, not belly!
(Cissy, sitting between Mother and Father because she claims *to get carsick, giggles.)*

FATHER: It got a little tummyache, not a bellyache, after all.

EMILY: *(alone in back seat)* It says "belly" in the Bible.
(She agrees with Mother, but possesses a fund of knowledge she feels obliged to demonstrate.)

MOTHER: The language of the Bible and the language of everyday life are two different things altogether.

FATHER: Your mother is correct, as always. The language of the Bible is not appropriate language for everyday speech.

MOTHER: *(ignoring Father)* Drive slowly when we go through Metropolis, so Emily can take notes for her theme.

CISSY: My belly feels funny.
(Consternation! Should they stop? Let Cissy out? Roll down the window? Buy her some chewing gum? It is decided to drive fast through Metropolis and go straight to the Peck Plot, where she can run about among the tombstones in the fresh air. This, of course, takes precedence over Emily's Original Research.)

I got an A, anyhow. "Emily has Literary Tendencies," Mrs. Wilson wrote across my theme, which I brought home to show to Mother and Father. They were both proud of me.

The phrase *Literary Tendencies* was taken up by them, and then by others.

"Emily has Literary Tendencies," people would say. They didn't mean it, I suppose, but they always made *Literary Tendencies* sound as if it were not so much a disease, maybe, as a kind of morbidity, a lack of normal health. They may have been right. I don't know. Perhaps it was like the New England conscience, which, as it turned out, I did inherit from Mother.

Certainly, Cissy didn't inherit it. The way she climbed upon gentlemen's laps, for example; climbed up and burrowed in and snuggled down, as if she were some sort of little animal; made a nest and curled up, peacefully, as long as she was being cuddled, patted, stroked—but, should the gentleman reach for a drink or a cigarette, or, simply pause for a moment, the burrowing and snuggling began again to remind him of his neglect, and did not stop until the neglect was rectified.

"Cissy, don't pester Judge Blair," or, "Cissy, I think Mr. Hefflinger would be happier if you were to get down at once," Mother would say.

"Oh, Cissy's my girl, aren't you, Cissy?"

"It isn't everyday an old codger like myself can hold a pretty blonde on his lap."

The pet names she was called. Cissy. Missy Cissy. Cissy-pie. Later, scrawled upon the Angel (a famous necking spot for the students at Norton High): *Hot Pants Cissy*. This was, fortunately, after Mother's breakdown. Aunt Dee took rubbing alcohol and scrubbed it off.

It was Father's fault. He spoiled her. Mother often said so.

THE DOGGIE DOO DOO

Latex. Fantastically realistic imitation.
Nauseating. Put on your hostess's best rug.
Watch her chide poor Fido.

MRS. HEFFLINGER: (*mother of Jimmy Hefflinger, with whom Emily is secretly in love, who has invited the Ryan family to visit them at their cabin at the Lake*) Oh, no!

FATHER: (*innocent expression in choirboy blue eyes*) Is something the matter, Mil?

MRS. HEFFLINGER: (*to Mr. Hefflinger*) Carl!

FATHER: Perhaps I can be of assistance?

MRS. HEFFLINGER: No, no, it's all right. I'm sorry, Bingo's made a mess. Where *is* Bingo? Carl? I'll get paper towels—
(*Cissy looks at Doggie Doo Doo; looks at Father, giggles*)
(*Emily, silent, dying of shame*)

MOTHER: John! John, you didn't—!

MR. HEFFLINGER: Well, I guess we better clean it up.

MRS. HEFFLINGER: I'll do it. You men take the girls down to the Lake. They want to go out in the boat. I'm afraid Bingo's been a very naughty dog.

MOTHER: (*pale-faced, weakly*) John?

FATHER: I, for one, intend to stay and help Milly. (*picks up Doggie Doo Doo, puts it casually in pocket*)

JIMMY HEFFLINGER: Hey—smooth. Let's see it!

EMILY: Let's go out in the boat!

CISSY: Show it to Jimmy, Daddy.

MOTHER: John!

MRS. HEFFLINGER: (*laughing*) Oh, John, it's one of your jokes!

FATHER: You know I never joke, Mil. (*takes out Doggie Doo Doo from pocket and hands it, proudly, to Jimmy. Jimmy and Cissy examine Doggie Doo Doo*)

MRS. HEFFLINGER: You certainly fooled me this time.

JIMMY: (*turning Doggie Doo Doo over in his hand*) Hey, this is great. (*to Cissy*) Where'd your father get it?

CISSY: (*giggling, looking up at Jimmy with big blue eyes*) He has this catalogue. (*coquettishly*) I'll show it to you, sometime. It's got lots of smooth stuff. Come on, you promised to take us for a boat ride.

EMILY: (*forever shamed, forever unable to forget her shame when she sees Jimmy Hefflinger at school*) I don't think I'll go. I brought a book to read.

(*Jimmy and Cissy run off, down to the dock. Mrs. Hefflinger fixes gin fizzes for the adults. Mother declines hers. She has a sudden headache; perhaps it is the sun, perhaps she had better lie down for a time with a cool wet washcloth on her forehead. Father fetches a cool wet washcloth, returns from the bedroom. Emily sits down with her book.*)

FATHER: I've been told my—ah—joke—was not in the best of taste.

MRS. HEFFLINGER: Nonsense! You wouldn't be John Ryan without your jokes. I'm going to tell her to come back out here.

FATHER: Better wait a bit, Mil.

MRS. HEFFLINGER: Well, you know best. (*looks at Emily*) Emily is quite a little bookworm, isn't she?

FATHER: (*proudly*) Her teacher says she has Literary Tendencies.

◆

———————— SNOW ————————

(*7:00 A.M. February morning. Emily is sixteen; Cissy, eleven. Mother, that winter, has "taken to her bed," a phrase of Aunt Dee's, taken up by others. Father sleeps on a cot in the hallway in order to be near her in the night. Cissy and Emily are still asleep. Father enters their bedroom.*)

FATHER: Girls! Wake up! We're going to give Mother a nice surprise.

CISSY:
(Emily, always an early riser, already awake, sits up, gets out of bed) *(burrows under covers, to Father)* Go 'way. *(Father pulls covers off Cissy's bed. Cissy shrieks. Both girls follow Father, reluctantly, arms across chests, shivering, in their flannel nighties. Father leads them into Mother's room. Mother is lying on her back, eyes open. She seems to be looking at something beyond, or perhaps through, her visitors.)*

FATHER:
(to Mother) Surprise! Surprise! We have a little surprise for you this morning. *(goes to window, peeps behind drawn curtain; faces Mother again)* Ready? *(clears throat, assumes theatrical stance)* Presto Chango! *(pulls curtain)* Snow! *(Father twinkles, beams.)*

(Mother looks at snow, expression does not change; she seems to be looking at something beyond, or perhaps through this sudden Winter Wonderland.)

CISSY:
(marveling at the magical metamorphosis produced by Father) Oh, Dad-dee!

FATHER:
(to Mother, trying again) Now we see it. *(draws curtain)* Now we don't. *(pulls curtain)* Presto Chango—snow!

MOTHER:
It's very nice, but the light hurts my eyes. Would you mind closing the curtain, again, please, John?

In 1949 I returned from Reed College to attend my mother's funeral. She had taken, it seemed, too many pills all at once. The funeral was private, but Miss Porter showed up, anyhow. Her sobs spoiled the lovely simplicity of the words from the Book of Common Prayer—the service Uncle Gideon had arranged. I considered her presence in the worst of taste.

After the funeral, Father, Cissy, and I sat in the living

room at 43 North Elm. Father was pale, solemn, still. The laugh lines in his face were etched more deeply; perhaps they were no longer laugh lines. He chain-smoked, dropping ashes on the Peck hooked rug. I fetched an ashtray.

Father said, "Well, I guess Mama is with Barnum and Bailey."

Cissy giggled; then burst into tears. Father wept with her. I stood, holding the ashtray—apart, alone, dry eyed. Being more Peck than Ryan, I could neither laugh nor weep.

This story is about my father's jokes. Father joked. Cissy was his Fall Guy. Mother had her pride. I have Literary Tendencies. I am writing this story. Everyone has his or her way of coping.

It's Not the Picture Tube, He Said

It's not the picture tube, he said.

He sat down at her kitchen table and took a receipt pad out of his shirt pocket and put it on the table. He was a short stocky man with pale-blue eyes under thick spectacles. He wore a baseball cap on his balding head.

You just needed some adjustment, he said.

I guess I'm lucky it's not the tube, she said. She left the sink, where she was working, and stood beside him.

Lot's of jokers would tell you it's the tube. You wouldn't know the difference, would you? He studied her face, waiting for her reply.

She laughed. No, you're right. I wouldn't. I guess I'm lucky to have found you.

Where'd you find me? he said.

Well, I'm new here, so I looked in the Yellow Pages. I suppose I could have asked a neighbor, but I just looked in the Yellow Pages for someone nearby—

—and lucked out, he said.

Oh, yes, I feel very lucky. Nowadays, there's so much people don't know. Scientific things. You can't keep up. It's like going to doctors. You have to trust them.

89

You trust many people? he said.

Well . . . I probably shouldn't . . . but what can you do?

What would you have done if I said it was the tube?

I guess I would have believed you. I'm not a repairman. I mean, it's not my field.

You would have wondered, though. You might have questioned my integrity.

You look honest, she said.

Honest Dan, Your TV Man, he said. But you would have wondered, just the same. You might have wondered in bed at night.

Well, I might have, she said.

You have many sleepless nights, wondering about things like that?

Oh, now and then. I guess most people do.

I never have a sleepless night, he said. I hit the mattress, and, bang, I'm out like a light.

That's wonderful, really wonderful. I wish I could. Will you take a check? she said.

You're new in town. Most servicemen wouldn't consider touching your check, he said.

I have identification, credit cards.

No tickie, no laundree—That's what most of them would say. But I'm not your typical serviceman, he said.

I feel very fortunate, she said. She took her checkbook out of a drawer and sat down opposite him.

Twenty-three yen, he said.

She began to write out the check.

You find lots of strange things in the Yellow Pages, he said. Like I said, you lucked out. Sometimes I read the Yellow Pages for the laughs.

I never thought of that, she said.

Laughter makes the world go round, you better believe it.

Yes, she said, and handed him the check.

You laugh much? he said.

Well. . . . as much as anyone, I suppose.

You never give straight answers. You aware of that? he said.

No, I guess I wasn't, she said.

I guess. I suppose. Probably. You don't seem sure of yourself, he said. He was examining the check, puzzling over it.

Did I get something wrong, she said.

You worry about being wrong a lot? he said.

She laughed again, nervously. You sound like a psychiatrist, she said.

His head shot up. You been to one of those creeps? he said.

No, she said. Well, yes, I did, once, she said. Just for a short time. Long ago.

I won't ask you why you went, he said. That's your business, not mine. I'm not the nosy type. But tell me this. Did it do you any good? he said.

I guess . . . I mean, I thought it did. At the time, she said.

At the time. But you're not so sure now, are you? I bet you lay awake at night, wondering about that, too.

It's very hard to tell about that kind of thing, she said.

You're damn right it's hard to tell, he said. Mucho dinero for the Shrink, and what do you get? Your TV repaired? A new picture tube? It's my personal suspicion you didn't get value received, he said. He was examining the check again, taking his time.

Do you want my driver's license or a credit card? she said.

What for?

I thought, maybe, well, you'd feel more confident, she said.

Confidence is not the issue. I'm interested in your handwriting, madam.

My handwriting?

It tells a lot about a person, he said.

Are you a handwriting expert? she said.

You might say it's a sideline. I'm particularly interested in your *t*'s, he said.

My *t*'s?

Look here, he said. He shoved the check in front of her eyes. See how you cross your *t*'s? he said.

Yes, I mean, I guess that's the way I cross them, she said.

I've never thought much about it. Does it have some meaning?

You're damn right it has some meaning, he said. You cross them this way. See. Your crossline slants to the right. Okay?

Well, it does, doesn't it? she said.

Know what that indicates? he said.

No, I'm afraid I don't, she said.

Hostility, he said. Terrible hostility. Your *t*'s tell the story. It's all right there in your *t*'s.

Don't most people have problems? she said.

You can say that again. Something's eating at you. Anybody ever tell you that? Your Shrink tell you?

Not really, she said. Not in so many words.

I didn't think so. I'm the first. Right?

Yes, you're the first, she said.

Well? he said.

Well what? she said.

What is it? Why the hostility?

Look, she said. I have an appointment. I can't really—I mean, right now isn't a very good time to—

You gotta face it, lady, he said. It won't do you no good to run away from it. He leaned back in his chair, shoved his cap back on his head. He looked at her thoughtfully. Anybody ever tell you this handwriting thing works both ways? he said.

No. I've never discussed the subject before, actually, she said.

Most folks haven't, he said. He leaned toward her now, dangling the check in front of her, displaying it as a lawyer might display evidence of a crime to a jury. It's all right there, but it works both ways. You change your handwriting, you change your personality, he said.

You mean—if I change the way I cross my *t*'s? You mean—?

He nodded, slowly. Go ahead, he said. Now, you're cooking with gas.

Go ahead? she said.

What you were saying, he said. If you change the way you cross your *t*'s, you'd get rid of what?

My hostility? she said.

Touché, Señora! Try it. See if it doesn't help, he said.

Yes, I will, she said. I'll try it. She stood up. I'll work at it. I'm really appreciative, she said.

I try to be of assistance when I can. It's no good just sitting around, all eaten up by hostile emotions. My name is Ray, he said. Be sure to ask for Ray when you call next time. Then we'll see how you're progressing, he said.

I will, she said. Ray. I'll ask for Ray.

And? he said.

And I'll work on my *t*'s, she said.

Good girl, he said. He took out his wallet and folded the check neatly once and put it in the wallet and put his wallet back into his pocket. He began to write out the receipt.

I don't need a receipt, she said. The check's the receipt. You don't need to bother.

Rules of the game, he said. My name and phone number will be on it, too, in case you forget.

I won't forget, she said.

Most people don't. I've been in the business for almost twenty years. I've got loyal customers. You better believe it.

I do believe it, she said. And thank you for everything, Ray.

My pleasure. Sayonara, he said.

As soon as she heard his truck leave the driveway, she sat down at the table again. She felt shaky, limp. She sat there for about five minutes. Then she reached for the receipt and turned it over on its blank side. She took her pen and began to practice her *t*'s, concentrating on slanting them in the opposite direction.

On the Desert

Earl C Bennet had integrity. He knew his luck would change one day; it had to on account of the Law of Averages; therefore, compromises weren't necessary. But even if he hadn't believed in the Law of Averages, he wouldn't have given in. That was the kind of man he was.

Earl C was forty-nine years old. The *C* in his name didn't stand for anything, but was just part of his Christian name given to him by his mother and daddy. He was six feet tall, almost, if he stood up straight. But for a long time now he had slumped. The slump had solidified into a little hump between his skinny shoulder blades; Earl C accepted the hump as matter-of-factly as folks accept a proper part of their body. His face was long and bony; his skin and hair were the color of the Mojave in late summer. He wore khaki pants and a white T-shirt. The only color to him was his eyes, which were the translucent blue of the bottles he collected out on the desert and kept on the windowsill, and which had a neutral expression, as if, like the bottles, they had been put there just for decoration.

Earl C lived in his place of business, which was called

Earl's Place. It was a three-room wooden shack with a tin roof, right next to the Highway, seventy-six miles from Vegas and twenty miles from "The Heart of America's Favorite Recreation Land."

The front room was the Café, where he served sandwiches and soft drinks and sold thunder rocks and other souvenirs; next to the Café was the storage room, where he kept his freezer and supplies. The other small room, beneath the sloping tin roof, was his bedroom. He used the outdoor public Gents for his toilet.

Five years ago the Highway had been busy, but now, owing to the new Freeway, it had turned into a frontage road, and only local traffic went by. Darlene, Earl C's wife for twenty years, had seen the Freeway coming and had tried to persuade Earl C to sell the place and buy a motor court on the Freeway. Earl C had refused.

It wasn't because he didn't think Darlene was right; she was usually right about things like that. It was just that he didn't intend to be pushed around by Big Shots in Government. He had voted against the Big Shots all his life. His favorite candidates for President of the United States had been William Lemke, Roger Babson, and Claude A. Watson.

"You slay me, Earl C," Darlene had said, her soft, fat body shaking with silent laughter.

Earl C thought he remembered she had been pretty once. But, imperceptibly, throughout the years, she had put on flesh; the flesh had smoothed out her features and other distinguishing parts of her body, so that it sometimes seemed every part of her looked the same.

"You really slay me," she wheezed helplessly wiping tears of amusement out of her little piggy eyes.

Then she had took off. With the money she had inherited from her first husband and had hoarded in the bank all the years of their marriage, she had bought the Cactus Motor Court. The Cactus Court had Beautyrest mattresses, air conditioning, wall-to-wall carpets, and a plaster burro out in front. Darlene had her own little unit, where folks registered. She had equipped it cozily, with a new sofa and two overstuffed chairs, plastic potted shrubs that looked real, and a color TV. During the season, her No Vacancy sign was on most of the time.

She had also gotten herself a divorce for what she called "business reasons." But this didn't stop her from dropping in every Saturday night during off-season to play casino and heckle Earl C about his lack of business sense.

"How's your smelly old zoo?" she would say, as she deftly shuffled the cards.

"Flourishing," said Earl C.

"That zoo just costs you time and money. You ought to go out there with your deer rifle and shoot them all."

"I like my zoo," said Earl C firmly.

"How many thunder eggs you sold this month?"

"Didn't keep track."

"You ought to get rid of this place and come over to the Cactus, Earl C. I'd put you up in the trailer. I could use somebody to do the night shift and work as handyman. You never were much good fixing things, but at least you don't drink. I fired that drunken Mexican last week."

"I like it here," said Earl C.

When Darlene was amused, which was most of the time, her eyes screwed up so tight they vanished inside the folds of her flesh. They did that now. "There's no fool like an old fool, Earl C," she said. "You ain't going nowhere. I was just out at your Ladies Rest Room. It's a filthy mess."

"I got a new idea," Earl C said slowly. "I got it in a place in Las Vegas." He showed her a verse he had copied down on the back of an envelope. "I was thinking of putting this up in the rest rooms."

Darlene read it.

Let no one say to your shame,
There was cleanliness here 'til you came.

Darlene rocked with soundless laughter. "You slay me, Earl C," she said.

Since business was slow, Earl C spent a lot of time sitting

on his tiny front porch next to the frontage road. On the other side of the road the desert stretched out until it reached the row of rocky hills in the distance. In the daytime, the hills were lavender; at night, black, craggy silhouettes. Somewhere up there, it was said, was a hidden uranium mine. In his younger days, Earl C used to go into these hills with a horse and search around in the dry gullies between the barren cliffs. He had not discovered the mine, but he had brought back many bleached bones of animals—skulls, pelvises, rib cages, and femurs of cows, horses, and coyotes. He arranged these bones artistically out in front of his place and planted cacti in and among them for a pretty effect. But he always examined them carefully first. He had heard that dinosaurs, in all sizes from that of a chicken to eighty-foot-long giants, had once roamed these parts; it was necessary to keep your eyes open; you never could tell when you might come upon a find. He also picked up interesting specimens of rocks and minerals, which he polished and labeled and placed on a bench beneath the bottle window.

Now he had arthritis, and horseback riding shook up his spine. But he liked to stare across the road to the mysterious hills. I'm not getting any younger, he would say to himself. I'm not getting any richer, either. But someday, something will happen. It's got to, on account of the Law of Averages.

Out in back of his place, Earl C kept his zoo. He had had, from time to time, a horned toad, two rattlers, a Gila monster, a deodorized spotted skunk, a sidewinder, a ring-tailed cat, a kangaroo rat, an iguana, a prairie dog, and two alligators (not indigenous), which he had ordered, against Darlene's wishes, from a shop in Florida. Most of the zoo had now passed away. The Mexican family down the road had stolen and eaten the iguana; Earl C could never prove this, but he knew it in his bones. The Gila monster had caught a chill during the rainy season, and passed, too; it was his favorite, and he had taken it to Kingman and had it stuffed and then returned it to its cage. But folks complained he had advertised a *Live* Zoo, and they weren't getting their fifty-cents' worth, so he put the Gila monster on the back of the counter, next to the live black widow in a Mason jar. The zoo now consisted of one rattler, one sidewinder, the kangaroo rat, which never came out of its nest in the daytime, and the ring-tailed cat, which was mangy and turning mean.

Earl C had advertised his Place for ten miles in each direction with signs he had painted himself and nailed to telephone poles. Each sign pointed out a different attraction.

10 MILES TO EARL'S—COOL DRINKS
7 MILES TO EARL'S—EATS
5 MILES TO EARL'S—LIVE FAMILY ZOO
2 MILES TO EARL'S—CLEAN REST ROOMS

When you got to Earl's Place there were many other signs, including a big one he had added after the Freeway went in. It said, IF YOU CAN'T STOP, WAVE.

Recently, Earl C had had bad luck about the signs. A young man with a crew cut and wearing a jacket and tie, who was from the County Planning Department, had stopped by and told Earl C the signs had to go; they didn't comply, were his words, with the county's new sign ordinance. Earl C felt gravely put upon by this Government man, but what could he do? Nothing! That was the way it was with those Big Shots. They made laws that suited only them. One day, about a month later, the signs vanished.

"I see your signs are gone," said Darlene on the following Saturday night. She kept up with things; nothing escaped her notice.

Earl C explained the situation to her.

"You're a dope, Earl C," Darlene said. "That county man just wanted his palms greased, that's all."

Earl C would never offer a bribe, on account of his integrity. Just the same he was curious about how you went about it. He asked Darlene how much money the county man would have expected. Darlene's fat body quivered and quaked with amusement. He asked her how you gave it to him; did you just hand it straight out, mail it in a letter, or leave it lying on top of the counter for him to pick up?

"There ain't no rules," she chortled. "You just have to have a business head."

There was one thing Darlene never could get through *her* head, businesslike though it was, and that was Earl C's conviction, based on scientific evidence, that things would change for the better. A taciturn man, he had a mind filled with images he could not express. They took the form of flickering, incandescent shapes, much resembling the neon splendor of Las Vegas, where he occasionally went to play keno.

El Dorado
Golden Nugget
Four Queens
The Mint

"Twenty-Four-Hour Excitement" was what they promised and Twenty-Four-Hour Excitement was what he dreamed about. One day, he knew, it would come about.

Earl C could recall the exact moment when it did. It was 10:22 A.M., November 15, 1967, at the Buy-n-Save Market in Kingman, where he went once a week to buy supplies. Darlene dropped in that evening, and right away she sensed the new look about him. It was the Twenty-Four-Hour Excitement look, which, though he tried, he could not suppress.

"How's business?" she said, as they sat at one of the tables in the Café, where they played cards. Her voice wasn't smug this time; it was sharp and suspicious, and her eyes remained wide open.

"Middling," said Earl C.

"How's that ornery bobcat?" she went on, fishing.

"Ring-tailed. Same as ever."

Still eyeing him cannily, she said, "Gin rummy or casino?"

"Don't know as I have time for either. I got to think."

"Think?" she said scornfully, but he detected an anxiety in her voice. "When did you ever think last, Earl C?"

"I have to find a good lawyer, not in Kingman, but in Vegas."

She put down the deck. "You're in trouble?" she said gleefully.

"Nope. Some Big Shots are, though. Some Big Shots back in Chicago."

"Earl C, you slay me." He could tell her heart was not in her words. "Now just what do you want a lawyer for?"

"I found something today," he said with dignity.

Her eyes were bulging out of her face, reminding Earl C of the Gila monster.

"Or maybe it kind of found me. The Law of Averages has come about."

"What is it, Earl C?" Her voice was threatening.

"Don't know as I better tell anyone until I see the attorney."

"If you need an attorney, you better tell me first. You don't have a drop of business sense in your head."

"I'll tell you if you can guess!" He thought for a moment. Then he put it another way. "I'll give you a hint, though. I found it in a cube of Vi-Rite Oleomargarine."

"I reckon you found a thousand-dollar bill," she said sarcastically.

"Might turn into more." He hummed under his breath.

"All right. Animal, vegetable, or mineral?"

His lips twitched. "Animal."

"What are you getting at, Earl C?" She appeared to have stopped breathing; her flesh barely rippled. He recognized the symptoms; she was in a real pucker.

"Animal," he said. "Maybe a mouse."

"For your Live Family Zoo, I reckon."

He hummed again, softly.

"I didn't come here to play kids' games, Earl C," she said between her teeth. "You tell me, or I hightail it out of here."

Earl C knew his teasing had gone far enough, because he had to tell Darlene; it was part of his Twenty-Four-Hour Excitement. He said, "Just a minute, you wait here." He went into the back room where he kept his freezer, and returned with a small plastic tackle box. Slowly and elaborately he opened the box and removed a small package wrapped in aluminum foil. Slowly, even grandly, he undid the foil, then the Vi-Rite wrapping, and held its contents up under the lamp for her to gaze upon.

She stood up and hung over his hand and stared.

"I see a cube of oleomargarine, Earl C. What's so special about that?"

"Look close." He pointed to a particular part.

She bent down to study it. There, smoothly encased in the pale yellow mold, was a darkish section; on close scrutiny it appeared to be made of a hairy organic matter.

"Well?" said Earl C proudly.

"Look here, Earl C, you've got something there all right, and you know it." Darlene was breathing heavily. "Yes, sir, you got a find."

"I'm pretty sure it's half a mouse. I'm fixing to get it scientifically analyzed, for sure."

"It's a something that doesn't belong there, no matter what it is," Darlene said. "Listen, Earl C, you better let me handle it. They'll make you a nice settlement if we go about it correct."

Earl C carefully wrapped up the oleo, fitted it back into its plastic box, and returned it to the freezer. He came back and sat down opposite Darlene.

"You got a lock on that freezer?"

"Yes, ma'am!"

"We could get a real good settlement if you don't bungle things."

"I ain't taking no settlement," Earl C said. His voice took on a kind of rapturous quality. "Those Big Shots in Chicago are going to fix me up with a place in Palm Springs, maybe, or I just might get me a Mobile Home and tour the world. I've always wanted to see the Yellowstone National Park, and New York City. They're going to arrange things for Earl C Bennet nice. I'll take it all the way to the Supreme Court if need be. This time the law's on my side."

"The Supreme Court takes money, Earl C, and you don't have none. But I know something about business. Those folks back in Chicago would make you a decent payment just to get that thing back."

"I don't settle," Earl C said again. "That ain't my way."

The attorney in Las Vegas, a young chap in a fancy office, wearing a bolo tie and expensive boots, said right away that Earl C had a case. "A case," he said, emphasizing the "a" part. "We'll take some photographs of that cube, then I'll get a letter right off, and we'll see what transpires. In this kind of action, they usually oblige by settling out of court. My fee will be a percentage of the settlement." He looked Earl C over. "Twenty percent," he said.

Earl C, holding on his lap the traveling styrofoam icebox with his find in it, shook his head. "I ain't going to settle for nothing less than ten grand."

"You may have set your sights a bit too high," the lawyer chap said easily. "But I think we could manage to get a few hundred for you."

Earl C hugged the icebox more closely.

"Those Big Shots sold me an inferior product," he said. "I got this here inferior product on my lap. I'm fixing to get ten grand, you can tell them that."

Two years went by in which Earl C made many trips into Vegas. He had turned down three offers from Chicago, the highest and last one being three hundred dollars. He had changed attorneys four times. The last attorney had a new letter in the mail right now.

Other things had happened, too. Busy with his cases, Earl C had neglected what was left of his business, and he was in trouble about his taxes. He had scarcely enough money left to keep him going for a month. The ring-tailed cat had passed, and the kangaroo rat had eaten his way out of his cage and run off. Thick dust had collected on his rock-and-mineral collection, and the bottles were so dirty they were no longer translucent. People drove by and stopped to use the rest rooms without patronizing the Café; Earl C was forced to padlock the doors.

But his spirits stayed high; he was still experiencing the Twenty-Four-Hour Excitement. Even Darlene's disgust at his turning down the offers did not dampen his dream. He sat in the evenings on his porch and looked out at the hills. "I'm not getting any younger," he said to himself, "but I'm getting richer, slow but sure." He was betting hard on the most recent letter, which the lawyer had made severe.

When the answer came it was a repeat of the last one, with an addition. The addition said this was a final offer; after that they would terminate the correspondence. The lawyer urged Earl C to accept it. Politely, but firmly, he declined. The fifth lawyer he went to see that same afternoon had already heard about the case and said he couldn't do anything more. Earl C packed up his find and headed home. "Right is right," he said to himself. "The law doesn't always serve justice."

That night Darlene stopped by. "What's that up in front of your place, Earl C?" she said. She was referring to the new sign he had made that afternoon in large letters:

ASK TO SEE WHAT I FOUND IN A
CUBE OF VI-RITE OLEOMARGARINE

"I've decided to handle the case myself," he told Darlene.

She sniffed, scornfully. "I just fired that Indian handyman," she said. "He was a no-good Indian. You're a no-good white man, Earl C, but if you accept that last offer, and give me half, you can still have the trailer in return for taking my night shift and some work around the motel. If you don't, the law's going to get you for your taxes."

"When word about my sign gets around, there'll be some activity," said Earl C calmly.

The sign did attract curiosity. Folks stopped by and asked to see what he had found; when he showed them, they looked and marveled. Earl C explained his position to them in detail. "I've been offered four settlements," he said. "I've got all the correspondence locked up in a drawer. But I'm holding out for ten grand. Those Big Shots ain't going to get away with it."

He could tell by their comments they approved of his stand. "That's right, that's the spirit, keep it up," they would say. Then they would drive on.

In late June, badgered by the tax man, Earl C put his Place up for sale. His only prospect, a car-wrecking-lot man, claimed the building was worth nothing and would have to be demolished.

Earl C sold out for peanuts. Then he released the rattler and the sidewinder and the black widow out on the Mojave, dropped his rock-and-mineral and bottle collections off at the Desert Museum in Kingman, took his stuffed Gila monster and the tackle box which contained his fortune, and went to live at the Cactus Court. The Gila monster decorated the small plastic-top table in the trailer; he put the tackle box in Darlene's freezer and added a lock. His agreement with Darlene was the night shift and doing cleanup and repairs. He didn't tell Darlene that he was just biding his time; he had a new secret plan concerning his litigation.

His new plan involved a lawyer in Phoenix who, he had been told, had special experience in personal injury cases. Earl C liked the sound of that; if there was anybody who had been personally injured, he had. The first chance he had to sneak away from Darlene he drove there with the tackle box. Though the lawyer asked for a higher percentage of the fee, on account of his specialty, he said he felt sure he could do something for him. He would let him know what transpired.

For this reason Earl C had difficulty putting his mind to the work Darlene demanded. He fell asleep on the night shift while Darlene snored in the back room; folks rang the bell, then drove off when they got no answer. The *No* on the No Vacancy sign stayed unlit more than usual when Earl C took over the desk. Darlene's temper took a turn for the worse.

She put him to whitewashing the rocks that bordered the parking lot; Earl C spilled the whitewash on the pavement and had to endure her wrath. While she puttered around in bedroom slippers and a muumuu and screeched at him to do this, do that, he just smiled to himself, knowing he would soon be rid of her. He had decided on the Mobile Home for sure. But, now, rather than New York City, he favored Southern California. He had never seen the ocean, except in movies and on TV, but he had heard it was much like the desert—shifting shapes, changing colors, and unexpected finds washed up on the shore. When Darlene popped her eyes at him, he blinked and looked right through her. Instead of seeing that massive blob of flesh, he saw the pretty California sea.

One day Darlene brought him a letter from Phoenix, which she had already taken the liberty of opening. She threw it down on the table and said, "There you are, Earl C. Take it or leave it."

The Phoenix lawyer had arranged for Earl C to be awarded $1,000 minus his fee. If Earl C didn't accept this, the lawyer wrote, it was all that anyone could do. Earl C read the letter several times over, then he put it down.

"Well?" said Darlene.

"I guess I'll have to get me another lawyer," he said.

Darlene began to control her breathing.

"I ain't going to compromise on a Once-in-a-Lifetime Opportunity."

Darlene began to yell. "You're more worthless than a Mexican or Indian, Earl C. You'd be better off if you drank yourself silly instead of having found that hunk of mouse! You take that offer, and you start paying me rent until you get down to business. You take that offer, Earl C, or you'll wish you had!"

Earl C said, "It ain't right, so I can't take it," and shut up.

Earl C knew Darlene was crooked, but he never realized how far her crookedness could go. Late that afternoon, purposely, and with malice aforethought, she took the tackle box out of her freezer, unwrapped the oleo, and set it on top of the plaster burro in the full sun in front of the Cactus Court. When she called it to Earl C's attention, it had already thawed. The oleo had slid down the burro's rump, leaving the bits and pieces of the hairy organic matter sticking to the plaster back.

Darlene stood there in her muumuu, watching Earl C.

Then her eyes screwed up and her body began to quiver; soon her shaking grew epic like a mighty earthquake. Her laughter wasn't silent this time: little snorts of amusement escaped from her compressed lips. She took the garden hose and sprayed the burro off.

Earl C walked slowly to the trailer and got his deer rifle and loaded it and came back and shot Darlene through her heart. Darlene slid softly to the ground, clutching the garden hose. She looked funny dead. She seemed to have deflated, all at once, like a balloon. Her heart's blood mingled with the water and was changing from dark red to pale pink.

Some people, who had heard the shot, came out of their units, but Earl C paid them no mind. He turned off the hose, then walked slowly back to his trailer. When he got there, he sat down. From his window he could see the desert shimmering in the distance; in the background were the hills. The light was such you couldn't be sure just where they were every moment; they changed their position like phantoms. Sometimes they looked real close up, sometimes faraway.

If luck was on your side, you could come on finds in those hills. But he had had his luck and used it up; it was too late now for him. Just the same, he enjoyed knowing the finds were there. He waited with quiet integrity, for the sheriff's men to come and hand him over to the law.

Señor Muerte

Amsterdam. The Rijksmuseum. "Rrrk-mu-zi-uum," says Daniel, making an embarrassing bullfrog noise deep in his throat. "*The Night Watch!*" he says. Christ, the place will be mobbed; it's the most important picture in the Netherlands. But you have to see it, once, he adds, in a slightly shamefaced tone, for it is also the tone that grown-ups use to explain necessary evils to the young, exactly the sort of tone that Daniel, himself, abhors. Joan is embarrassed for her father—caught as he is, between Principle and Principle.

Daniel, who has already been exploring Europe for four months on what he calls his "sabbatical," is showing his daughter Western Civilization, in which he no longer has much faith, but still—one must examine one's heritage before one can go from there. Twelve is a good age for this; how he wishes he had had her opportunities at twelve.

Twelve, he continues, is just the time to get a Foundation, following which, one can begin to practice the Art of Traveling, which is a subdivision of the Art of Living, to which—after much sad experience, after many mistakes, owing to a

Success-Oriented education, which tricked him into designing residences for the Undeserving Rich, and perhaps also because there are so few Undeserving Rich who hire architects these days (a profound example of the ephemeral nature of worldly ambition)—he has decided to devote his days.

Twelve is not a good age to examine your heritage, particularly if, once examined, it must be discarded. At twelve you have already suffered brain damage. Your mind is rigid; you would much rather be at home with what your mother calls your "peer group." You are a ready victim for Cultural Shock. But this is Daniel's summer—arranged, signed for, and sealed in Chambers, and, anyhow, Mother is on a honeymoon.

"Well, what do you think of the hirsute embellishment?" Daniel asked Joan, when he met her at the airport, shyly fondling a new, shaggy salt-and-pepper beard, gazing at her with his big blue wistful eyes.

But there is not only the beard, there is the entire New Look, as if Daniel is a fugitive in disguise. Instead of the elegant corduroy suits he used to wear, there are the faded Levi's and the faded blue work shirt, the Vibram-soled Alpine boots, the very large silver Navajo belt buckle. Instead of Brooks Brothers ties, he owns a collection of bandanas—pink and orange and yellow and *purple*—which he knots about his neck. More unsettling than his costume are his habits. He has taken up Autogenic Therapy, which he practices twenty minutes in the A.M. and twenty minutes in the P.M., squatting in the Lotus position, counting backward from one hundred as he emits his Alpha brain waves. In addition, he does ten minutes of Royal Canadian Airforce exercises and jogs in place for five minutes twice a day beside his bed—an earnest, almost grim expression upon his face. It is Daniel, not this foreign land, that produces the Cultural Shock.

"It's very nice," she told Daniel about the beard. Primness has become both a refuge and a defense.

In Amsterdam, she sulks primly, stuffs on Dutch chocolates, writes long, far-from-prim letters to her peer group, describes the bidets, the sex shops, the whores sitting in their doorways. Daily, she shampoos and brushes her long straight ironed-looking blonde hair. She is not in the least interested in seeing *The Night Watch*; she has already seen it, anyhow, on the backs of matchboxes and candy boxes and in miniature framed reproductions in the souvenir shops, along with the miniature wooden shoes, the miniature windmills, the miniature chocolate Delft plates. Tourist trash, Daniel calls the souvenir-shop merchandise, as he waits impatiently on the sidewalk while she browses. It is one of the few activities she enjoys.

The Night Watch is at the end of an enormous, crowded room.

"Christ Almighty!" groans Daniel, staring at the tourists.

The room is so crowded, in fact, that Joan, who is five feet three, cannot see *The Night Watch* at all. She stands on tiptoe, and the crowd, like a great warm wave, pushes her backward and forward. There is a shortage of oxygen, a strong odor of sweat and mildewed rain apparel. Joan, who has delicate spells, feels faint.

"Poor old Rembrandt," Daniel is saying; "the Establishment—the burgomasters, they were called—really put it down. No way, they said, after he painted it. To hell with them, said Rembrandt, and died in poverty, doing his own thing."

Joan finds the educational tour guide speech, seasoned with out-of-date argot, as embarrassing as Daniel's pronunciation of Dutch. She spots a hole between two pairs of trousered legs, bends down and slips through it, sideways, and pops up, at last, in front of the twisted silken rope that, along with two uniformed guards on each side of it, guards the most important treasure in the Netherlands. It is mostly black. The light bounces off its varnish, making it difficult to distinguish any details. It is much better, she decides, on the backs of match folders and candy boxes in the souvenir shops.

"Well, now you've seen it," says Daniel's voice in back of

her. "It's only called *The Night Watch*, you know. It's really
not a night watch at all. It's actually" (he is reading from a
guidebook) " 'the Company of Captain Frans Banning
COCQ and Lieutenant Willem Van Ruytenburgh in 1639,
on the occasion of the visit of Maria de' Medici, widowed
Queen of France, to Amsterdam, when the civic guard had
acted as her escort.' Shall we get out of this hell hole and
treat ourselves to an ooo-tees-myter?"

London. A Bed and Breakfast lodging across from the Brit-
ish Museum. Daniel is very proud of the way they travel.
He has blacklisted all travel agents. Instead, he reads
books, studies maps, consults the kind of people who will
understand just the thing they want. No Tourist Traps for
them. In England, they will stay where the English stay; in
Italy, the Italians, et cetera, et cetera.

At breakfast, over brittle toast, gummy marmalade, and
lukewarm tea, a Ms. Christy MacPherson, not English,
from the Island of Oahu. Blue eyes and tawny skin and long
black hula-hula-girl hair. A male Scottish ancestor mated
with a native Polynesian—a Princess Royal. "The most ter-
rific merger in all of history," says Daniel, with an appreciative appraisal of Ms. MacPherson in her tight tank top.
Ms. MacPherson is nineteen, does Modern Dance as well as
native Polynesian numbers, and is passionate about Art
and Architecture. Most people think she's flipped out on account of this devouring passion.

"We," says Daniel, speaking like a king, "are not most
people." He deftly pours her tea. "It depends upon your
definition of 'flipped out' anyhow," he says.

They have a long talk, very tedious. "Jung," says Daniel.
"Thank God you didn't say Freud," Ms. MacPherson
breathes in great relief. "Freud's a dirty word, as far as I'm
concerned—male chauvinist pig. If you'd said 'Freud'!" She
giggles, takes a sip of tea. "I'm sure you've read *The Be-
trayal of the Body*?" Daniel nods soberly. "Western Civilization," he says, "has degraded the body. Dualism. The
wicked body, the pure transcendent soul." "If that's what
Dualism is, well"—she gives Joan a sideways look—"if cir-

cumstances were a bit different," she says, "I could use a *very* unladylike expression."

"Always say what you feel!" says Daniel grandly. "Then stuff Dualism!" cries Ms. MacPherson. "Your pagan blood has saved you from a fate worse than death," says Daniel. "My dear Miss MacPherson—" "Christy." "My dear Christy, do us the honor of accompanying us on our drive to the Cotswolds tomorrow. I know of a particularly charming fifteenth-century church with brass rubbings. We don't have to be Dualists to enjoy it. We have splurged and ordered a car for the occasion. I'm showing my daughter about, giving her a Foundation, as well as renewing our acquaintance. Her mother and I are divorced. We would be so happy, would we not, Joan, if you would join us as our guest."

Joan smiles *primly*.

Christy leans forward for a match, a movement that provides her with the opportunity to wiggle her supple jeaned butt. Daniel, appreciative of this treat, rises, takes the match from her, and lights her cigarette. "The church I was discussing is a particularly fine example of the Romanesque," he says, looking into the Polynesian's blue eyes.

"Romanesque is my very favorite type of architecture," says Christy. "In the Islands," she says, "we say '*Mahalo nui*.' Which means, 'many thanks.'"

The fifteenth-century church, the Cotswolds. Rain. They pick their way through the soggy graveyard, Daniel sheltering Christy with her umbrella. The church is cold and damp. Chipped statues stare hollow-eyed from niches. The brass rubbings have been taken over by uniformed schoolboys and their Master. Up in front of the altar rail, a custodian, an old man with a dry cough, is polishing a large bird with spread wings perched on the top of a long brass pole. Joan suppresses a rainy-day yawn and joins Daniel and Christy. Daniel is conversing with the custodian.

The custodian puts down his rag and addresses Christy.

"In all the seventeen years I've been polishing this ere bird," he says, "this gentleman 'ere"—he points his rag at

Daniel—"is the first one to recognize what he is. Most folks, now, they think he's an eagle. Well, he's not an eagle, he's a Phoenix. The gentleman is correct!"

Christy gives Daniel a wide-eyed, wondrous gaze. Daniel assumes a modest man-of-the-world air, slips the man a tip. He strokes his beard to conceal his pride.

They leave the church, Christy clinging to Daniel to avoid slipping on the wet stone path.

"The Phoenix—" says Daniel. "I've looked a bit into iconography," he says. "It is the symbol of Resurrection, of Eternity, Rebirth. We don't have to be religious in the conventional way to appreciate that. It fits in nicely with the Eastern philosophy as well. I'm quite sure you can find such a concept among the Polynesians, although I must confess my ignorance when it comes to primitive art. But why primitive? The word implies a lack of something—of what?" he cries, suddenly coming to a stop, so that Christy has to back up in order to return to the protection of the umbrella. "We ought to reexamine our values," he says, "before we stick things with names like that!"

"The missionaries destroyed most of ours," says Christy. "They persuaded the natives to push their idols over the cliffs. Sometimes I feel this awful guilt, my great-great-grandfather was a missionary."

"No one would ever guess it," says Daniel, squeezing the Scottish-Polynesian's arm.

Madrid. The Prado Museum. Joan's feet ache. They did the Spaniards yesterday. Today, they are taking in the paintings that Spanish kings collected from other countries. In front of them: *The Garden of Love.* Courtly revelers in a pretty, rustic setting. Musicians. Lovers. Bacchantes. The sensuous glint of satin gowns.

"Rubens. He was fond of life's pleasures, and why not?" says Daniel, his arm resting lightly on Christy MacPherson's shoulder.

"With your permission," says a melancholy voice in back of them. The voice belongs to a soberly dressed, hawk-nosed, skinny old codger, leaning upon a gold-headed black cane. A

Spaniard, speaking English with an English accent. He
bows arthritically in the direction of the ladies. "I have
been observing this particular painting for many years, and
I should like to make a correction," he continues, without
anyone's permission at all. "The masterpiece you see before
you is not about love, not about earthly pleasures, not about
life; it is about death." He points toward the painting with
his cane, almost topples over, recovers his balance, pro-
ceeds, "Rubens was playing—how shall I express it—a little
private joke. Naturally, you will comprehend, the people
who wanted a picture by this great artist desired a happy
courtly scene. The Master had other ideas. He had buried
his mother, his father, his wife, his children. He was familiar, also, I am convinced, with the prints of the Early Middle Ages, which depicted life's brevity—prints, often named,
ironically, *The Garden of Delights*. The Dark Ages, as we
know, was a time of disasters. The Black Plague. Corpses
piled in the streets. Life and its delights were, indeed, brief.
You have only to compare those prints with Rubens's picture and you will notice a similar composition. The figure in
the foreground"—he points again with his cane—"is in the
same position as the Death Figure, usually a lurking skeleton, in the medieval prototype. Rubens has depicted himself
with his new young bride. Youth and old age. And, there, as
I have shown you, is Señor Muerte himself, grinning at the
frivolous scene before him. He knows that all the merry-
makers will soon be underground, no? This is what Señor
Muerte is thinking. This is the real picture the Master has
painted."

The old bore bows again, reaches for Christy's hand,
makes a kissing gesture above it, and vanishes. Christy
stares at her hand—still outstretched—then rubs it against
her skirt, as if she is washing away germs.

"Creep!" she says.

"Probably jealous of my fair companions," says Daniel,
stroking his beard nervously.

Nobody is looking at the picture anymore. There is an
awkward silence.

Daniel breaks it. "Shall we go have a sangria?" he says in

a jolly voice. "Followed, perhaps, by some flamenco?" He hurries them out down the long passage. "I've been given a name, a place where tourists don't go, the Real McCoy, so to speak." He strokes his beard again with a gesture that has almost become a tic.

Venice. "The greatest municipal show on earth," says Daniel. A city of dreams and merchants. Half European, half Byzantine. Now a museum city. Preserved. Of course, if you didn't preserve it, it wouldn't be here. That was always a problem. Still, there was an unwholesome quality, like an additive in food, an unreal look, like artificial coloring that makes hot dogs redder. Daniel has many interesting things to say about Venice, though, of course, he always adds, he is only here to show it to Joan and Christy. When you come right down to it, it has become a Tourist Sideshow.

Joan and her father no longer take adjoining rooms. That stopped in Madrid. But it is a small pensione, and, going to the WC in the hall one night, Joan hears Christy and Daniel arguing through the thin walls of Christy's room. In the daytime, Christy seems restless. She returns to her room after breakfast to write letters. She refuses to give them to the concierge, insists on taking them to the *posta* herself. At lunch, in the Piazza San Marco, she complains to Daniel that the servants in Venice get on her nerves. They pop right into her room without knocking. They seem to hover, lurk. There is always the outstretched hand. She is convinced they have gone through her luggage, though nothing is missing for sure.

After lunch, they go by gondola to the Accademia to see Venetian art. The air is muggy, the sky dark. Candy wrappers, a Coke bottle, and a Number Two float past them on the choppy water. Joan averts her eyes. Christy compares the polluted water to her native crystal sea. She asks Daniel if he has a Valium. Her head hurts. Daniel expounds on the virtues of Autogenic Therapy compared to pills. Christy pouts.

At the Accademia, Joan leaves the quarreling lovers to

themselves and wanders about alone. Nymphs, goddesses, and plump pink naked ladies recline on sofas, in gardens, bathe in pools, their hands upon their crotches. A large white bull, with a garland of flowers about his neck, carries one of them off upon his back. The resistance she puts up, all squirming arms and legs, appears phony to Joan. She walks on. Dimpled-bottomed cupids float on fleecy clouds. Chariots wheel through the skies. Gondolas glide by with masked revelers. Popes and Doges in scarlet gowns march in processions, under canopies. God, the Father, with a white beard, pokes his head out of a lightning bolt.

Too much! She sinks down on a bench to recover from the visual pandemonium. In front of her is another large picture. She glances up at it and spots a familiar figure. It is Jesus. Jesus, in a Venetian piazza. And there, all around him, are the servants of Venice, dressed in different clothes, of course—old-fashioned clothes. But they are doing the same things Christy complains about. They hover, lurk. They lean over balconies, peer from in back of pillars, peep through grated windows. They remind Joan of curious little boys, spying on the goings-on. Spying on Jesus! If Jesus had a suitcase, she thinks, they probably would be going through it. She smiles at the thought. She thinks of telling the great-great-granddaughter of a missionary that Jesus had to put up with Venetian servants, too. Prudently, she decides against it.

Pompeii. They take a guide. Daniel does not believe in guides, but it is the only way to see the famous sex room Christy has read about and is dying to see. When, however, she discovers that Daniel intends to include Joan, her missionary blood surfaces. She is, she declares, shocked!

"I'm not going to make her stand outside and wait for us, for God's sakes," says Daniel. "Can you imagine a better way to make sex seem dirty to an impressionable young girl? What happened to your pagan heritage?"

"You have to stop somewhere," says Christy, tight lipped.

"Where and why?" shouts Daniel, yanking at his beard.

"You know what I mean," says Christy. She holds her head erect, her eyes flash indignation. There is something a little *insincere* about this sudden concern for Joan's morals, Joan thinks. She is reminded of the fat lady being carried off by the bull. At the same time, there is something *sincere* about it. The pursed lips and righteous posture transform the lithe Hawaiian into one of her Scottish ancestors. It is not difficult to picture Christy throwing idols off the cliff into the sea.

They start off, following the guide—Christy with her disapproving air, Daniel, fingering his beard, Joan, walking *primly* in back of them.

The guide is an old man. He has three moles on his dark, wise-looking face. Despite the July heat, he is dressed in a brown business suit, vest, and fedora. He has been a merchant, he tells them. His work as a guide—three days a week—is a kind of semiretirement. He has two sons and a daughter. One son lives in Detroit. He walks slowly on the shady side of the high pavements. Everyone knows him, everyone greets him: he is a very popular old man.

He shows them the Antiquarium, with the moldings of people and animals in contorted postures, caught by the holocaust, suffocated by the fumes. He shows them the Forum, adorned with statues, the Great Theatre, the baths. He explains the sewage system—very advanced for those days. His customers listen politely, but there is a pecular tension among them. Suddenly, the moment arrives. The guide whispers something to Daniel. Daniel looks at Christy. Christy gives a haughty shrug of her shoulders. The guide looks at Joan. Daniel nods, yes, and slips the guide some extra coins. The guide takes a special key out of his pocket, opens a side door next to the sidewalk, and ushers his party into a small room.

It is dark and cool. The guide gestures toward the walls, which are covered with black-and-red frescoes—people fucking in funny postures. This is the lovemaking room, he tells them. Do the ladies find it objectionable?

Christy, judging from her expression, does. She glares at Joan, refuses to look at Daniel. Daniel looks hurt. It is obvi-

ous to Joan that Christy wanted to view the acrobatics on
the wall alone with Daniel, perhaps review them with him
afterward in Daniel's room, late at night. Not being a
parent, Christy does not understand that some things come
before one's own personal sexual pleasure. Not being a parent, she does not appreciate the trauma that could occur to
an impressionable young girl of twelve, left standing outside the Lovemaking Room. Christy, thinks Joan, has read
Laing—whoever he is—but she is uninformed on Dr. Spock.

"I think the frescoes are extremely beautiful," says Joan
trying to help Daniel out.

The guide looks pleased; Daniel grins; Christy makes a
huffing noise.

The Pope, says the guide, has closed this room to the public. To see it one must make private arrangements, as they
have done. The Pope does not want tourists to misunder-
stand, to think badly of their history. The guide thinks this
is silly. People, he says, in his wise, grave way, are the same
everywhere. He winks at Joan, who nods solemnly in agreement.

"Are you interested in seeing what else the Pope thinks
you should not see?" says the guide, pushing out his lower
lip, comically.

Daniel looks uncertainly at Christy, who says nothing.

"Yes, please," says Joan.

Daniel, caught between the two protagonists, strokes his
beard uneasily.

The guide excuses himself for a moment, returns carrying a small box.

It is like a dollhouse with doors on hinges. Joan remembers toys like this when she was a child. You opened the
doors, and there was an amusing scene—a bear dancing
with a ballerina, or a family of mice, dressed in Victorian
costumes, sitting cozily in their parlor.

The guide stands before them, assumes a theatrical
stance. He opens and shuts the box fast, like a magician.
Christy gives a definite shudder. Joan suppresses a giggle,
then nods, graciously. Daniel laughs out loud.

Pleased with the majority response, the guide opens and

shuts the box again and again. Each time Joan has only one second to glimpse what the Pope thinks she should not see. Before he is finished, Christy has marched off. She sits down on a stone bench and waits for her sexually depraved companions to tire of the performance. Daniel—uneasy again—leaves Joan and goes to sit beside her. He talks to her in a low, rapid voice. Christy stands up abruptly and sashays out of the room. The upper portion of her body expresses outraged dignity, the lower part is hula-hulaing. Daniel, looking helplessly at the guide, follows her out.

"The lady doesn't like it?" says the guide, tucking the box under his arm.

"She has missionary blood," Joan explains.

"But you like it, young lady?"

"It's a particularly fine example of a sex room," Joan says. She decides to stay for a few moments so the guide's feelings won't be hurt. She wanders over to the bench and sits down and studiously reexamines the murals. The guide sits down beside her.

"It's better than the drains, eh?" he says.

Joan nods in agreement. She begins a little conversation with the guide. "Does it ever give you the heebie-jeebies working with all these dead people?" she asks him.

"Dead people?" says the guide. "No, no, I feel, after a while, very close to them." He puts his hand over his heart, then lays it lightly upon Joan's bare knee. "They are dead, we are alive; but they are like us, not so long ago, no?" He squeezes her knee—a gentle little squeeze.

Joan likes the warm touch of his hand inside this cool sex room. She likes the guide very much. She *hates* Christy.

Florence. Their pensione, on the working-class, nontourist side of the Arno. An ancient palazzo, according to the dour Signora who runs it. "If it is," says Daniel, "it must have belonged to a very third-rate nobleman." Just the same, he is delighted with his "find." They are among the People—far from the hordes of tourists who fill the outdoor cafés, cluster on flights of steps and around monuments, or follow their tour guides in docile rows across the piazzas. When they cross the Ponte Vecchio to visit the Duomo or the Campanile, they always know they can return to their sanctuary, humble though it may be. It is a knowledge that gives Daniel a sense of euphoria. This, he tells them, is the Art of Traveling.

They are there for two days when Christy drops by the American Express and picks up a letter. She is reading it as she comes out, drops it into her purse, and does not divulge its contents.

The next morning a gleaming BMW motorcycle arrives in front of their palazzo. Its driver is a broad-shouldered, bronzed young man with tendrils of yellow hair curling out from beneath his helmet. He is wearing a nail-studded black leather jacket, a studded leather belt. Joan and Daniel watch from a window as Christy hops on, straddle-legged, in back of him, her arms clutched around his leather waist. Then like the white bull in the Accademia, the abductor carries her off. The last they see of her, before the BMW rounds the corner, is her long black hair floating behind her in the breeze.

Exit Christy MacPherson. Good riddance, as far as Joan is concerned. But, though Daniel makes a brave show of not caring, though he tells Joan that Christy is a very mixed up young woman who hasn't the least notion of what she wants out of life, he is obviously moping. Joan decides it is important to keep him company as much as possible.

During Pranza, she sits cross-legged on the *letto matrimoniale* in Daniel's room, brushes her hair, and watches Daniel do his laundry. He has stripped to his jockey shorts. His belly, despite the Royal Canadian Airforce exercises, swells above his shorts, white and squishy. He washes out his miracle-cloth shirt and nylon socks in the tiny basin, then sets up his traveling clothesline. Each end of the line has a rubber suction cup. He fastens one to the wall, the other to the armoire. He hangs up his wash with miniature plastic clothespins. His domesticity has a sadness to it. Joan brushes her hair with fiercer strokes.

"Voilà!" cries Daniel, stepping back and gazing at the arrangement with pride. Then he clutches his stomach and doubles up with a groan. When the seizure subsides, he stretches out on the floor and takes his pulse, counting to himself. He tells Joan he believes the bad air of Florence is undermining his health. He takes his pulse again. He tells Joan he is looking forward to the good food of Paris, where their trip will end. "Not 'haute cuisine,'" he says, wincing with another cramp, "but plain bistro-type fare." He takes his pulse a third time with an air of serious concern.

That evening after supper Daniel comes down with a high fever, which he labels La Grippe. For five days, Joan brings him broth and toast and tea from the kitchen. In the afternoons, while he sleeps, she crosses the bridge and attends the cinema. She sees John Wayne, Al Pacino, Jane Fonda, and an old Jerry Lewis, speaking Italian, their lips moving to the language of the U.S. of A. It is as if they are imprisoned up there on the screen, forced to say "*Ciao*" instead of "Howdy," and are trying to communicate to her secretly. It is a moving, personal, patriotic experience, and she feels homesick.

Every day, when she returns, Daniel has improved, but La Grippe has left its mark. He is no longer the same man. His face sags. Little pockets and pouches have appeared. His eyes are weaker and he sends her out for a pair of stronger nonprescription spectacles. He has not trimmed his beard, which now has more salt than pepper in it. He has stopped wearing the bright bandanas, and she can see the gray hair on his upper chest. He is touchy about trivialities. He wants the shutters closed, complains about the street noise, the taste of the Signora's broth. Then, overcome by remorse, he apologizes.

"Flu is a depressant," he explains. "When we get to Paris, everything will be different."

"Paris will be the pièce de résistance for you," he says. "We'll go shopping. I'll buy you something pretty to take home."

He pats her hair in a paternal way. "It hasn't been too bad, has it?" he says. He answers the question for her. "It has been an experience," he says, "which you will find meaningful in later life."

They go for short excursions to build up his strength. They visit the Conventa di San Marco to see the Fra Angelicos. Daniel falls in love with the cool cloisters, the whitewashed walls, the peaceful garden. Catholicism, he decides, has its points. A retreat room, like Lorenzo de' Medici kept there, would be useful when the press of everyday life overwhelms you. He confesses to Joan that he can no longer meditate successfully. During the height of his fever something happened to his Alpha brain waves. They are badly out of whack.

The day before their departure, they enter the Signora's dining room for the midday meal, seating themselves at their usual table—Daniel facing the door. The dining room is quiet, sedate. The only other occupants are an elderly Italian gentleman, who lives in the neighborhood and takes his meals here, and a Danish couple, who come every summer. The Signora puts their soup and house wine in front of them. Daniel's appetite has improved. He eats all his soup, looks forward to the pasta, lifts his wine glass and toasts the trip to Paris. Then he sets the glass down and stares with a look of disbelief at the door.

The Tour enters. They swarm into the dining room, taking it over. They are fellow countrymen, all old, a noticeable majority of women. The men wear knitted sport shirts, open at the neck. Their bright colors have the effect of making them seem even older. The women are dressed in pantsuits or print dresses. Like female birds, their plumage is more subdued. Most carry cameras. Each bears a plastic tag upon his or her breast.

THE XYZ CLUB
SYLVAN SPRINGS, SOUTH DAKOTA
ANCIENT CITIES TOUR

Their voices resound throughout the room—flat, unmodulated.

The Signora's son brings Joan and Daniel's pasta. Daniel looks at it with glazed eyes and does not pick up his fork.

The Tour Director, a sturdy young man with slicked-back hair, wearing a dark suit, white shirt, and modest tie, is seating his flock.

"Mrs. Fox, why don't you sit next to Mrs. Conroy today? Miss Wood, if you'll sit here, please, out of the draft? The acoustics are better next to the wall, Mr. Bennet. Mrs. Henry, do you want me to take your camera? Here are your pills, Mrs. Carlson. Good girl. There is a choice of fish or beef. Shall we have a show of hands for fish?"

Joan begins her pasta, hoping to encourage Daniel to begin his. She listens to the voices at the table in back of her.

"Memory isn't what it used to be, but—"

"The guide said they were pure gold, made before Christ!"

"I don't see how they can leave all those precious things out like that! Of course, it's their business, not mine!"

"I'll never forget how beautiful they were!"

"Yes, you will, Lil. You forget everything. You thought we were still in France."

The Director taps upon his glass. The room becomes silent. The members of the XYZ Club Ancient Cities Tour turn toward him, as he begins his announcements.

They will spend three nights here. They should be in the bus at 9:00 A.M. They should dress coolly—the ladies might bring a light sweater. Color film is suggested. Their luggage is now in the hallway, but no one is to worry. It will be in their rooms as soon as possible after lunch.

"And, now, we have a very special occasion this afternoon," the Tour Director says. "A birthday! Mr. Sorenson is twenty-one, or is it Sweet Sixteen?"

Laughter. A woman cries out, "It's Sweet Sixteen and he's never been kissed!" More laughter.

"Mrs. Hallstead, President of the Xtra Years of Zest Club, will now take over our podium. Mrs. Hallstead—!" The Tour Director makes a playful bow and sits down.

Mrs. Hallstead arises. She is large, white-haired, full-bosomed. She wears a dark nylon ensemble. Her cheeks are rouged, her lipstick bright, her posture betrays no insecurity. She smiles cheerily at her audience, glances at some notes she holds in her hand and begins to sing. She is a soprano.

> *George Sorenson, it is your birthday,*
> *Which one, it matters not.*
> *Your merry spirit and joking*
> *Has contributed to our happy lot.*
> *We, the members of the XYZ Club,*
> *Wish you joy a thousand fold.*
> *From you we learned a lesson—*
> *There is no such thing as 'old.'*
> *Happy Birthday, George Sorenson,*
> *Happy Birthday to you.*
> *Back in Sylvan Springs*
> *You'll tell your grandchildren*
> *The marvelous tales of your European debut.*
> *Your birthday in Florence, Italy,*
> *Will go in your book of dreams.*
> *And now it is the momemt*
> *For the cake and the ice cream!*

Applause, cheers. Mrs. Hallstead sits down with the manner of a duty well done. George Sorenson, next to her, beams bashfully. Daniel plays with his pasta, puts down his fork, asks Joan if she would mind if he excuses himself: he suddenly remembers he has not confirmed his train tickets. He rises, strides across the room, almost colliding with the Signora, who enters, bearing the birthday cake. He zigzags around her and makes his escape. Joan sighs gently and finishes her pasta.

That night, Joan has a dream. She is back in Madrid, in the Prado Museum, with Daniel and Christy. They are standing in front of *The Garden of Love*. Suddenly a skeleton, carrying a gold-headed black cane, appears. He makes a courtly bow. Then he points with his cane at the rollicking lovers in the picture (who bear a strong resemblance to Daniel and Christy), bends over Christy's hand, and with a ghastly, knowing grin, departs. It is Señor Creep, Señor Muerte, Mister Death himself. Joan wakes up. The room is suffocating. She throws off the blankets and opens the shuttered windows and leans out into the humid night, gasping for air.

Twelve is not a good age, but Joan will be thirteen in a month. The next morning, while Daniel is at the bank, seeking the best rate of exchange, Joan borrows a traveling iron from one of the Tour ladies. She presses Daniel's bandanas and leaves them, neatly folded, on the *letto matrimoniale* in his room. This is all she can do for him. But who knows? Perhaps, with luck (she is keeping her fingers crossed) there will be a Ms. Somebody—a Christy, a Becky or a Linda— traveling by herself to Paris on their train. A Ms. Somebody with a passion for Art and Architecture, who will find a middle-aged man with blue wistful eyes and an appreciation for youthful, feminine charms, a pleasing companion, the pièce de résistance, she hopes, for the remainder of their journey.

A Happening at Cheerful Corners

The storm broke just before tea. George and Evan, on their way up from Retreat Cottage, ran crazily across the soaked lawn, collecting the garden chairs that had tumbled into the Grotto. They stacked them under the eaves in back of Big House, then scurried—raincoats over their heads—up the flagstone path, almost colliding with Miss Stengle, who was just returning from town beneath a straining umbrella. In one damp gloved hand she held aloft the bamboo windbells she had plucked out of a forsythia bush, and tinkled them triumphantly.

"Bravo!" cried George.

"Turmoil and Disaster!" shouted Evan.

The three of them rushed up the porch steps. The door was opened for them from the inside.

"Sanctuary! Sanctuary!" Hoppy called out, and ushered her three dripping friends into the vestibule, where they removed coats and rubbers.

Colonel and Mrs. Bliss were descending the stairs from Crow's Nest. The Colonel stopped on the landing to consult the barometer.

"We're in for a good one," he said, "the glass is dropping."
"Do I hear Colonel Bliss's cheery voice?" said Hoppy.
"I said, 'We're in for a good one,' " said the Colonel, and
escorted his wife down into the parlor.
"I have an announcement," said Hoppy.
"Hear! Hear!" cried George and Evan.
"I say: Let's ride it out and enjoy our tea!"
There were more Hear! Hear!'s, and applause from Miss
Stengle.

Sixty-nine years ago, in New Haven, Hoppy had been chris-
tened Margaret Canning Hopkins; to the merchants in
downtown Carmel, she was "Miss Hopkins"; to her paying
guests at Cheerful Corners, she was "Hoppy." Her white
hair was cropped short in a Dutch bob; a pince-nez dangled
on a black ribbon over her still erect bosom. Her voice was
hearty; her step, sure. She was dressed, this afternoon, in
one of her several "good" worn-tweed skirts, a shirtmaker
blouse fastened by an agate brooch at the neck, and a tan
Shetland cardigan. She was not only the owner of Cheerful
Corners, she was also its spirit. Her announcement produced a sense of calm. While she went into the kitchen, the
five Regulars took their accustomed places about the blazing fire.

Miss Stengle sat in the wicker armchair, which had a
wicker pocket on each arm, filled with old copies of *National Geographic*. She had been staying at the Corners,
now, for two months—ever since her retirement from the
San Mateo Public Library. She occupied Seascape, in the
downstairs left wing; she spent her mornings writing a book
about her experiences as the child of missionary parents in
China. George and Evan, down for the weekend from the
City, where they had a flourishing Art Import business, sat
on the chintz sofa. Mrs. Bliss took the wing chair; Colonel
Bliss, proud of his posture, the straight-backed chair—part
of an old dining-room set. Colonel and Mrs. Bliss lived in
Palo Alto; they were spending two weeks. Ever since the
Colonel's retirement, Mrs. Bliss had done her Christmas
shopping in Carmel.

Over the years, other guests had come and gone; the Regulars were what Hoppy called her "family." Cheerful Corners was not just a business; it was a creation; a work of art to these fortunate five. They loved its hostess; they loved every inch of its grounds; they loved the cozy parlor where they met for breakfast and tea.

Only someone with a gift for the Personal, such as Hoppy had, could have managed to have crammed so many meaningful mementos and curios and furniture into so small a space and still leave room for people and their comfort.

Knickknacks, souvenirs, objets d'art, filled every surface, every nook and cranny. The mantelpiece held a clock made of shells; a stereopticon and its collection of slides; ceramic animals in playful poses, and a convoluted lavender-and-orange Art Nouveau glass vase containing poppies made of faded colored tissue paper. Over the mantel was a framed photograph of Cheerful Corners, showing it as it was when Hoppy purchased it thirty-five years ago; there was the same brown shingled exterior, the same view of the sea, but the wisteria vine and the plum tree, from which Hoppy made her famous plum jam, had, like Hoppy, flourished with age.

The two desks, the six odd end tables, the three coffee tables—all of various vintages and style—were loaded with trinkets. There were the treasures cast up from the sea— the sand dollars, the polished agates, the abalone shell, the Japanese fishnet float, the pieces of twisted driftwood. The bookshelves held, besides old books, a souvenir plate from the 1915 San Francisco Exposition, two American Indian baskets, and a miniature pair of gold glass slippers. The windowsills were crowded with pots of African violets; an avocado seed suspended by toothpicks in a glass of water, and rows of succulents in tiny pots, which belonged to Sam—Miss Samantha Robbins, Hoppy's helpmate of twelve years.

On the dark paneled walls hung a cuckoo clock, which worked, and a ship's clock, which did not work (despite Colonel Bliss's resolute attempts to repair it); a watercolor of Point Lobos, executed by Miss Stengle; an assortment of postcards, including one from Venice from George and Evan, and one from Hawaii from the Blisses. There were also two calendars—a new one, illustrated with California wildflowers, and an old one, which Hoppy could not bear to discard, illustrated with Pacific Coast lighthouses. There were numerous photographs of friends—former Regulars, some who had moved to far parts of the country or the world but who still "kept up," some who had sadly departed from the world altogether. There were photographs, too, of long-dead dogs and cats, and a photograph that Evan had taken last Christmas of Hoppy, Sam, the Blisses, Miss Stengle, and George in front of the Tree. There was a Sampler—GOD BLESS CHEERFUL CORNERS—embroidered by Mrs. Bliss; four Japanese prints, which had come with the house; a Chinese gong the Colonel had brought back from the Orient, and which Hoppy used to call stragglers into breakfast or tea. On the floor beside the fireplace was a white ceramic cat—and the squashed Moroccan red leather hassock, where Sam always sat; next to the hassock was Buster, Hoppy's ten-year-old deaf, fat, asthmatic pug, asleep and snoring.

The kitchen door swung open; there was the fragrant odor of Hoppy's orange-nut bread, of Sam's cinnamon cookies; and Sam entered, backward, guiding the wicker tea cart. There were polite ejaculations of pleasure from the Regulars.

Sam was nineteen years younger than Hoppy. She had arrived one day twelve years ago—pale, thin, and spinsterly—and had remained as Hoppy's Right Hand. She was now, also, Hoppy's heir. She had grown pudgy and pink cheeked. Never, for one moment, did she forget the good fortune that had led her to Cheerful Corners. Though Hoppy had insisted on having a proper will drawn up so that there would be no nonsense from some unknown relative, after Hoppy's death, Sam still thought of herself as the most humble and least worthy of Hoppy's "Family."

The wind howled down the chimney, sending little sparks out on the grate; the sea pounded against the shore like a giant drum. Hoppy took her place in her chair at the tea cart—a small red lacquered chair with a three-cornered seat—and did the honors, pouring the tea into an assortment of English-bone-china cups. Sam passed the tea and orange bread and cookies. Miss Stengle gave a little sigh of contentment; George stroked Buster's back with one foot; Evan rose and stirred the logs.

"We did not expect this in November, did we?" Hoppy said. "What a pity for the Christmas Bazaar! The ladies have worked so hard. I shall go tomorrow, if I have to swim. They make such lovely things out of pine cones, Styrofoam, ribbon—bits of this and bits of that. I only wish I were as creative."

"Ah, but you are!" said Mrs. Bliss.

"No one but a Hoppy could have created Cheerful Corners," said Miss Stengle, shyly.

"I wish to second; any thirds?" said the Colonel, smearing plum jam on his bread.

"Here! Here!" said George and Evan together.

The colonel cleared his throat—a signal that he meant to say something of importance.

There was a silence.

"What," said the Colonel to Hoppy, "is the condition of your roof?"

"We did the North side a year ago," Hoppy said. "We had the cypress in the grotto staked at the same time. Cheerful Corners has survived many storms. It will survive more." She nodded at Sam, who was now seated on the hassock with her tea.

Sam returned the nod.

"Everybody happy?" said Hoppy.

There was a chorus of "Yes"'s, and a "Perfection!" from Mrs. Bliss, who had just bit into the bread.

"I only hope our new guest isn't in any trouble out on the highway," Hoppy said.

This time there was a longer silence.

Then the Colonel said, "New guest?"

"I didn't know we were expecting anyone," said Mrs. Bliss.

Miss Stengle shifted on her chair, uneasily. A new guest was, for her, both an adventure and a cause for anxiety.

George and Evan moved slightly closer together on the sofa.

"A Mr. Charles Montgomery from Hillsborough," Hoppy said. "He called last evening. Sounded very pleasant, I must say. We were going to put him in the Snuggery, but, with the storm, I think he might be more comfortable upstairs in Lookout."

"I've put fresh towels in both," said Sam.

"How . . . did he find out about us?" said Miss Stengle.

"Word of mouth is the only way we advertise," said Hoppy. "We have never been disappointed, have we, Sam?"

Sam nodded in agreement.

"Let those who will stay at one of the hotels in town, or at one of the new atrocities out on the highway," Hoppy said. "Our own kind seeks us out, and finds us."

An invisible wave of tenderness enveloped the Regulars; Miss Stengle bowed her head, as if she were in church.

"If money were my motive, I would have sold Cheerful Corners long ago to one of those real-estate people that pester me."

Miss Stengle drew in her breath sharply at this thought; the others listened with a quiet reverence.

"It does get tiresome. A very pushy gentleman stopped by the other day. He mentioned a handsome figure. He seemed quite taken back when I informed him that there were more important things than money. I told him what I always tell them. I said this was not just an ordinary commercial venture, it was my home, where I received my guests. No, there won't be a Holiday Inn or a Hilton built on this land in my lifetime—or, in Sam's. I can promise you that!"

This speech, which all had heard before, had the same reassurance that the repetition of a litany does for the devout. Miss Stengle's breathing grew quieter. Mrs. Bliss shut her eyes briefly in order to hide the tears that had suddenly filled them. It had been a year since her Radical; should she go, before the Colonel, where else but at Cheerful Corners would he find the admiration and respect that was his due?

She blinked and picked up her knitting from the floor. She was working on a scarf for the Colonel's Christmas present, which she had told him was to be a sweater for their grandchild in Venezuela. Who else but Hoppy, thought Mrs. Bliss, would be able to cajole this lovable, but stubborn man into wearing it to protect his delicate chest when he took his constitutional? George and Evan had begun to help Sam collect the cups and plates; both paused at Hoppy's familiar words. What they lacked in the City—the warmth and closeness of a larger family life—they had found and cherished here. Cheerful Corners had rescued them from eating out on the holidays that most people shared with relatives. Hoppy was like a mother to them—the right sort of wholly accepting mother—which neither had had. The Colonel patted his stomach and opened the local *Pine Cone.*

"We shall all have to curl up with a good book this afternoon," Hoppy was saying. "No one must dream of going into town for dinner. Sam and I will rustle something up. It will be simple, though—I warn you!"

"Emergency rations," said the Colonel, and everyone laughed.

The front door burst open. The wind blew into the room; the fire leaped; the Colonel's newspaper rattled. All heads turned to watch as the stranger struggled with the door to keep it from banging shut. All remained watching as, having succeeded, he stood a bit uncertainly in the vestibule, gazing into the parlor.

"I'm so terribly sorry," he said. His voice was low and pleasant—what Mrs. Bliss thought of as "cultured." "I'm afraid," he said, "that I may have tracked in some mud."

"As long as you're safe off the highway, a little mud won't matter." said Hoppy, rising to greet him. "We don't fuss over a little mud at Cheerful Corners. Our concern here is with people."

Sam—ahead of Hoppy—was beside him to receive his wrinkled Burberry.

"Thank you so much." He seemed intensely grateful for this simple courtesy.

"Now," said Hoppy, "into the parlor. I'll do the honors

while you warm yourself at the fire. Sam will bring you some tea." She turned to the Regulars. "Mr. Montgomery," she announced.

George and Evan and the Colonel were already standing. Mrs. Bliss and Miss Stengle sat erect. Miss Stengle could once again feel the palpitations in her breast that she always experienced when meeting someone for the first time.

Mr. Montgomery was a man in his middle fifties, tall and slender, with sandy hair and blue eyes.

Nice, sensitive eyes, thought Miss Stengle.

He was dressed in gray flannels and a handsome tweed jacket and a black wool knit tie.

I wonder if he might join the Colonel in his golf game when the storm blows over, Mrs. Bliss thought.

It occurred to George and Evan, simultaneously, that he might make up a fourth for bridge; neither Miss Stengle nor Mrs. Bliss played and Hoppy was always too busy.

"Carlton Bliss, here," said the Colonel, extending his hand.

Mr. Montgomery responded with a firm handshake.

Yes, this chap would do, thought the Colonel.

Buster awoke and lumbered stiffly over to Mr. Montgomery and sniffed at his trouser leg.

"And we mustn't forget Buster," said Hoppy.

Mr. Montgomery smiled and bent down to pat Buster's back. Buster's fat body quivered in appreciation; then he returned to the fire.

The Regulars all felt relief—both for Hoppy and themselves. Sam, who had disappeared into the kitchen, returned with a tea tray. Hoppy gestured toward the sofa; George and Evan moved over to make room,

"Thank you, I'll stand, if you don't mind," Mr. Montgomery said. He accepted the tea, with a polite bow of his head; politely declined the bread and cookies.

"They look delicious, but I'm afraid I'm not really hungry," said Mr. Montgomery.

"You won't get out of here without trying Hoppy's plum jam," said the Colonel. "Rules of the house!"

"Tomorrow, dear," said Mrs. Bliss, "Mr. Montgomery will

be hungrier tomorrow. Tomorrow," she added merrily, "is another day."

Mr. Montgomery gave her a grateful smile.

"To use Colonel Bliss's expression, I shall give you a small briefing," said Hoppy. "Breakfast here in the parlor between seven and nine. Tea at four. Ordinarily, my guests go into town for lunch and dinner, but tonight we're going to rustle something up in the kitchen. I can't have my guests going out tonight."

"Emergency rations," said the Colonel. The Regulars laughed. Mr. Montgomery smiled again.

"I think, if you don't mind, I'll just sack out tonight. I had a bite on the road. I hope that you'll excuse me, Miss Hopkins."

"Hoppy to my guests," said Hoppy. "We were going to put you in the Snuggery, one of the garden cottages. But, with the storm, we think you'd be happier upstairs in Lookout."

"Actually, I rather enjoy storms. I think I'd enjoy the cottage," Mr. Montgomery said.

"Then, the Snuggery it is. We can even provide you with an umbrella. At Cheerful Corners, everyone is free to do as one pleases. We have quite a varied library, if you'd like to take a book down with you."

"Oh, I brought a book, but thank you so much," Mr. Montgomery said.

"We soon hope to add Miss Stengle's work to our collection. She is writing a book about her experiences as a child of missionary parents in China."

Miss Stengle blushed.

"I'm sure I would find it very interesting," said Mr. Montgomery, inclining his head toward Mrs. Bliss by mistake.

"Was it bad out on the road?" said the Colonel.

"Bad?" said Mr. Montgomery.

"Not fit for man nor beast, eh?" the Colonel said.

Mr. Montgomery looked a bit bemused. He put his teacup down on a table. "Perhaps, if you don't mind . . . ," he said to Hoppy. "I shouldn't want to inconvenience you, but I am a little tired . . ."

He does look fatigued, thought Mrs. Bliss.

"Sam will show you to the Snuggery at once," said Hoppy. "If you don't change your mind about supper, we shall see you at breakfast."

"Plum jam. Rules of the house!" the Colonel said.

"Sam, take the extra flashlight. There are matches and candles in the drawer beside your bed. We may be in for a blackout."

"You have all been so kind," Mr. Montgomery said. "It was so pleasant to meet all of you ..." His words faded into a murmur.

"Sweet dreams!" called out Hoppy, as Sam led Mr. Montgomery away.

The Colonel was certain he was a corporation executive; he had played golf with corporation executives; on the whole, they were not unlike the military: you could count on their understanding of protocol. George inclined toward a lawyer; Evan, someone high up in Investments. Miss Stengle thought it possible he might be a professor. Mrs. Bliss, with a glance at Miss Stengle, said it was highly probable he was divorced or widowed.

"Well, we know he's a gentleman, and that's what counts," said Hoppy. "He'll fit in, one way or the other."

Mrs. Bliss put down her knitting and laid a hand on the Colonel's knee. "I think you could do with a little catnap, dear," she said to him.

"Sometimes I think my wife considers me a child," said the Colonel. " 'Take your pill. Wear your warm socks. Take your nap.' Et cetera Et cetera. Of course, I'd be the first to admit I couldn't manage without her."

"Of course you could, dear," said Mrs. Bliss

The storm raged all night. But by morning, like some mysterious and exotic visitor, it had vanished—flown away, out to sea; the sky was sunny; the sea, calm once more.

George and Evan, threading their way among fallen tree boughs and soggy piles of leaves to Big House, reported that the damage was minimal.

"I'll stake up the forsythia bushes, and George will rake the ground and replace the chairs," said Evan to Hoppy.

"Barometer's up," called out Colonel Bliss from the landing.

"Do I hear Colonel Bliss's cheery voice?" said Hoppy.

"I said, 'barometer's up,' " said Colonel Bliss, and he descended the stairs with Mrs. Bliss on his arm.

"It will be interesting to see what treasures can be found on the beach this afternoon," said Miss Stengle. She had rouged her cheeks and put on her best cardigan.

"I'm happy for the Christmas Bazaar," said Mrs. Bliss, who was making plans to attend it.

"I'm happy for Mr. Montgomery," said Hoppy. "We aren't responsible for the weather, but we're always pleased when the sun shines for a new guest. We won't ring the gong, Sam. He may want to sleep late. We'll keep his muffins warm in the oven."

Over his coffee, the Colonel described a storm in the Aleutians during World War II, in which he had played a heroic part. Mrs. Bliss, who had heard the story many times, listened with the fervor of a bride.

By 10:00, the Regulars had finished their breakfast, but they lingered on in the parlor, both out of courtesy and curiosity, for Mr. Montgomery to appear. By 10:30, a forced and hearty conversation covered up a slight uneasiness.

After all, he didn't show up for supper, either, said the Colonel to himself. Did this show a lack of common courtesy, an inconsideration of his hostess as well as, perhaps, the others—himself included? He would have enjoyed telling Montgomery the Aleutian story. Was it possible the chap wouldn't pass muster after all?

At 10:45, Hoppy took matters in hand. "We might just check," she said to Sam. "He ate no supper and seemed so tired. He could be ill. Why don't you take a breakfast tray down to him?"

So it was Sam who found him. She described finding him to the police, and, later, to the shaken Regulars at tea time.

She had knocked several times and received no answer. Perhaps, she thought, Mr. Montgomery had gone out for a walk. Timidly, she tried the door. It was unlocked! Timidly, she had opened it and, with lowered eyes, called out. She no longer could remember what she had said. Probably she had said, "Good morning," or simply, "Mr. Montgomery?" It didn't matter what she had said, anyhow, for there was no answer. She had peered into the room. Mr. Montgomery was lying on his bed. Just lying there, she told them. Fully dressed, except for his jacket, which was folded neatly over a chair.

"I saw his shoes first," said Sam. "He still had his shoes on. I saw the soles of his shoes, sticking straight up!" She had paused. The memory of Mr. Montgomery's shoes seemed to fill her with awe.

After that, she had seen the pill bottle on the floor. The empty bottle. Then the empty glass—it had contained whiskey—on the bedside table. Then, the notes. One, a sealed envelope, the other, just a piece of paper—both pinned to his blue cashmere sweater.

"I knew at once that something was not right," Sam said.

She had tiptoed in. Mr. Montgomery's eyes were wide open, but unseeing.

"Staring up at the ceiling," said Sam, as if someone might be in doubt.

Those nice sensitive blue eyes, thought Miss Stengle, and she began to tremble all over.

Sam had read the notes. At first, she was not certain that she ought to read them, but, after all, there they were—undoubtedly meant to be read by whomever found him. Yes, she had decided that that had been Mr. Montgomery's intention.

Written across the envelopes were the words: *Instructions for the Police.*

Written on the piece of paper—a message: *I'm so terribly sorry*, it said.

"Rotten thing to have done," said the Colonel.

"He seemed so kind, so mannerly," said Miss Stengle.

"Perhaps," said Mrs. Bliss, "he was suffering from an incurable disease."

"Or a disappointment," said Miss Stengle.

"Gives the place a reputation. It's not what a gentleman would have done," the Colonel said.

"But why here?" said George.

"Yes, why here?" said Evan.

"I thought he was a decent chap, but I've changed my mind," said the Colonel, dropping a forbidden sugar lump into his tea.

Then Hoppy spoke. "I do not concur," she said. Her voice was firm; her manner assured. She commanded everyone's attention.

"The fact is, I consider that Mr. Montgomery has paid us a compliment."

There was a murmur of surprise.

"Who among us," said Hoppy, "would choose to spend his last night on earth at a Holiday Inn or a Hyatt?"

Miss Stengle opened her eyes wide.

"Cheerful Corners would be precisely the choice of a gentleman of taste. He chose us because we are nice."

"I can second that, at any rate," said the Colonel.

"He showed consideration. Not only were his instructions to the police complete, so that there was nothing for me to do but answer a few simple questions, but he also added a monetary gift for what he called "the trouble he caused." He made it quite clear it was a gift—not a tip—that it was to be used for something special that all of us at Cheerful Corners might enjoy."

I must remember to do something like that, thought Mrs. Bliss. Yes, for the Colonel's sake—I must remember.

"At the moment, I am considering new slipcovers for the sofa. However, I am open to suggestions."

Memorial slipcovers, thought Evan.

The old ones are getting shabby, thought George.

"And so I repeat, that I feel flattered and humbled by Mr. Montgomery's decision, and this is how I intend to view the whole sad affair. Sam, I believe the Colonel might enjoy more jam."

The little group of Regulars looked at Hoppy with love and admiration. They felt soothed and steadied, as if they had drunk a nourishing broth. Miss Stengle's breathing was steadier. Mrs. Bliss patted the Colonel's knee and picked up her knitting. The Colonel nodded his head thoughtfully, as if the sentiments just expressed had been his all along. George and Evan rose to help Sam with the cleaning up.

"It's four-thirty," said Hoppy, consulting the cuckoo clock. She turned to Mrs. Bliss. "If we are brisk about it, we shall just have time to make the Christmas Bazaar."

The Little Pub

It was January. Night fell abruptly, shrouding the oak-studded hills of Vista Verde in deep shadows. Only a few lights were visible from the picture window where Mrs. Jessup stood having her Happy Hour, her first—or was it her second?—vodka martini in her hand. She stood at the window in her house on La Floresta Lane, looking at the lights far below. They were the lights, she said to herself, of the Little Pub. The lights of the Little Pub twinkled cheerily in the darkness. Smoke would be curling out of its chimney in tidy loops like the chimney smoke in a child's drawing. Big Bill has lit a fire, she thought. Perhaps I should call Ruff and walk down there. But would we be able to find our way in the dark? There were no sidewalks and no streetlights in Vista Verde, very different from Chestnut Hill, where she and Mr. Jessup had lived before moving here. The lights were visible from the house, but would they be in the darkness, on the lane? Probably not visible, she decided. Probably we would lose our way. And, anyhow, I have the cards to finish. First things first, she told herself. Sacrifices are always entailed whenever people put first things first, as they must if they want to do things worthwhile.

That morning Mrs. Jessup had driven to the city to attend a Seminar for Executive Wives at the Hyatt Regency, sponsored by Mr. Jessup's corporation. It had been an extremely rewarding session. A Social Anthropologist had spoken to them on "Developing Inner Resources Through Creativity." Or was it a Social Psychologist? She must try to remember to tell Mr. Jessup when he returned. Distinctions of that sort were important to him, and rightly so, though she was not absolutely sure why.

The Social Anthropologist or Social Psychologist had traced the forces that made up the Modern World. The old-fashioned sort of Community Life, which was extolled in magazines and films and on TV, and about which so many people were foolishly nostalgic, was archaic—a thing of the past. It was particularly a thing of the past for dynamic men who set high goals for themselves. The world, not just their tiny community, was their milieu; mobility their Life-Style. It was important, he said, to face facts. But this did not mean that their wives need lack fulfillment. It was, he had pointed out, really up to them. There were endless avenues open in which to be creative. He had enumerated some of these open endless avenues—foreign-language lessons, decorating and art and gourmet-cooking courses, working as a docent in a museum, volunteering to help the handicapped, entertaining graciously, bringing up children, graciously volunteering to entertain graciously, even, and perhaps most important of all, providing a serene and loving atmosphere for the executive husband. They—the executive wives—should think of their job as a part of a Team Effort. Sacrifices were, of course, entailed, but sacrifices were always entailed whenever people did things worthwhile. The rewards would be their own personal growth and their husbands' gratitude.

Mrs. Jessup had explored most of these avenues at one time or another, but she had not explored them lately. For the last six months, ever since they had moved into Vista Verde, she had really stopped exploring altogether. Almost the moment she had the furniture arranged and the new curtains up, Mr. Jessup had told her, in his proud, quiet way, that another Transfer was in the air, this time a very important one; the Chairman of the Board was about to retire, and he was in line for this position. It would be—now was—the culmination of his career. She had therefore done nothing in the way of exploring or making new acquaintances, and for this reason she was grateful to the Social Anthropologist–Psychologist for reminding her of what he called her "potential." As the wife of the Chairman of the Board, Inner Resources through Creativity would be more useful than ever.

After the seminar, she had gone to the city's largest stationery store and searched through the cards, hoping to find a more original one than the ones she had sent so many times before. She had not succeeded, and had to hurry home in order to be there when Mr. Jessup, who was at a conference at the Airport Hilton—or was it the Airport Sheraton?—would phone her. There was three hours' difference, and with three hours' differences he always called at three o'clock to be present at the conference's Happy Hour before dinner. On the way, she had been struck by an idea. Perhaps she could make a card herself? During an art class she had taken once, in a past exploration of avenues, she had learned how to make a block print with a raw potato. Various designs and messages occurred to her. Cartoon figures? An old-fashioned script? Black-and-white? Colors? She had suggested the idea, somewhat shyly, to Mr. Jessup when he phoned.

"Make one?" said Mr. Jessup. "What did you have in mind?"

"I don't know yet. Something humorous, maybe. I thought it might be fun."

"Oh, let's keep it kosher," Mr. Jessup said.

"You mean, buy a card?"

"It seems to me you have enough to do, just addressing them," he said thoughtfully.

As soon as he hung up, Mrs. Jessup drove down to the

Vista Verde shopping center, below their house, and bought the simplest card she could find. It was then almost four. She had called Ruff to feed him, but Ruff had crawled out from under the fence again and was gone.

The nice young Vista Verde patrolman will bring him back, Mrs. Jessup said to herself.

Whenever Mr. Jessup was out of town, the private patrol car stopped by in the early evening, and the nice young man rang her doorbell and asked her if everything was all right. This was something Mr. Jessup insisted upon. Mrs. Jessup didn't mind because she liked the young man. He reminded her, somewhat, of her younger son, an engineer, now married and working in Saudi Arabia. She also liked the nice relationship the young man had with Ruff. He either brought Ruff back from the shopping center, where he liked to go, or, if Ruff came to the door with her, he would pat Ruff's gray fat back, while Ruff wriggled all over in ecstasy.

"I guess you can't be too lonely with old Ruff." the young man would say.

"Ruff is a good companion," Mrs. Jessup would tell the young man. "Of course, if a burglar came, he wouldn't be much help."

"Oh, we all know Ruff. He'd show the burglar around the house," the young man would say.

"Would you care to come in and have a drink?" Mrs. Jessup had said once.

"I'd sure like to, ma'am, but we're not allowed to when we're on duty."

"Of course, how silly of me," said Mrs. Jessup.

"Now, you take care of yourself, ma'am. Just call us if you've any problems."

"Thank you, it's good just to know I can," Mrs. Jessup said.

The view from the picture window was of the wooded hills, now black shadows against the sky. Except for the lights of the Little Pub in the distance, you would never guess there

were other homes around. The Vista Verde Neighborhood
Association reviewed the plans of each house before it was
built to be certain that no one's view was obstructed. The ad
for the Jessup house, which was running in the Vista Verde
Crier now, was similar to the ads the real-estate people had
run the last six times they had moved:

> Spanking new executive mansion in exclusive
> neighborhood. Secluded, three-acre, wooded re-
> treat. AEK. Pool, three-car garage. Country Club.

Except for the lights of the Little Pub, one might think
one was stranded, alone, perhaps the last person alive in
the whole world. Mrs. Jessup had once read a book like
that; the memory of it still made her feel funny. She mixed
herself another cocktail at the wet bar, then she went into
the kitchen and opened the oven and looked at the frozen
Stouffer cheese soufflé she had put in before her first drink.
Then she returned to the living-room window. If she did not
have the other cards to do, she decided, she would definitely
call Ruff and walk down there; they would, somehow, find
their way in the dark. How pleasant it would be, if she did
not have the cards to do, to sit in her favorite chair beside
the Little Pub's fireplace—the old, sprung, cracked leather
chair—or was it the old, sprung, chintz chair? It didn't matter. The chair was not the important thing. What was important was the general ambience.

The general ambience of the Little Pub was very agreeable. The credit for this went to Bill. Big Bill, the regulars
called him. Mrs. Jessup was a bit too reserved for this; it
was not her style. She left off the "Big" and addressed him
simply as "Bill." Bill called her "Sugar."

"The usual, Sugar?" Big Bill would say to her when she
had settled herself down in her favorite chair.

She would smile—a bit coquettishly—and nod. With anyone else, she might have been offended, but not with Big
Bill. Big Bill, she thought, could call the Duchess of Wind-
sor "Sugar" and get away with it. He had such a nice, easy

manner with the ladies, and everyone else, too, for that matter.

"One vodka martini on the rocks for my little Sugar," Big Bill would sing out, as he mixed the drink himself. This was a little joke they had together. He would then bring the drink on a tray to Mrs. Jessup and present it with a comical flourish. "And what is Ruff's pleasure?" he would say, looking down at Ruff.

Mrs. Jessup would laugh. This was another joke she shared with Big Bill.

Mrs. Jessup sipped her cocktail and thought about the Little Pub. About her chair, the crackling fire, about Big Bill. About the general agreeable ambience.

"I'm leaving; Mr. Jessup is being transferred," she would tell him.

She could imagine Big Bill's regret at hearing this. "He's Chairman of the Board," she would say. "It's quite an honor, of course, but I shall miss the Little Pub."

Big Bill would, undoubtedly, present her with a drink on the house; perhaps he would even toast her and Mr. Jessup's future. Certainly he would ask about Ruff. "What about Ruff?" he would say. "How does he feel about this?"

"I'm afraid Ruff doesn't care much for Transfers," Mrs. Jessup would tell him. "The last one made him so upset I had to give him some of my tranquilizers."

Mrs. Jessup looked at her watch. It was 5:30, almost time for the patrolman to bring Ruff home. In the meantime, it was pleasant to think about the Little Pub.

At the Little Pub you were surrounded by people of all ages and sexes. People of all sexes, including men. Yes, even though she was no longer nubile, as they said somewhere, perhaps in Japan, though she was of a "certain age," as they said in the Scandinavian countries—or was it France?—or "over the hill," as the common folk saying went, she still enjoyed a room with men, now and then, on a lonely evening during the Happy Hour.

She liked, she thought, the way men looked. The way their jackets scrunched up in back and their trousers wrin-

kled at the crotch; the way they talked sometimes in mono-
syllables or little grunts. Their laughs—their hearty men
chuckles—she liked this, too. There were, of course, men in
her life. The check-out clerk at the Vista Verde market, the
pharmacist, her doctor, the hardware man, the nice young
patrolman; Mr. Tanaguchi, the gardener. She had an especially warm relationship with Mr. Tanaguchi, who possessed an amazing understanding of plants. It would be re-
sourceful—even creative—to go to the phone right now and
call him up and invite him and Mrs. Tanaguchi over for a
cocktail. But what if Mr. Tanaguchi didn't drink? Or, suppose he drank only sake? She had no sake in the house.
Or—worst of all—suppose Mrs. Tanaguchi, whom she had
never had the pleasure of meeting, misunderstood her
warm relationship with Mr. Tanaguchi? No, this particular
avenue was not open; she could not be the cause of any
embarrassment to Mr. Tanaguchi.

The doorbell rang. Mrs. Jessup went to answer it. The
young patrolman was standing on the doorstep. Mrs. Jessup
smiled at him. Just seeing him there gave her a nice feeling.

This time the young man did not smile back. His face, she
noticed, was serious, actually quite pale. Could he be ill?
Mrs. Jessup wondered.

"Ma'am, I have something to tell you," he said. His voice
was not as hearty as usual, and he cleared his throat nervously. "Maybe you'd like me to come in, and you can sit
down?"

Mrs. Jessup led him into the living room. She sat down,
but the young man remained awkwardly standing.

He cleared his throat again. "It's about Ruff, ma'am. I
don't know exactly how to say it, but—we found him this
evening. He was run over by a car on the road. I'm afraid
there was nothing we could do. He was already—gone."

Mrs. Jessup's first thought was of the young man. How
kind he was! How apologetic! But it was not his fault. Silly
old Ruff was always digging out from under the fence and
roaming around, which was against the Vista Verde leash

law. Mrs. Jessup tried very hard to think of something to
say to cheer him up.

"Dogs," she said after a moment, "are incapable of sac-
rifice."

The young man looked at her in an odd way. He seemed
almost frightened, the way he stood there, clutching at his
cap. Mrs. Jessup was determined to get her point over in order to reassure him.

"Dogs enjoy an old-fashioned community life; they are
foolishly nostalgic," she said. "New neighborhoods—new
and unusual odors and noises—fill them with a kind of
frenzy. They forget their house-training, chew things up,
dig under fences—and get run over! They lack inner resources and are not at all creative!"

"Mrs. Jessup, I have Ruff's body out there in the truck. I
didn't know . . . Do you want us to take care of it, or would
you prefer to?" He was stammering slightly, backing toward the door as he spoke.

Mrs. Jessup pretended not to notice his nervousness. Instead, she considered his words carefully. It would be nice,
she thought, to bury Ruff in the backyard, with a little monument of some sort over his grave. RUFF—A GOOD DOG.
Something like that. But she could not expect the people
who bought the house to keep up a grave. "It would be very
kind of you . . . to dispose of it," she said.

The young man put out his hand, and Mrs. Jessup shook
it. "Take care of yourself, now," he said, and left hurriedly.

Mrs. Jessup returned to the picture window. Should she
go down to the Little Pub, she wondered, and tell Big Bill
about Ruff? "Ruff is dead," she would say. It was important
to face facts. It was important, too, to stop thinking about
the Little Pub. There was no Little Pub. This was another
fact that needed to be faced. No Little Pub existed in Vista
Verde, and never would. Imagine the Neighborhood Association permitting such a thing! It would be against the zon-
ing regulations, which did not allow Commercial Uses—
only executive-style houses with proper setbacks and shake
roofs on three acres. Worst of all, a Little Pub would attract

Undesirable Elements. Undesirable Elements, sitting in old squashed leather—or chintz?—chairs (it did not matter), smiling coquettishly at Big Bill, letting Big Bill call them "Sugar."

One could not have that. She finished her drink and went into the kitchen and took out the soufflé and put it on the dining-room table in its foil container. It was limp and sticky, but she managed to get most of it down. Then she went into the den and began, again, upon the cards.

Helen and Bill, she wrote, filling out the blanks, ARE MOVING TO *4 Old County Lane, Greenwich, Connecticut.* There was a drawing of a doormat, and under that it said, THE WELCOME MAT IS OUT.

She finished all of Mr. Jessup's list, which Mr. Jessup's secretary had sent her from his office. Tomorrow she would begin the list of their friends. It was then ten-thirty. She made herself a nightcap and took it into the bedroom with her and flipped on the TV. She lay in bed, watching the middle of an old movie, sipping the drink, and thinking how surprised and grateful Mr. Jessup would be that she had accomplished so much in his absence.

The Crazy Day

Estella went into the Fun House with Vern and came out with Buddy. Estella and Buddy walked out of the clown's mouth, giggling and clutching at each other; they didn't even bother to look around for Vern, who had come out first and was waiting for them in front of the Super Dog Stand. They scampered away hand in hand down the Boardwalk, like two escaped lunatics.

Vern was really graveled. What the hell, I brought Estella, and I was dumb enough to bring Buddy, too, Vern thought. Buddy had spotted them when they stopped at the Texaco Station on El Camino Real, where he hung out on weekends. He had just invited himself! He hadn't even offered to pay for any of the gas, either. Vern had brought them both down here in his Chevy and paid for Estella's ticket to the Fun House, and what did they do? Screw them!

Estella was getting too fat, anyhow, he thought. She was beginning to look like her mother from behind in those orange pants. Well, not quite like her mother, her mother was at least forty. And Estella wasn't fat, exactly, she just had a naturally plump ass. Her boobs were big, too, which he approved of, and one kind of went with the other. But anyway, what did he care?

What did he care about the way she *or* her mother looked? Well, he certainly didn't care about her mother. The only thing he could say was that Estella's mother had brought up Estella very careful in Baptist Sunday School; she would be extremely disappointed to see how her daughter was behaving now. Well, tough shit, thought Vern. She and Bud could thumb a ride home for all he gave a damn.

He walked fast in the *opposite* direction. He walked right through families, dodging strollers and little kids holding spun sugars; he barged between couples and through concession lines. Somebody shouted, "Hey, watch it, Buster!"

"Screw you, too," thought Vern, and went into the Sportatorium to play the machines.

It was crazy how it happened. Estella couldn't have explained it, herself. She and Vern and Buddy were on the Platter, skidding all over Christmas, arms and legs sprawled out like unrelated bits and pieces of people. Estella was screaming at the top of her lungs. She had never felt so helpless in her life. Then, suddenly, she and Buddy flew off into one heap into the mattresses. It was crazy, lying there, all tangled up with Buddy. She didn't even realize for a while she was still screaming. They just lay there while she screamed; then she stopped and the giggles started. It seemed like they hadn't stopped since. Buddy had to pull her to her feet. She was so dizzy and so weak she just plopped right back into his arms. Buddy propped her up again, and they stumbled, like two old drunks, over the mattresses into the Hall of Mirrors.

Estella had to cling to Buddy for support. Her eyes were filled with tears; she couldn't see. She tried to get her purse out of her pants pocket to get a Kleenex, but she couldn't even manage that; Buddy had to help her. On account of the fit of her pants the pocket had practically disappeared; it was necessary for Buddy to dig around to find it. In the process, he tickled her until her tears turned into shrieks. She knew she was making a scene in the Hall of Mirrors, but she couldn't help it; she simply didn't have the strength to care.

The purse popped out suddenly, like a cork out of a bottle; Buddy wiped at her eyes with the Kleenex; Estella's shrieks turned into little sobs. They staggered around, looking in the mirrors. They looked at each other tall and skinny and fat and squatty and just went on getting nuttier and nuttier. Estella had to bite her lip to keep from getting hysterical all over again.

After this, they scrambled up the ladder to the top of the Big Slide. Estella went up first. At the top, they arranged themselves with Buddy's legs squeezed tight around Estella's thighs for support; then down they went, swoosh, up and over the bumps, and fell into another tangled heap at the bottom.

Buddy put a hand on Estella's breast. Ordinarily, she would not have allowed this. Her mother had warned her about boys trying things. First, they try a little thing, then you end up pregnant; then they leave you to support yourself and your kid. Estella's mother knew what she was talking about; she had worked her guts out ever since Estella's father had split so that Estella could have a better life. Estella appreciated this, though sometimes it got a little boring hearing about it all the time. Estella was acquainted with some rich girls at school whose mothers gave their daughters the Pill. Estella sometimes wished her mother was rich and sophisticated in this way. It would be nice, she thought, to have a mother who did that. It was an excellent idea to take the Pill, not because you necessarily intended to go around having sexual intercourse, but in case somebody slipped you some dope in a Coke and you would be at that person's mercy. Imagine waking up and finding yourself pregnant. Her mother would never believe it, not in a thousand years; still it was the kind of thing that happened everyday.

Buddy's hand was really fooling around, now. But she was just too far gone to stop him. It took energy to put

Buddy in his place. With Vern, it was different. Vern wasn't bold like Buddy. In a way, she had to admit, she admired Buddy's boldness, even though he was a nut. The way he hung around that Texaco Station, you'd think he owned it. Everyone knew him, everyone called him by name; they even let him wash windows and fill tires for free. He went there straight from school, when he bothered to go to school at all, and stayed on until they closed. He had a real crush on the Texaco Station. Oh, God, what a nut! She shook off his hand and got up; Buddy followed her. With his assistance, she tottered onto the Boardwalk. Out here, in public, she forced herself to act more dignified, though she still felt giddy and had to cling to Buddy for support.

Well, that's the way things are, she thought. *C'est la vie.* She had learned this expression from a customer at the Beauty Bar where she swept up after school. It meant, That's life, That's the way it goes. It was a French expression, the customer had explained.

"You got the nerve for the Dipsy Doodle?" said Buddy.

If he'd asked her to jump off the wharf into the Pacific Ocean she probably would have gone right ahead and done it, it was that crazy.

In the Sportatorium Vern bought a beer, then he wandered around contemplating the different attractions and trying not to think about Estella. He couldn't help thinking just a little, though. That bitch, Estella, he thought. That bastard, Buddy. All the way down in the Chevy, Buddy had sat in the back seat and made his animal noises: first he was an ape, beating his chest and making ape sounds; then he was a goat, a cow, an owl, and two cats mating.

Vern and Estella had just sat there, listening to the radio, and purposely paying no attention, so as not to encourage him. At least, Vern had thought Estella wasn't paying attention. She took off her scarf and removed her pink curlers and back-combed her hair and applied spray to it. Estella's hair was real pretty, a kind of reddish blonde, and she took extremely good care of it. Then she did her face. She put on the foundation, then sprinkled powder over the foundation, and followed that with liner and shadow and mascara. Estella's eyes were large and blue, and she had naturally long lashes. After she did her eyes, she studied her face carefully for zits; her skin was soft and clear, and she took excellent care of that, too. If she found a zit, it was always a disaster.

Estella was busy all the time up there in front, seemingly happy and content. No one would have guessed coming down the turn events would take when they got here. Vern tried not to think about it. He concentrated instead on what to do.

He decided against viewing the Lord's Supper in life-size wax figures and he decided against the peep shows and the For Men Only. His mood was more for an attraction that required skill. The Electric Shock Machine was in this category, and he considered it. Ordinarily, just the idea of an electric shock gave him the willies, but today was different; today it had an appeal. Still, he wasn't sure. While he stood in front of the Machine and pondered, this pip-squeak sailor with a button nose came over to watch. This somehow settled matters in Vern's mind.

He put his beer can down on the floor and put a dime in the box and grasped the knob, firmly; an uncomfortable quiver went through him, but he hung on. The gauge at the top of the box, which resembled a thermometer, moved up slightly.

"Just a Sissy," said the sailor, reading the gauge.

The quiver turned into a sharp tingle right down to Vern's toes. The gauge crawled up some.

"You're Getting There," read the sailor.

The tingle was now a mean jolt; Vern screwed up his face, hoping to reach "He-Man," but a sudden feeling he was bolted to the box made him panic; he broke away.

Then the sailor stepped forward. He put in his dime and grasped the knob and hung on, coolly. The gauge shot up to "Super He-Man" at the very top. A bell rang. The sailor hadn't even winced.

Vern moved over to the pinball-machine area and began to play the Miss-O. To his regret, the sailor followed him right along. He watched Vern play; then, after a while he started up a conversation. He said his name was Bryan Smith and he was from Logan, Utah, and did Vern know any place around where you could find a broad? The ones he had tried picking up on the beach were the stuck-up kind, and he didn't put up with that. He was willing to pay for value received, but he wanted value.

Vern concentrated on his playing and just shook his head, no. He didn't go in for that kind of business, anyhow. It might be all right for Bryan Smith, but it wasn't for him. He preferred a genuine relationship, based on a mutual attraction. At least, he had. Which was maybe his trouble all along. Probably Bryan Smith had a point, but Vern wasn't in the mood to discuss it.

But this didn't stop Bryan Smith. He just went right on with his conversation. He informed Vern about the kind of woman he approved of and the kind he didn't. He liked them with pointy tits and swishy asses. There couldn't be too much goo on their faces, and he wouldn't stand for back talk. That was Bryan Smith's religious background. He didn't go in for threesomes, daisy chains, or other perverted stuff, either. He wanted one trick at a time, and he wanted it straight.

"Well, that's how it is," he said; "that's my philosophy, anyhow. You could push harder on that machine and still not tilt it."

Vern released the ball and pushed harder and hit the Mystery Spot, which won him one hundred points.

"See, just like I told you," said Bryan Smith.

After the Dipsy, Estella was so exhausted she could hardly stand. Buddy bought them each a Fish Stick and a Kandy Korn and they sat down together on a bench across from the Merry-go-round. The Merry-go-round's crazy music kept them from talking, which was all right in the condition she was in, Estella thought. What was there to talk about anyway? Well, she guessed they *could* talk about Vern. She could say, "Where's Vern?" for example. "Do you suppose maybe we ought to look for Vern?" But she didn't imagine Buddy would have any original ideas on that subject, and even if he did, she didn't feel like hearing them at this particular moment. Sometimes it was better not to bring certain things up. Sometimes it was better not to even think about them.

So they just sat there, eating the Fish Sticks and the Kandy Korn and watching the folks on the Merry-go-round. There was a middle-aged lady in a red wig Estella wouldn't have been caught dead with, riding a camel and waving at somebody in the crowd. There was a young couple, who didn't look much older than Junior High age, riding on the high-backed gilded bench; they sat up stiffly, like two statues, staring straight ahead; they were the most serious of any of the riders. Then there was this sassy little girl, riding a pink pig, who, every time she came around, stuck out her tongue at Estella and Buddy. Estella pretended not to notice. She and Buddy finished their snacks, and Buddy took out his package of Camels and lit one and passed it to Estella; she took a drag and passed it back. Then she sighed wearily. Buddy took her hand.

Then this fantastic old man came over and sat down on the bench next to Estella. He was hard to believe. All he had on was a pair of those disgusting swim trunks that weren't much more than a diaper. They were bright blue. He was so skinny, his skin hung in loose, wrinkly folds. But the main thing about him was his color. He was the color of burnt molasses all over, except for his hair, which was long and white as snow. He had a bottle of baby oil in his hand, and he began to oil his legs and then his arms and then his chest, like he was some kind of precious antique. Well, it was hard to keep a straight face; she and Buddy got the giggles again. The man didn't seem to notice, he just went on oiling and polishing.

Christ Almighty, he's old and wrinkled up, thought Estella. She tried to smother her giggles, but they just kept coming out in little spurts. She gave Buddy a nudge to help him smother his, but he was having the same difficulty. So they just had to pick up and leave.

They walked on down the Boardwalk. Buddy sneaked a hand around her waist and quickly, before she guessed what he was up to, pinched her derriere. Estella squealed and gave him a slap. Not a hard one, though. She was as weak as a newborn infant.

"You want an ice-cream cone?" said Buddy.

She couldn't answer him.

"Well, do you?"

She gave him a mysterious smile. Let him figure out what I want, she thought. Anyhow, how do I know? It's all just too insane. You go in with one fellow and come out with another.

Buddy took her arm and guided her to the Ice-Cream Cone Stand.

Vern left the Sportatorium and walked on down the Boardwalk with Bryan Smith tagging right along. Bryan Smith was about a foot shorter than Vern. When he talked, he just talked straight ahead. Vern had to stoop to hear his conversation. Bryan Smith's conversation still ran to women. He had forgotten to say that, where women were concerned, he confined himself to the Caucasian race. He believed this was intended by God. But outside of this, and outside of the other conditions he had mentioned, he wasn't particular, because all broads were the same, especially in the dark. The fact was, you couldn't trust them with the time of day.

Vern thought about Estella, whom, up till now, he had considered to be in a special category all by herself; sadly he realized that Bryan Smith had a point.

They stopped at Bump-a-Cars to look in the window; Vern contemplated Bryan Smith's beliefs. Suddenly, he saw Estella and Buddy. Estella was in a little blue car; Buddy, in a red one. They were going at each other like a bull and a cow in heat. First they bumped back fenders, then front ones.

Their eyes were glazed; their faces like maniacs. It was such a revolting sight, Vern wanted to puke. It helped the situation to listen attentively to Bryan Smith. It took his mind off his upset stomach.

Bryan Smith was now telling Vern about this dream he'd had where he had single-handedly won a whole war with all the Gooks in the Far East, where he had been stationed, and had been decorated for it by the President on the White House lawn in front of the TV cameras; his mother had been present, and she had cried, but Bryan Smith hadn't moved a muscle.

Vern listened hard, but he couldn't keep his eyes off the Bump-a-Cars. Then it turned out the couple he thought was Estella and Bud were two other dudes. Hey, I guess I'm starting to space out, he said to himself. He walked away, fast, with Bryan Smith still at his heels.

Two hippie types passed them. A boy and a girl. The next thing Vern knew Bryan Smith had stepped right in front of them, blocking their way. "I really like long hair," Bryan Smith was saying. "My mother and sister have long hair. I think it's real pretty."

"Hey, man, slack off, man," one of the hippie types said.

A black dude in an Afro and tight striped silk pants joined them.

"Which side you on?" Bryan Smith asked the dude.

The dude laughed and went on walking.

"That's the trouble with them Spades," said Bryan Smith. "You can't trust them."

The hippie types had taken this occasion to disappear. Bryan Smith swung around smartly, but it was too late. He was convinced, though, they had gone into the Tilt-a-Whirl. Vern wanted to go on, but Bryan Smith took him firmly by the arm—though he was a pip-squeak, he had a lot of strength—and led him beneath the ride.

"You can help me spot them," he said to Vern. "I'm going to get them when they come down."

The pastel cages hung suspended in the air; then they would swing a notch, stop, and pick up another passenger or passengers. Suddenly, they were full, and the whole contraption began to revolve, slowly at first, then at full speed, until the cages were spinning at the far end of their cables like yo-yos.

Vern didn't let on he was looking for Estella and Buddy, not the hippie types. He imagined how Bryan Smith would respond. Bryan Smith had balls. He would be brave in battle. He had a definite philosophy of life. *You couldn't trust a woman with the time of day.* How could Vern argue this fact after what had happened? Still, you couldn't be sure. Maybe when Estella had flown off the platter she had cracked her head and was suffering from a concussion; maybe Buddy had offered her some of the dope he bought at the Texaco Station or persuaded her to drink an alcoholic beverage and she had passed out. Maybe, though probably not. He didn't let on to Bryan Smith, but he kept on looking. Once he caught a glimpse of orange, the color of Estella's pants. But the cages whirled by so rapidly, he couldn't be positive.

After a while, the Tilt-a-Whirl began to lose momentum, the cables drooped, and the whole contraption slowed down. Bryan Smith informed Vern if the hippie types weren't on it, don't think he was going to give up; maybe Vern had caught on by now to the fact that he wasn't the kind of guy who gave up easy. No hippies were going to get away from Bryan Smith from Logan, Utah; he was going to hunt them down!

He said all of this as he watched the passengers disembark; his eyes were narrowed, his hands were on his hips; he was so intent on his project he didn't even notice Vern edge away.

Vern edged away, then ducked into Trader Joe's. Trader Joe specialized in African art objects, souvenir T-shirts, beach equipment, sexy postcards, exotic shells, and furry animals in neon colors—oranges and greens and reds and purples. Estella would have enjoyed an animal, he thought. She liked cuddly things to decorate her room. He got to wondering if she would have preferred a green panda or a purple poodle dog. He thought of how she would have held it, making a big fuss over it, kissing it, and patting its fur. They were expensive, but still he might have bought her one if things had gone differently. Well, things hadn't. As soon as he was certain he had given Bryan Smith the slip, he went back out again upon the Walk. He couldn't face Bryan Smith learning about his situation.

Estella and Buddy studied the flavor board on the Ice-Cream Stand. Buddy picked Rocky Road. Estella always took Chocolate—that was just the way she was. But today, for the life of her, she couldn't make up her mind. She considered Burgundy Cherry, then Peppermint Fudge Ribbon, then Butter Pecan. She considered all these; then, when she had rejected one, she would sigh and start all over. She could tell Buddy was getting impatient, but what could she do?

"I can't help it, Bud; I know it's nutty, but I just can't help it," she said.

Finally she gave up and blurted out, "Chocolate Mint on the bottom and Peppermint Fudge Ribbon on the top in a sugar cone."

The second Buddy came back with it, Estella knew she had made a mistake. But she didn't have the courage to admit it. Buddy, she thought, would probably flip out. Still, it depressed her. For the first time all day she felt depressed.

It was getting to be late; the sun was fading over the sea; she shivered. She licked the Peppermint Fudge Ribbon all over, slowly, so it turned into a smooth hump, but she couldn't bring herself to take a bite. She had made a mistake ordering it, and maybe she had made a few other mistakes too.

Oh, well, *c'est la vie*, she thought, trying to cheer up.

So much had happened, how could she be expected to think sensibly?

Sunbathers were coming in off the beach, and the families with little kids were starting to leave the Boardwalk; there was a chill in the air. The colored lights came on. The Roller Coaster was outlined in blue, making it look like some giant prehistoric monster.

This gave Vern an idea. He had planned to take Estella on the Roller Coaster, even though she had informed him that was one thing she would never, never do, in all her life. He had planned to tease her on to it; then, when he got her up there, he would have held her hand to give her courage. Well, thanks to certain people, he thought ... Well, he could take a ride himself, for hell's sake. He could take a ride and then get into the Chevy and go home. Certain people could thumb, for all he gave a shit.

The Roller Coaster was three-fourths empty. It started up almost as soon as Vern sat down. Suddenly he was hurtling at breakneck speed through the dusk. A crescent moon hung in the sky and was reflected in the dark water. He could see the lights on the wharf and some blinking lights out at sea. He could see the lights on the cars heading home. He didn't feel scared or even excited; he just felt lonely and cold. If things hadn't turned out like they had turned out, Estella would be sitting next to him, warm and soft and bellowing, clutching at his hand. But things had turned out the way they had; why couldn't he get this straight? Estella hadn't hit her head or been drugged; she was just untrustworthy. It was time he stopped thinking about it any other way.

How did you think about it then? You thought about it like Bryan Smith would think about it. They were all the same, especially in the dark. This was how Vern would think from now on. This was the useful thing that had happened today. This new outlook would change his whole life. It would even carry over into other areas. He would go into the military instead of Junior College; if there was a war he would be brave and do a lot of killing and win a medal like in Bryan Smith's dream. All in all, he would be a stronger, better person. He was extremely grateful to Bryan Smith for this philosophy.

As soon as the Roller Coaster stopped, Vern made

straight for the Chevy; his new outlook causing him to walk a jaunty stride, without looking either to right or left.

The Chevy was parked three blocks away. When Vern got to it, he found it hard to believe his eyes. There was Estella, sitting there in the front seat, back-combing her hair, just as if nothing had happened! The shock of this sight almost made him forget his new resolution. His knees felt funny and he could feel the beat of his heart. Some people, he thought shakily . . . Some people have their nerve.

Then he got hold of himself. He thought the same thought over again, only this time he thought it differently. Some people have their nerve, he thought, in a cool, careless kind of way. He walked casually around to the driver's seat without giving her another glance.

As he walked around, he spotted something else. It was a big lump in the back seat. That Mother Fucker, Bud, was lying there, all curled up like a baby, fast asleep. This time he had more control. Some people, he thought, think they can get away with murder. He hesitated beside the car. Should he pull Bud out and knock his teeth down his throat? In his mind he could see Bud—a limp and bloody blob upon the pavement. He could hear Estella's screams. It would be satisfying, looking down at that blob, hearing the screams. He would have liked to have had Bryan Smith see that particular sight.

But why let Estella know he cared what she and Buddy did? Why let her think he gave a shit, when he didn't anymore, anyway? He would just give both of them the freeze. He got into the car, put the key into the ignition and started up, exactly like neither one of them was there.

"Where've you been, for Christ's sakes?" cried Estella in a funny, high, trying-to-sound-innocent kind of voice.

She was going to be in for a few surprises, Vern thought. He edged the car out into the traffic without responding.

"We lost you in the Fun House. We looked all over Christmas for you. We figured you gave us the slip."

"H'mmm," said Vern. After a moment, he said, "I bet."

"Honest Injun, cross my heart. Didn't we, Bud?" She turned around and looked into the back seat. "Old Buddy's asleep," she said with a nervous giggle.

Estella looked at Buddy, sleeping. His mouth was open and his T-shirt had come out of his pants, exposing his belly button and a patch of white hairy skin. He looked ugly and crumpled and dumb. It was hard for her to imagine she had spent the whole day with someone as unrefined-appearing as that.

It was hard even to remember the day; it was just a sort of blur in her head, like maybe it was a day that had happened a hundred years ago. She could recall the crazy feelings she had had; she would never, in all her life, forget those feelings, but they certainly had nothing to do with that stupid oaf in the back seat. She gave a little shudder of distaste and put her hand on Vern's hand for comfort.

Estella's hand was soft and warm and pleasurable, but this didn't cut any ice with Vern. He just went on driving, slowly, in the long traffic crawl, ignoring her hand.

"I'm glad Bud's asleep, aren't you?" Estella was saying. "He's such a nut. Honestly, I don't think I could put up with his animal act right now. Especially the ape. It's so juvenile, don't you agree?"

"I never did see anything in that act," Vern said, in a stony Bryan Smith kind of voice.

"He made me ride the Dipsy. Kid stuff. Then we got us some ice cream."

She was stroking his knee gently with her fingers, but, for all he cared, she might as well have been in Timbuktu.

"What did you do, honey?"

"Who, me?" What had he done? Not much! Except develop a whole new attitude about life, thanks to a certain Bryan Smith! But he didn't need to tell Estella that; she'd discover it, herself, soon enough.

"Maybe you found yourself another girl?"

"Maybe."

"Maybe she was more attractive than yours truly." Estella took her hand away and opened her purse and took out a little spray bottle and sprayed some of its contents to her wrists and onto the back of her ears. It smelled like carnations. "Well, *c'est la vie*," she said.

"Say la what?" said Vern, and wished he hadn't.

"It's just an old French saying. You wouldn't understand." She flicked on the radio and began to hum to the music.

The only noise in the car was Buddy snoring in the back seat and the music and Estella humming. Estella smelled like carnations; he wished she didn't; she moved closer to Vern and laid her head on his shoulder. Vern made his shoulder stiff.

"I'll tell you what it means if you'll be real sweet and nice," Estella said.

Vern grunted.

"It means, well, you know, like that's life. Sometimes funny things happen and you can't do anything about them. They're out of your control." She sighed as if maybe she knew something more, something sad and mysterious that Vern could never hope to understand.

Some people, thought Vern, shaky again.

"Old Bud sure snores."

"I never did see what anyone could see in that dope," said Vern in a careful, tentative way. He let his shoulder relax; then stiffened it again.

"I feel the same way exactly," said Estella.

Estella's soft, carnation-smelling body made Vern ache with longing for her; it also made him ashamed of his own weakness. He knew, now, he could never be like Bryan Smith no matter how hard he tried. It was a depressing thought, but what could he do? Run them all off the road? Wait until he got home and commit suicide? Neither alternative seemed to fit his personality. He let his shoulder relax. Well, he couldn't drive with his shoulder all stiff, anyhow.

It was warm inside the car. Estella felt drowsy. She snuggled closer to Vern. All she knew for sure was that she'd gone into the Fun House with Vern and come out with Buddy and now she was with Vern again and that was the way things were.

"Oh wow," said Estella, in a whispery voice, "what a crazy old day."

Landmarks

It was early November, past the tourist season, and cold for this place. Around seven o'clock, a new black Chrysler New Yorker drove up. A man got out, an older man, middle-aged. He was wearing a hound's-tooth Scottish hat and a plaid muffler.

"You can fill it up, and just get the front windshield," the man said. "Everything else is okay." His voice was friendly. He had a nice, friendly manner. He stood around as if he would like to help, but couldn't, because of the way he was dressed.

Then the front door on the passenger side opened, and a woman hopped out. She was a tiny middle-aged woman, with gray hair and dainty features; she had the kind of face that probably had been pretty once when she was young. She was dressed in a long plaid skirt and high-heel shoes, and a short furry jacket. She still had a good figure. She was spry, too; she moved like a young girl. She skipped around the station, rubbing her little hands to keep them warm.

"You ought to have my jacket," she said to the attendant,

while he put the nozzle in the gas tank. Her voice was girlish and friendly. She followed him around while he attended to the windshield. "It's so cold," she said. "It's so cold, it could snow. Does it ever snow down here?"

"It did once," the attendant said. "A long time ago, when I was little."

"How little?" said the woman. She sounded interested.

"Five. I was five years old, I guess."

"I bet you really remember that day," the woman said.

The attendant had the squeegee in his hand and was starting back toward the pump, where the man was still standing, but the woman maneuvered around in front of him, so he had to stop. She looked up at him with big violet-colored eyes and smiled. She had a friendly smile. She was a friendly little old lady, the attendant thought.

"Sure do," he said. "It hasn't snowed down here since."

The man was holding out his credit card. The attendant went to take it, with the woman hopping along after him.

"Ask him directions," the woman said. "Ask him how to get to the yacht harbor. We're going to visit our son," she said. "He's living on a boat, and we're going to take him out to dinner. We've been there at least a thousand times, but this fellow always gets lost." She laughed cheerfully.

"I don't always get lost," said the man, giving the attendant the card.

"I'd like to know the day he didn't get lost," said the woman. "He gets lost going around the block at home."

"It's easy to find the harbor," the attendant said, while he punched the card. He handed the slip to the man to sign. "You just go straight down this street to the first light and turn left."

"I'm listening even if he isn't," said the woman.

"I'm listening," said the man as he signed.

"You go one block, turn left, and then keep on going. You'll run right into it. You can't miss it."

"He could," said the woman, with her cheerful laugh. "He could miss anything. He always has to consult a map, but he still misses everything. I'd hate to go into the woods with him. You'd read about us in the papers. They'd find our skeletons!"

The man said, "Her instincts are not reliable. She doesn't take one-way streets or off-ramps into account. She can get you good and lost listening to her instincts. 'Straight down this street to the first light,'" he said, rehearsing the attendant's directions, "'then turn left and you run right into it.'"

"He'll probably run right into the harbor," the woman said. She seemed overcome with amusement at the thought. "But it's all right, because I'll be on the lookout. I have an excellent memory for landmarks."

"She may have an excellent memory for landmarks, but it's hard to tell," said the man. "She pulls the sun visor down, so I can't see the street signs. She doesn't look for landmarks, she looks at herself in the mirror. We're going to have a wreck one of these days if she keeps this up. I'm considering having the mirror taken out." He took the receipt and credit card from the attendant. "I don't know what she's looking at, anyhow," the man said.

"If he has the mirror taken out, I'll get another one put in," the woman said. "He likes to make a big fuss over nothing. He likes to have everything . . . just so. His way, if you know what I mean. I'm not the only one who thinks so. My son—the one we're going to visit—has suggested he just relax. Do you relax?" she said.

The attendant said he'd never tried it, but maybe he would someday.

"You ought to start now, before it's too late," the woman said. "It's hard to get an old dog to change his spots."

"She means it's hard to get a leopard to change his spots," the man said. "She gets everything mixed up like that. You can see what I mean by relying on her instincts. My son—the one she just referred to—has had certain suggestions for her, too. Courtesy prevents me from mentioning them."

The woman giggled. "I'd like to know when courtesy prevented anything. He has a tendency to be overcritical. He's used to bossing people around, so he has the idea he can act that way with me. You've probably seen people like that in your line of work. I imagine you see lots of people who drive in here and order you about like you're some sort of slave."

"I try not to notice," the attendant said.

"It must get on your nerves, though. You must want to pour oil in their gas tank, or vice versa. It must rankle. That's what I mean about him. But I don't let him get away with it. I speak up."

"You know what she does?" said the man. "If you don't jump at her beck and call, she takes revenge. Once, in Spain, she threw one of my shoes out of the hotel window. She has a violent streak in her. And she's filled with ancient grievances. They're bottled up inside of her. She suffers from gastritis as a result."

The man held the door open for the woman. He did it in an old-fashioned, courtly way. The woman stepped in, daintily. She turned and smiled at the attendant.

"You ought to have a nice warm jacket on a night like this," she said.

The man closed her door and got in on his side.

"I remember the directions. Ten to one he doesn't," the woman said through the window.

"Her gastritis takes the form of diarrhea," the man said. "She has diarrhea almost everyday."

He started up the engine. "Once, in Hawaii, it got so bad, she went in her pants," he said as the car rolled away from the pumps.

The woman stuck her head out of the window. "Guess what?" she called out from the moving car. "For the last two years, he's been practically impotent. He tries to get it up, but he can't! It's because he has his nose to the grindstone and can't relax! All he cares about is his work!"

The man stopped the car at the curb. He stuck his head out of his window. "That's a lie! And she knows it!" he shouted. "She'll say anything! She has no scruples whatsoever!" He edged the car out into the street, and it picked up speed.

She was leaning halfway out of her window, yelling at the top of her voice as the car moved away. "That isn't the half of it!" she yelled. She still sounded cheerful and friendly.

"There's plenty more I could tell you! But he's rushing off, so I won't! But I could tell you things that would make your hair curl!"

The Chrysler moved away into the night. The attendant watched it go. The man was driving in the slow, relaxed, leisurely fashion in which older folks drive. They appeared to be chatting in a relaxed, leisurely, middle-aged-couple way.

A Special Occasion

Mr. Moore knew he was dying. It would be stupid for him not to know, being eighty-seven, or was it eighty-eight—somewhere, anyhow, in the late eighties—and with all the hoses and various other contraptions fastened onto him, having suffered his third stroke. He had thought, once, it would be nice to live to be one hundred. He had had an uncle and a grandmother who had made that age; it had an honorable tone to it, like winning an athletic contest. If you lived to be one hundred, a fuss was made, your picture was in the newspaper, and the President sent you a telegram. But, now, in his late eighties, his wife dead, his sons scattered about the country, his friends mostly gone; the changes in the world, none the better, and the changes in his body, certainly worse—he no longer saw the sense in it. When it came to important matters—and dying he thought was important—he had always been sensible, though he had often fumed and fretted and kicked up a storm, making things hard on those around him, until an issue was firmly settled in his mind.

His mind, on the issue of dying, was clear and settled. He

knew what he was about, even though it did not always come out that way in his speech. The facts that he sometimes called the fat nurse Lillian—Lillian had been his wife's name—and that he sometimes confused the hospital room with the bedroom of the small house in Idaho, where he had grown up, and, occasionally, with the bedroom of the railroad hotel, where he and Lilly had spent their honeymoon, were of no consequence. What was of consequence, and annoying in the extreme, was that no one else—neither the doctors nor the nurses nor his daughter, Sheila, nor his two sons, who had spent good money to fly all the way across the country to be at his deathbed—had the grace to make an occasion out of it.

Mr. Moore had a ceremonious nature. He set store by the observations of occasions. He didn't believe in extravagance or making a fuss, but occasions were the landmarks of a life and should be recognized. At Christmas, Lillian had trimmed a large Tree; many widowers, like himself, no longer bothered with a Tree, but on Christmas Eve, when the Trees were marked down, Mr. Moore always bought a small one for his tabletop and trimmed it with some of the ornaments Lillian had kept in a box. He wrote down the dates of the birthdays of his children and grandchildren, after Lillian was gone, and never neglected to send them a greeting card. He flew the flag on the Fourth of July. There were other events, too, such as Graduations and Retirements. When he had retired from the Railway Express, they had had a party for him and presented him with the gold watch. Then there were births—and deaths. Each seemed to him of special importance, marking, as they did, the beginning and the end of things. His dying, he thought, should be properly observed in some special way.

For example, it would be suitable to be asked for a statement. Some personal comment on his opinion of what had transpired, as well as a general one, on the nature of existence itself. "Last Words," or a "Deathbed Speech," it was called. These Last Words were noted, taken down and remembered, long after the dying person who had uttered them was gone. Mr. Moore had practiced some Last Words but whenever he roused himself and began, as best he could with all the hoses in him, to repeat them, they hushed him up.

"Now, Father, there's no need for that sort of talk," his older son, the Professor, would say. "I didn't come all this way to listen to nonsense."

That was like a Professor, Mr. Moore thought. Professors talked nonsense all day, but when it came to an important last statement, they didn't know it from a horse's behind.

"If you're going to go on like that, Dad," said his younger son, who was in Public Relations, whatever that was, "I'm going to take the next plane back. I came to have a nice visit with you, not to hear morbid talk. All those drugs they give you have made you morbid. The chances are, you're going to outlive all of us, so let's not have any more foolishness."

Mr. Moore did not think the Last Words he had practiced were either morbid or foolish; they were, in fact, trenchant and to the point; certainly, far more worthwhile than the junk his Public Relations son put out. But what could he do, when everyone turned a deaf ear?

His daughter, Sheila, who lived in the same town with him and visited him regularly, was as bad as the rest. "When I die," Mr. Moore said to her, "I want the cheapest coffin you can get. Don't let them talk you into any fancy, satin-lined casket. They're crooks, all of them, those morticians."

"There's plenty of time for that kind of arrangement, Daddy," said Sheila. "Wait until you're back home and on your feet, and we can discuss it then."

"I'm not going back home. I'm not getting back on my feet," said Mr. Moore, but he might as well have been talking to the air.

"Daddy, I have to go now. I have a dentist's appointment. Gilly said she would drop in on you after school." Gilly was eight years old, his favorite grandchild; her real name was Lillian, after his wife. "I hope you aren't going to talk that way in front of Gilly," said Sheila. "She's just a child, and it would upset her. She's planning on having her grandfather around for a long, long time."

Well, she'll be in for a surprise, then, thought Mr. Moore.

When Sheila left, the fat nurse, whom he sometimes called Lillian, came in with a plant.

"Look what the Good Fairy has brought you, Mr. Moore. A beautiful azalea," she said. "I'll put it here where you can see it. You can plant it in your garden when you get home."

"I won't be going home," said Mr. Moore.

"Now, now," said the fat nurse. "When you plant it, be sure you put it in a shady location, and cut off the old blossoms, first. Don't you want to know who it's from?"

He nodded.

The fat nurse opened the card. "It's one of those comic cards, the expensive kind," she said. "I'll read it to you: There's a picture of a bedpan." She laughed. "Then, it says—are you listening?"

Mr. Moore nodded, again. What else could he do, but listen?

"There's a funny picture of a bedpan, and it says:

BECAUSE OF THE FUEL SHORTAGE,
YOUR BEDPAN HAS BEEN TURNED DOWN SIX DEGREES

I get a kick out of those comic ones," she said. "It's signed, 'Get well soon. Love, Edith.' Is Edith your sweetheart?"

Dying men of my age don't have sweethearts, thought Mr. Moore. He knew that, though he could not, at the moment, recall who Edith was.

"I bet she's your sweetheart. I bet you have a lot of sweethearts," said the nurse, and she bustled out.

It was late afternoon of the same day—at least Mr. Moore assumed it was the same day, though Time, here in the hospital, both merged and expanded in peculiar ways. He woke up from a catnap, and there was Gilly, standing beside his bed. He recognized her, because she had come very close, and was staring down at him with curiosity. Despite her closeness, he could no longer see her quite in focus. He knew very well, however, what she looked like. She had clear, steady gray eyes, like Lillian's eyes; a pert, freckled face; short brown hair, cropped close to her head; and a nice upright way of carrying herself, which he had always admired; so many young girls slouched, nowadays.

"How are you, Grandpa?" said Gilly. Her voice was steady, like her eyes. She was a steady, direct, no-nonsense little girl, which was why he had always favored her over the others.

"Not bad, for a dying man," he said.

Gilly pulled up a chair, very close to the side of his bed, and sat down. A young nurse came in to take his pulse and temperature. "Doesn't your Grandpa look chipper today?" she said to Gilly, while Mr. Moore had the thermometer in his mouth.

Gilly studied Mr. Moore's face before she answered. She was like that, he thought. There was nothing flippant, or frivolous about her. When she was asked a question, she answered it only after serious consideration.

But the nurse did not give her time to answer; she whipped the thermometer out, jotted down her findings, and hurried out.

"Chipper!" said Mr. Moore. "The words they use! Would you say that was the right word to use for a man in my interesting condition?"

Gilly giggled. "It's a dumb word," she said.

"I'm cheerful enough, but not chipper," Mr. Moore said.

"You're old and sick," said Gilly. "Do you hurt?"

"No, no, thank God. I'm not in pain. Dying people often are, but I've been fortunate."

"That's good." She paused. "Is it scary? Dying?" she said.

"Scary? Now, I'm glad you asked that. Nobody else has. I've been wanting to comment on that very subject. Scary? No, it's not scary, exactly. It's different. It's strange. You always know you're going to die, but it comes as a surprise, just the same."

Gilly listened intently, as she always did.

"Even at eighty-eight, or eighty-seven ..." said Mr. Moore.

"You're eighty-eight, Grandpa."

"Even at eighty-eight, it's a special occasion."

She nodded gravely in agreement.

"It makes you think of things. Go over your life, you know." He managed to prop himself up a bit on his pillow. He cleared his throat, which was difficult because of the tube in his nose. "I've had a good life, as lives go," he said. The tube made his voice hoarse. "Some regrets," he said. "I might have done a few things differently." He tried to think what he might have done differently; he had had a list of small regrets in his head, but they had vanished. "On the whole, no regrets to speak of," he said.

"That's nice. Some people do, I guess," Gilly said.

"Some people should," said Mr. Moore. "Some people—I won't mention names, out of consideration for your feelings—but some people—" He choked, and could not go on.

"Grandpa, how long does it take for the skin to fall off the bones?"

"When you're dead, you mean?"

She nodded.

"Well, it depends. In my case—look at my arms. I shouldn't think it would take too long. A month, at best."

"Would it be okay, when you die, for me to have your skeleton?"

"My skeleton?" Mr. Moore was interested. "What do you want with my skeleton?"

"I could remember you when I looked at it. And I could show my friends."

"Show your friends my skeleton?" He lay back upon his pillow, exhausted. It was not, however, an unpleasant exhaustion; it was quite different from the tedium he experienced with the doctors and nurses and his children. "Yes, I can see it might be interesting," he said, after a moment. "But you can't have it. It wouldn't be seemly."

"I just thought I'd ask. It's all right."

Mr. Moore gave up trying to think of the trenchant, worthwhile remarks he had practiced for his Deathbed

Speech, and which no one had permitted him to make. It was the spirit of the occasion more than the particular words that mattered, anyhow. Gilly, he thought, seemed to understand the spirit of the occasion, and this gave him comfort.

"I think," he said to her, when he again recovered some strength, "that you have inherited the common sense I have always been known for. It heartens me to think I've left something to Posterity, something that will be carried on, when I'm in my grave and forgotten."

"Thank you, Grandpa."

"You won't hold it against me about the skeleton."

"No. Mother probably wouldn't let me keep it, anyhow."

Mr. Moore closed his eyes. He dozed for a time. When he woke up, Gilly was still there.

"I'm grateful to you for coming," he said to her.

She smiled at him. Then she leaned over and, manipulating her head in among the contraptions, kissed him upon his cheek. "If you're still alive, tomorrow, after school, I'll come back," said Gilly.

Mr. Moore dozed off again. When he awoke, the fat nurse was opening the curtains, letting the morning sunlight flood into his room. He no longer remembered Gilly's visit.

"Is it another day?" he asked the fat nurse.

"It's a fine, beautiful morning, and you've had a fine sleep," the fat nurse said. "You were a good boy and didn't wake up once. I just looked at your chart."

"I dreamed," said Mr. Moore.

"It must have been a nice dream. I can tell from the way you look. I bet you dreamed about one of your sweethearts," she said, thrusting the thermometer into his mouth and reaching for his pulse.

Mr. Moore tried to remember his dream, but he could not. The fat nurse must be right, though. It must have been a nice dream, because he felt strangely comforted, as if something had occurred—something special and ceremonious, befitting the special occasion in which he was the most important performer.

Norwegians

This time Mr. and Mrs. Jessup just concentrated on one country—Norway. "Norway isn't ruined by tourism, yet," Mr. Jessup said. "Let's do Norway before it turns into a Venice."

"The country of Norway is extremely picturesque and not yet ruined by tourism," Mrs. Jessup dictated into her husband's portable dictating machine as she sat in the bedroom of their inn. The tapes were mailed to Mr. Jessup's office in Evanston, typed and Xeroxed by his secretary, and distributed to relatives, friends, and business associates. The letters were Mr. Jessup's idea. Mrs. Jessup had done it in the Orient, too, and everyone had commented favorably. The first time she felt shy, but now she had developed more facility. Mr. Jessup said he thought it was good for Mrs. Jessup. Since their two sons had grown up and married he had detected a lack of purpose in her life. Recently, he had had a physical by their family doctor. The doctor had inquired after Mrs. Jessup; Mr. Jessup had mentioned that this was a difficult time in a woman's life.

Mrs. Jessup told the machine about the fjords, the curious little Lapps, the stave churches, the Viking ships, the Munch Museum, and their visit to the home of a Norwegian couple in Bergen. The man had a connection with Mr. Jessup's firm. Sometimes Mrs. Jessup used a little book for help, which Mr. Jessup had purchased for her in Oslo. It was called *Facts About Norway*.

"The predominating trees in Norwegian forests, which cover nearly one fourth of the land, are fir and pine, but birch and other deciduous trees are found even in mountainous districts," the book said.

Mrs. Jessup changed this when she talked to the machine, to make it sound more like her own style. "*Most of the trees are fir and pine,*" she told the machine, "*but there are also some birch and other deciduous trees.*"

After seeing what Mr. Jessup called the "main attractions," Mr. Jessup had gone to a "simpatico" traveling agent in their Oslo hotel and told him they wished to settle down for a week in a small country village with its own industry, unconnected with the tourist trade, a place where they could rest and "walk among the people." "This," Mr. Jessup said to Mrs. Jessup, "is the way to end a trip."

"*We are now in a quaint rustic inn in a small fishing village, unconnected with the tourist trade,*" Mrs. Jessup said to the machine, while Mr. Jessup unpacked. "*It is not a fancy resort. Far from it! Papa, at his desk; Mama, in the kitchen; the children helping out. Here we will rest and walk among the people, which is the best way to end a trip.*"

After a simple lunch in the inn's sedate dining room, they went back up to their room again. Mr. Jessup always lay down for a half hour after his noon meal; the doctor had told him this was one of the best ways for men with responsibilities, such as he had, to avoid getting into trouble. Mrs. Jessup continued with her letter.

"*The room in our inn looks out upon the water,*" she said to the machine. She spoke in a low voice so as not to disturb her husband. "*The water is gray, dotted with gray rocks.*

*Gray rocks, gray gulls, a gray sky. An ancient lighthouse
stands on the rocky promontory across the water in all its
pristine glory. Picturesque—"*

She stopped, remembering she had used that word before
lunch. She erased the tape and went on. *"Fishing boats,
straight out of an impressionistic painting, bob up and down
beside an empty wharf."*

Mrs. Jessup glanced at Mr. Jessup; his eyes were open.
"Is the water a fjord?" she asked him.

"We've seen our fjords," said Mr. Jessup with an encour-
aging smile. "It's more of a bay."

"Having had our fill of fjords, the water is more of a bay,"
said Mrs. Jessup to the machine.

When Mr. Jessup had finished his rest period, they both
put on their new Norwegian sweaters. Mr. Jessup put on
his Tyrolean hat, which was decorated with a perky little
brush, and slung his camera bag over his shoulder. They
went downstairs again. Mr. Jessup asked Papa at the desk
if there was anything especially worthwhile seeing in the
village. They were particularly interested in old architecture, he said.

There was a long silence. "Well, that depends," said Papa.
"What I might consider worth seeing you might not consider worth seeing. People differ, you see."

"The Norwegians are not servants," said Mr. Jessup as
they went out the front door for their walk. "There's no
'yes, sir; no sir.' No bowing and scraping. No spit and polish,
like the English."

"The English do a lot of polishing," Mrs. Jessup agreed,
recalling the glowing silver tea sets and the shining brass
hardware.

"It has to do with courage in the face of adversity," Mr.
Jessup said.

"Polishing?" said Mrs. Jessup.

"Keeping up appearances, despite all," Mr. Jessup said.

"The Norwegians don't seem to polish," she said. She
thought for a moment. "But Norwegians are courageous,
too, aren't they?" she said.

"We know that they are," said Mr. Jessup. "Their Vikings, their Resistance, their brave battle with the sea. It's another tradition, that's all. That's why we travel. The Norwegians are a proud and independent race."

Mrs. Jessup made a note in her head of this last phrase for her letter. Though the Norwegians do not polish like the English, she said to herself, they are a proud and independent race.

It was a cool September afternoon. "A hint of winter in the air," said Mr. Jessup, buttoning up his sweater. They were walking through a small park. A young woman in a miniskirt and boots sat on a bench beside a baby buggy. Mrs. Jessup, thinking of her new grandchild, hesitated for a moment beside the buggy, then peeped inside it. Mr. Jessup, who liked to walk briskly—the doctor had told him this was the best sort of exercise for men who spent their days at their desks—was already some paces ahead of her. When he noticed that Mrs. Jessup was not beside him, he stopped; he waited with a courtly patience as she admired the infant and congratulated the mother. Suddenly, Mrs. Jessup sensed his absence. She scurried to catch up with him, as if she had been caught daydreaming in school. Mr. Jessup took her hand in his and squeezed it tenderly.

There were two statues in the park. One statue, on a pedestal, was a bronzed, bearded gentleman in a frock coat, with a watch and chain dangling from his vest pocket; the other—made of white stone—was a slim young girl, naked, with small, high breasts and flowing, snakelike hair. The girl stood, proud, under the gentleman's sober gaze.

Mr. Jessup stopped in front of the man. He studied the inscription on the base of the pedestal. "Henrik Ibsen," he said. He glanced at the girl. "The nude was obviously done later," he told Mrs. Jessup. "I must say, it's a curious juxtaposition."

"Maybe somebody was playing a little joke," said Mrs. Jessup.

"Ibsen," said Mr. Jessup, "is one of their national heroes."

"That's what makes it funny," Mrs. Jessup said. "It wouldn't be funny if he wasn't."

"You don't make jokes with public money," Mr. Jessup said. "I would guess it was just bad planning," he said.

They walked on. School was just out, and the streets were alive with children. Two large boys were tussling, while a circle of their companions cheered them on. A tiny girl, with a mass of curly yellow snarled hair, stuck out her tongue at Mrs. Jessup. When Mr. Jessup wasn't looking, Mrs. Jessup stuck out her tongue at the girl. A small boy picked up a rock and pretended he was going to hurl it at Mr. Jessup. Mr. Jessup gave him a stern look. The boy laughed and made an obscene gesture with his finger. Mrs. Jessup giggled.

"Rowdy bunch," said Mr. Jessup, taking Mrs. Jessup's arm.

A few blocks further, they found themselves in front of a small military installation surrounded by a stone wall. Its gate was guarded by a young soldier with long hair hanging out from beneath his helmet. Mr. Jessup looked past the soldier through the open gate. "There are some interesting old buildings in there," he said to Mrs. Jessup. "I wonder if the fellow speaks English."

He went up to the guard. "We are Americans," he said.

The guard nodded solemnly.

"My wife and I would like to take a look at the old buildings in there. Would this be possible?"

"Sorry," said the guard, "it's against the rules."

At that moment, a hatless officer, wearing three stars on his epaulets, strode out of the gate; Mr. Jessup waited until he was out of earshot of the guard and then approached him. "Excuse me, sir," he said respectfully.

The officer stopped.

"We are Americans. We are traveling in your splendid country. I happened to notice the fine old buildings in your presidio. They appear to date from medieval times."

"Yes, yes, very old," said the officer.

"I wondered if it would be possible for my wife and I to take a look at them?"

The officer pulled a billfold out of a pocket and removed a card and handed it to Mr. Jessup. "My card," he said affably. "Just tell the guard at the gate that I said you may go in."

"That's extremely generous of you, sir," Mr. Jessup said.

"My pleasure," said the officer, with a little bow of his head; then he hurried on.

Mr. Jessup looked at the card, then smiled at Mrs. Jessup. "It's usually simply a matter of approaching the right person," he said. He went up to the guard again and presented the card. The guard gave it an indifferent glance and handed it back. "Your General said we might see the old buildings," Mr. Jessup said.

"Sorry," said the guard, "it's against the rules."

Mr. Jessup's voice took on a slight edge of exasperation. "But you saw me, just this moment, talking to him!" he said.

The fellow grinned. "Yes, but you see, it's like this," he said. "The General isn't here now, is he? I'm the boss now."

"It's easy to see how the Germans took over if their Privates make up all the rules," Mr. Jessup said to Mrs. Jessup as they left.

Mrs. Jessup remembered seeing a church when they had entered town. She knew Mr. Jessup liked taking photographs of churches. She led him around another gang of loitering, noisy youths, down a narrow street of small shops and across a plaza. "Voilà!" she said proudly, pointing to a small yellow wooden building with a cross on its top, surrounded by a graveyard.

"It's not a stave church, is it?" Mrs. Jessup said, a bit apologetically.

"We've seen our stave churches," said Mr. Jessup. "They resemble Siamese temples. Siam. Thailand, now. Remember?"

"Oh, yes," said Mrs. Jessup.

"Still—it has a nice simplicity." Mr. Jessup walked up the steps and tried the door. It was locked. He backed up a few steps, unzipped his camera bag, and began to tinker with his equipment, measuring the light with a meter, adjusting the lens. "You stand on the porch," he said.

Mrs. Jessup knew how long it took Mr. Jessup to set things up properly when he took a picture; he took great pride in his photography. She would try to look bright and alert, but her mind would often wander. Standing on the steps of Nôtre Dame, she had seen a dog trot by and was reminded of a dog she had loved as a child; in front of the Taj Mahal, the warm, muggy air had taken her back to a summer evening and a boy. She had laughed out loud, remembering. Mr. Jessup had caught her laugh in the picture. After their trip, when they had presented their usual slide show for their friends, there she was—laughing—and everyone had remarked how much Mrs. Jessup seemed to be enjoying her exotic adventure.

"I haven't had my hair done for days," she told Mr. Jessup now. "You take the picture, and I'll go for a walk in the graveyard."

Mrs. Jessup walked around the church on a path that led through the graves. An old woman was bent over one of them, busily pulling out weeds from around a flat stone marker. Mrs. Jessup stood quietly in back of her and tried to make out the words carved on the stone. They were in Norwegian, but she could read the name and date.

OLAF OLAFSON

1923-1940

Olaf Olafson had been seventeen when he died, Mrs. Jessup thought. Danny Plummer—that had been the name of her old boyfriend—had been twenty when he was killed on Guadalcanal.

The woman looked up at Mrs. Jessup. Mrs. Jessup smiled at her shyly. "Your son?" she said, rocking an imaginary baby in her arms.

The old woman nodded. She picked up her black pocket-book, which was on the ground beside her, and stood up. She opened the bag and took out a photograph and showed it to Mrs. Jessup.

"He was very handsome," said Mrs. Jessup, hoping that by her tone and expression the old woman would understand.

The old woman put her pocketbook back upon the ground. She stood up. Her body stiffened in a mock military posture and she extended one arm in a Nazi salute. Then she dropped her arm, put both hands around her thin neck and twisted them; her face grew contorted, her tongue hung out.

Mrs. Jessup gasped. Olaf Olafson had been hanged, she thought. Danny Plummer's body had been shattered by a mortar shell.

Mrs. Jessup took the old woman's hand and shook it. She walked slowly back around the church, wiping tears from her eyes.

Mr. Jessup was still tinkering with the camera. "I've been waiting for you," he said jovially. "I need some human interest."

Mrs. Jessup took out her comb and combed her hair and posed for him on the church steps.

"You look like you just lost your last friend," said Mr. Jessup. "Let's have a little smile. Come on, now. Say cheese."

Mrs. Jessup said "cheese," and Mr. Jessup snapped the shutter.

"That could be a good one," he said, putting his camera equipment away. "The light was perfect."

"The people of Norway are a proud and independent race," Mrs. Jessup said into the machine, while Mr. Jessup took his shower before dinner. She paused. She could not write about Olaf Olafson—not in this kind of letter. It was not what people would expect. Nor did she think Mr. Jessup would approve. She had not, in fact, even told Mr. Jessup

about Olaf. She was not sure why she had not told him. He was a kind and thoughtful man. He would certainly have been sympathetic.

"*Norwegians differ from the English, another proud and independent race, in that they do not spend their time polishing.*" Mrs. Jessup told the machine. "*Despite this, it is a clean country. Handsome statues adorn its plazas. Architecture, of a simple design—*"

She had never told Mr. Jessup about Danny Plummer, either. She had told no one at all. When he died, nobody knew she had lost a lover. She was not the same person who had loved the dead boy, anyhow.

"*Architecture of a simple design—*" she repeated to the machine. She seemed to be bogging down. Perhaps it would help to look at *Facts About Norway* again. This time she talked directly from the book: "*Rich grave finds from the Viking age around* A.D. *1000 show that even at that time Norwegians had a great sense of beauty, color, and form, and liked to surround themselves with beautiful things.*"

Mr. Jessup came out of the shower, wrapped in a towel, all pink and steamy.

"*This afternoon,*" Mrs. Jessup was saying in her own words now, "*we went for a pleasant walk. There is a hint of winter in the air.*"

Mr. Jessup smiled at her approvingly.

Mrs. Jessup showered and put on a simple black dress and the pearls Mr. Jessup had given her for their thirtieth wedding anniversary. Mr. Jessup complimented Mrs. Jessup upon her appearance. They were about to go down for an early dinner when they heard a commotion below their window. Mrs. Jessup looked out. "Something is happening on the wharf," she said. "Another boat has come in."

"I could stand more of a stroll before eating," Mr. Jessup said.

The whole town seemed to be on the wharf; it was like a carnival. They surrounded the boat, which had just arrived; its decks were filled to the gunwales with tiny silver fish.

"It's a herring catch," said Mr. Jessup.

The fishermen were shoveling up the herring and dropping them into crates. The kids had gone wild. They swarmed over the boat, balanced on the gunwales, climbed the rigging, and threw themselves recklessly into the shining, slippery catch. A few older boys, mimicking the men, were trying to help out. No one seemed to mind.

"Someone should stop those kids. These are busy men," said Mr. Jessup.

Mrs. Jessup did not answer. She was looking on in amazement. As she looked, the same little girl she had seen in the park poked her head out of the herring; her tousled hair glistened with fish scales. She saw Mrs. Jessup and stuck out her tongue again, with a grin. Mrs. Jessup stuck out her tongue in reply.

The Northern waters being so frigid, the local custom here is to swim in herring, Mrs. Jessup said to herself, as if she were talking to the machine. I felt a bit timid at first, but soon I, too, slipped off my shoes and stockings and joined the natives. The sensation is unique, one might go as far as to say "indescribable." I have experienced nothing like it in all my travels throughout the world.

Maybe I'm going cuckoo, she thought, as Mr. Jessup led her back down the wharf through the noisy crowd.

It was now very cold. Mrs. Jessup shivered and put up the collar of her coat.

"Chilly?" said Mr. Jessup with concern.

"A bit," Mrs. Jessup said.

They were passing a pub next to the inn. It was crowded with people from the wharf and soldiers from the army post. Loud voices and the clinking of beer mugs came from the open door.

"A drink would warm you up," said Mr. Jessup.

They entered the pub. The tables were all filled. Two

young men, noticing their predicament, beckoned the Jessups to join them.

"Thank you very much, gentlemen," said Mr. Jessup in a hearty voice as the Jessups sat down between them.

The young men spoke English; they were from Bergen; they were in the army reserve, spending two weeks here on compulsory military duty. "We are here to save our country," one of them said. They both laughed; they seemed to be a little drunk. The General the Jessups had met that morning was at a nearby table; he greeted them with a loud, "Hello, my friends!"

Everyone seemed to be enjoying himself immensely.

The second young man—an exceptionally handsome young man, thought Mrs. Jessup—spoke to them. "You are Americans?" he said.

"Tourists," Mrs. Jessup was about to say; then she remembered that Mr. Jessup did not care for that word.

"We are Americans here to see your country," Mr. Jessup said. He signaled to a waiter. "May I offer you gentlemen two more beers?" he said.

"Thank you," said the first young man.

Mr. Jessup ordered a glass of sherry for Mrs. Jessup, and three beers.

"And what do you think of our country?" the second young man said to Mrs. Jessup.

"We think it's very beautiful. We like it very much." She looked at Mr. Jessup for confirmation, but he was busy paying the waiter for the drinks.

"Yes, we Norwegians are very fortunate," the second young man said. "I went to school in your country, by the way. I went to the University of California. Every weekend, I drove up to your Sierra to ski."

"Did you ever consider staying there?" said Mrs. Jessup.

The young man laughed, as if at some secret joke. He said, "I'm a Norwegian. Perhaps if I were a Dane or a Swede I might have considered the—ah—business possibilities. But I'm a Norwegian, you see."

"It must be like belonging to a private club," Mrs. Jessup

said. She felt oddly envious, as if she were standing by a window looking in at a nice party to which she had not been invited.

"Yes, yes, that's an excellent analysis," the young man said to her. His eyes, she noticed, were incredibly blue and fringed with long curly pale lashes.

"If it's so satisfactory being a Norwegian," said Mr. Jessup, "—I'm only asking out of an intellectual curiosity, you understand—how do you explain your high suicide rate?"

The young man smiled. He had a charming dimple on his left cheek; Mrs. Jessup almost had to keep herself from reaching out to touch it. The sherry, she thought, must have gone to my head.

"Perhaps you are confusing us with the Swedes," the young man was saying to Mr. Jessup. "Still, we Norwegians commit suicide now and then." He tipped his chair back, took a swallow of beer, then put the mug down. He leaned toward Mr. Jessup. "You know what they say of us Norwegians? They say, 'You only get to know a Norwegian—up to a point.'"

Mrs. Jessup wanted to ask, "At what point *don't* we get to know you?" but she was afraid that this might sound forward.

"In other words, you can't explain it," said Mr. Jessup, genially.

"Everything cannot be explained," the young man said. "Some say it's lack of sun. Others say we live, then we die, on our own, so to speak, when it suits *us*."

"I hope it suits *you* to live!" Mrs. Jessup said, with sudden feeling.

This time the young man smiled at her—a sweet, strangely compassionate smile.

Norwegian men have incredibly blue eyes and sweet smiles, Mrs. Jessup said to herself, as if she were dictating again. They are also extremely compassionate and understand the secret heart of woman. How do I know this? Shall we just call it my little indiscretion?

Oh, dear, I really must be tipsy, she thought. She put her glass down, hurriedly.

"Ready?" said Mr. Jessup to her.

Mrs. Jessup stood up.

"It was most kind of you to ask us to join you, gentlemen," said Mr. Jessup, shaking hands with both young men.

As they left, the General rose and gave them a salute. Mr. Jessup nodded briskly at him, then guided Mrs. Jessup in a different direction toward the door.

"*Norwegians*," Mrs. Jessup said to the machine that evening after dinner, "*are very proud of their nation.*"

Mr. Jessup was already in bed, reading, but Mrs. Jessup had not yet undressed. Her memory was not as good as it used to be, and she wanted to get her impressions down before she lost them.

"There's something all over your shoes," Mr. Jessup said.

Mrs. Jessup glanced down. Her black suede traveling shoes glittered with shining dots, like sequins. She stared at them for a moment. "I think it's the herring from the wharf," she said.

"Better get them off now," Mr. Jessup said.

She got up from her chair and went to the armoire and took out her suede brush. She slipped off her shoes and brushed them carefully. The silver scales flew off and disappeared into the rug. Again, Mrs. Jessup felt the same peculiar sadness she had felt in the pub. She returned quickly to her job.

"*It could perhaps be compared to belonging to an exclusive club*," she continued. She paused, considered for a moment, then went on. "*There is an old saying: 'You only get to know a Norwegian up to a point,'*" This last sentence bothered her. She decided to play it back for Mr. Jessup.

"Sounds fine to me," Mr. Jessup said.

"But you could say it about anyone, couldn't you? Not just about Norwegians?" Mrs. Jessup said.

"I would say it applies to Norwegians very well," said Mr. Jessup. "No one would say it about you, for example, would he?"

Mrs. Jessup thought for a moment. Then she decided that Mr. Jessup was, as usual, right.

Love Letters

My sister, Jean, has sent a fifteenth birthday card to my daughter, Rebecca. On it, she writes, "It seems I have among my effects your mother's love letters. Am sending them on."

"I can hardly wait," says Rebecca.

"What makes you think you are going to read *my* love letters?"

"They'll be rated Family Entertainment. Hot Stuff."

"You're quite right not to get your expectations up. The fact is—I can't imagine what they are. I was never much of a letter writer, and your father and I met in graduate school, so we never corresponded."

"Maybe you had a flaming passion for some pimply kid in the fifth grade."

"Maybe."

My husband—I shall call him "Richard"—is a well-known Social Scientist with a well-known Foundation on the San Francisco Peninsula. He is an authority on Urban-Suburban Problems and, particularly, the modern "nuclear" family. He has written many books and papers, including a

Best-Seller, which, for a time, was a topic of much discussion among bright young people who are now middle-aged. It dissected and analyzed the sort of existence we lead here in Vista Verde, a subdivision of homes on wooded three-acre lots. For this reason, I know what is wrong. The big thing that is wrong, of course, is that there is no Focus, no Foundation. All the old mainstays—to which we once turned for guidance and comfort—no longer work. Church. Patriotism. The Family. The Boy Scouts. Pride in Craftsmanship. Excellence in Plumbing and Termite Inspection, et cetera. I am not, I hope, diminishing my husband's accomplishments by pointing out that others have foreseen the Apocalypse. "Things fall apart; the center cannot hold." W. B. Yeats. To mention one. The question is, what to do about it? Poets are no more helpful here than Social Scientists.

When Richard hears about my love letters he asks me if I know that, according to a recent study, 65 percent of married women who had premarital affairs with not more than two other partners other than their husbands had happier marriages than those who had more than two premarital affairs or those who had no premarital affairs.

I asked him how you measured happiness?

"You set up certain criteria and select a control group. There was a similar study done with rats—"

"Do rats get married?" I say.

"You're not being serious," he says sorrowfully. He is a nice man and enjoys sharing his ideas with me. I cannot tell him how deadly serious I am.

"Anyhow, my only premarital affair was with you," I say. "What does that make me?"

"We're not talking about you," he says. "As far as I'm concerned, everything to do with you is dandy. But we're talking about the Norm."

"I don't care about the Norm," I say. "I just care about me."

My two sons, Adam and Andrew, are tall and blond. This year they look like sheriffs. They have drooping mustaches, wear cowboy hats, heavy metal belt buckles, and boots that scar our hardwood floors when they visit. They walk with a lazy grace, talk without moving their lips, and have quaint, courtly manners. They are both utterly lovely. Yet, as they grow older and nicer, they become less real. Did I give birth to them, or are they some kind of changelings? I know, now, all the mistakes I made bringing them up, but they aren't on hard drugs, have spent no time in jail, and people tell me I am lucky because we "communicate." Is this fair of them to have remained untouched, pure in heart, despite my blunders? Perhaps, casting no shadow, I am the one who is unreal. When we "communicate" they seem to be gazing through me as if I am transparent. I feel spurned, rejected.

When they hear about my love letters, their lips twitch in an almost-grin. How can a phantom have had love letters? Still, their reaction is suitable to the occasion and makes me feel comfortable. It is Rebecca who makes me uneasy; scornful as she is about the contents of the letters, I suspect she harbors some vestige of hope, and that, as usual, I shall disappoint her.

Rebecca has had all the advantages of a third child, of my experience as a mother. But, again—I feel the lack of any influence; she isn't nice at all. She uses a platinum rinse on her hair and frizzles it with an electric curling iron. It smells of chemicals and singe. Her lips are scarlet; there are tubercular-looking patches of rouge on each powdered cheek. Sickly colored "frocks" from an antique-dress boutique have replaced her jeans. She has scarcely been out of doors all summer. She sits on the living-room couch, the curtains drawn, plucking her eyebrows to a fine line, watching TV or listening to bad reissues of songs from the Roaring Twenties, the Nostalgic Thirties, the Swinging Forties. She is waiting for something to happen. So far, nothing has. There is the implication that I am to blame.

Life is not wholly dull; there are constant surprises. Last year, our best friends, Libby and Jack Coleman, were divorced. We had considered them the most devoted couple we knew. We don't see the Thompsons anymore, or is it that the Thompsons don't see us? This needs to be analyzed, explained. When Rebecca grows up (perhaps I should say "comes of age"), should we move to the Country or the City, or is it too late for a change?

"Remember this song?" says Rebecca.
    "I've heard it, I guess."
    "Did you shimmy to it?"
    "I didn't shimmy."
    "You were a Vamp, weren't you?"
    "That was before my time."
    I have taken up French and Yoga to escape her. Proper breathing, my Yoga teacher says, is the Answer to Everything.

Our street, La Floresta, has changed since we moved here twenty years ago. It is filled with strange little kids. When I drive down the block I toot my horn; they jeer and don't move. There is a fat boy who throws pebbles at my windshield.

"Remember this one?" says Rebecca.
    "Sort of."
    "You were a Flapper. Right?"
    "You seem to have a feeling for history, but you lack the facts."
    "Well, you had to be *something!*"
    "It was wartime," I say. "Most of the boys were gone. I was just a healthy American girl. I helped my mother and kept my room clean and studied hard and excelled in outdoor sports." My voice is priggish, to cover up my deficiencies. Still, I cling to some integrity. I refuse to provide her with a labeled and packaged Past, complete with period costumes, period slang, the names of "classic cars," scraps of old songs to which I fell passionately in love. Maybe some people had a Past like that, but it does not represent mine.

My past seems as unreal to me as the present has begun to feel. I am not going to pass out bonbons. I am uncompromising.

"You were a Wimp. I thought so," says Rebecca.

Our friends, the Abbotts, have bought a twenty-five-year supply of dried food in case of disaster. A millionaire acquaintance of theirs is putting all his money into Swiss banks. The chic young couple across the street are getting rid of their possessions. They have put their stuffed eagle, their collection of old cigar labels, and an Art Deco statuette of a nude girl into the pickup bin in front of their driveway. The fat boy has run off with the eagle.

"Have you ever considered cosmetic surgery?" asks Rebecca.

" I intend to age gracefully," I tell her.

"You could just have your eyes done. And those little lines above your mouth. Nothing ages a woman so much as those mouth lines."

"Americans," I say (quoting Richard), "put too much emphasis on youth."

"Well, you're not an Italian or an Arab," she says.

I look into the mirror. It is true that the Warp of Gravity has had its effect. I decide to buy a pair of those new tinted glasses and some scarves to hide my neck. I shall age—ungracefully.

Adam and Andrew drop in. They cannot bear to look at their sister. Their pure sheriff hearts are dismayed by her. I want to apologize for the aberration on the couch, which I am harboring, but it would only embarrass them. They have come to tell me they are moving to Oregon, before the Oregonians seal off the borders. They will live in a commune modeled after the Early Christian communities and support themselves by organic farming. They hope, they say, with a compassionate look at me, to avoid the Rat Race.

"Do you need money?" I ask them.

They look shocked, but accept a hundred dollars as a donation to the farm.

Richard is in Chicago, at the Airport Hilton. He is attending a conference on Urban Life. I would go with him were it not for Rebecca. She is too old for a sitter, but how can I leave our home in charge of her? Cigarette ash might smolder under the sofa cushions, burst into flame in the night. The house plants would wither; the dog, starve. Burglars could ransack the premises, and she would not notice.

The paper Richard will deliver at the Conference is called "Urbanity as Differentiated from Modern Urban Living." One of the things that he points out in this paper is the lack of street life in Suburbia; there are few places where all types of people, of all ages, can meet on a casual friendly basis, such as, for example, a neighborhood Pub. All the entertainment on the Peninsula is done in homes in a grand archaic manner as if "there were still a servant class." Gourmet cooking is much admired. If someone did want to open a neighborhood Pub in Vista Verde, the Vista Verde Neighborhood Association would fight the application; it would not be considered a good influence for young people and would attract doubtful elements. Would Richard and I fight the Association on this issue? Who knows, we may still decide to move, and there is no question—given the present climate of opinion—that a Pub would lower property values.

Rebecca has changed her name to Maxine.

"Could it be that you are having an Identification Problem?" I ask her. It would not do to reveal the fact that I am suffering from the same malaise. Perhaps daughters inherit this disease from mothers.

Richard is still gone, and I miss him. I mix myself a martini before dinner. (Rebecca-Maxine does not eat meals; she nibbles like a rabbit all day long. The sight of a full plate fills her with revulsion.)

It is dusk. The view from our picture window is of the hills. One would never guess, from the careful way we oriented our house, that there are other homes around.

> Older, single women, or widowed, [wrote Richard in his Best-Seller] are often ostracized from mixed, middle-class society. This problem was handled in various ways at various times in different cultures. At one time, in Europe, single, gentlewomen were sent into convents, not to take religious orders, but to assure them of protection. In India, a woman of a certain caste was expected to throw herself on her husband's funeral pyre. . . .

I think of calling up Libby Coleman, but it is too late. She has a drinking problem and turns mean after five o'clock.

"Why do you wear dark glasses indoors?" says the woman who sits next to me in my Yoga class.

"They're not dark glasses. They are specially tinted," I say.

"Didja ever see *The Great Gatsby*?" says Rebecca-Maxine.

"I read the book."

"It was a book?"

"A very good one."

"Didja carry a flask in Prohibition times?"

"I was too young to drink then."

Rebecca-Maxine looks at me with disgust.

A letter from Richard. He has heard an interesting paper on the Marital Problems of ex-priests and nuns. A Woman's Liberation group is picketing their conference, demanding more women in the Social Sciences. A colleague of his was hit by a tomato. Police were called. He is sympathetic to the women's causes; something, of course, needs to be done. But

he was also, he has to admit, a bit frightened by their faces.
"Their faces," he writes, "looked like the Furies, contorted
with rage and a lust for revenge." He hopes all is well at
home.

I am doing poorly in French Conversation. I am unable to
make the right sounds. "Stick out your lips until they touch
mine," says Madame Cozier. I assume this is just a figure of
speech. Just the same, I become stiff, numb, paralyzed by
the inhibitions of my linguistic background. Americans do
not do things like that with their lips. Madame Cozier is impatient with me. She is at least ten years older than I; her
vitality and confidence oppresses me.

I return from Yoga. Rebecca-Maxine is, as usual, on the living-room couch. But, instead of lying down, chewing on the
yellowed-ivory cigarette holder she picked up at St. Vincent
de Paul's, she is sitting up! The curtains are open; the living
room has less of the hothouse atmosphere surrounding a
kept woman waiting for her lover. I detect a sparkle in her
eyes, a new vibrancy in her voice.

"Your love letters have come!"

No use asking her if she has opened them; letters and envelopes are scattered about on the cushions; the manila
envelope in which they arrived is on the floor.

"You could have told me," she says accusingly.

"Told you—what?"

"Well, about—everything." She is looking at me with a
new look—one of grudging admiration. "I thought you were
just a Wimp," she says.

"Wasn't I?" I try to sound indifferent to hide my curiosity.

"You never said you were a Glamour Girl. Sweetheart of
the Ninety-first Division. Miss Pinup of 1943."

"Rebecca—what on earth? Maybe Jean made a mistake.
Are you sure they're *my* letters?"

"Lissen to this—It's from—wait a sec—Private First
Class John 'Skipper' Schneider, Army Air Force Flexible

Gunnery School, Las Vegas Army Air Field. Who was he?"
I try to remember. "Rebecca, there was an army camp
near my college. Whole divisions were trained there. Men
came and went—"
"You're telling me!"

> Sweetheart of the 91st Division, Miss Emily Abott
> My dear Miss Abott:
> Was it real? Time: A summer's Saturday night.
> Scene: The USO. Song: *As Time Goes By*. Charac-
> ters: A brand new Private; gauche; awkward;
> speechless. The Prettiest Girl in the World. An
> Honest-to-God Glamour Girl. [I shudder.] Mood:
> Sexy. Seriously, Emily dear, when I think of you, it
> makes this ol' War almost seem worthwhile. . . .

"What does 'Flexible Gunnery' mean?" says Rebecca.
"I don't know. Something awful." I think of Adam, of Andrew. Pvt. John "Skipper" Schneider was probably Andrew's age.

> In the meantime, *Please* write. A letter from you
> would mean more than I can tell you.

"Did you write?" says Rebecca-Maxine.
"I'm sure I must have. It was our patriotic duty."
"Was he cute?"
"I . . . of course."
"I guess he'd have to be, you were so popular. There are
lots more."

> Ensign R. E. Lidwick, USNR
> USS *Todd*. AKA 71
> c/o FPO
> San Francisco

"Oh, Ricky Lidwick. He went to high school with me. He
married . . . let's see . . . Esther Smith."

"Must have been on the rebound, judging from this:

> Emily, will you reserve what time you can spare in the Christmas holidays for a love-sick sailor, who . . .

"It's all cut out, here," says Rebecca-Maxine.
"Censored, probably. He was going to tell the position of his ship or their destination."
Rebecca looks puzzled. Then, "Oh, yes, like on TV," she says.

> Captain F. R. Browne
> MP School, IRTC
> Camp Robinson, Ark.

> Emily Dearest—
> My leave seems more like a dream than reality. Well, it was certainly worth the trip across the continent to see a certain girl (initials E. A.). I know your picture is hanging over bunks in both Theaters of War, but do you think you could manage to send me one, too? Make a real effort, huh? Until my next leave, if there is one—I think of you constantly.
> > All my love,
> > Frank

"Here's 'Skipper' Schneider, again," says Rebecca-Maxine. "This one's kind of a joke, I guess."

> War Department Directive 3 67/8 L.
> Army Air Force Flexible Gunnery School
> Las Vegas Army Air Field

> To Miss Emily Abott;
> Subject: Wanted, a date during furlough over Christmas holiday by Army Gunner 319134006.

My Dear Miss Abott:
The War Department requests that you contribute
your part to victory by making one of the Army's
new aerial gunners happy over the holidays by going out with him for several dates while he is home
on furlough—Hoping you will comply with our direct order,

we remain

G 2 Staff
Skipper Schneider
by Private Schneider

The afternoon wears on. I should be starting dinner. Instead, I sit, transfixed—and listen.

First Lt. Jimmy Olson, on maneuvers with the 11th Ar-
mored Division, would prefer to be looking into a fine Pi Phi
fire with me—to the music of Jan Garber, Alvino Ray, the
King Sisters. (The Pi Phis, he adds, could use a few new
records. A little Benny Goodman, or some Artie Shaw.)
Anyhow, it was great seeing me, especially since there will
undoubtedly be a *slight interlude* before he gets up to the
University again. His morale is low, so—let the Infantry-
man hear about the good old life—and especially Miss
Emily Abott.

Midshipman Carl "Buddy" Grant can't decide what to do
when he gets out of the Navy. Should he run a hand laundry? Be a scrubwoman? Clean toilets? He signs off "Love
and all those Indoor Sports."

Ensign Harry Long, of Yale University, is still at Staten Island on a "cruise." On his one liberty he went to Brooklyn
and watched the Dodgers play the Cardinals. He doesn't
know if this has any interest for a pretty Pi Phi, he doesn't
want to bore her, so he'll stop. But I did say I would write
and I had promised to send a picture . . .

Rebecca-Maxine shuffles through the letters. "No, that's not the one," she says. "I wanted Private Schneider again." "Oh, yes, how is Private Schneider?" I say. "Well, not so hot. Here it is."

> We are doing the following things—firing rifles, jumping with life jackets, rowing whaleboats, going through gas chambers, studying torpedoes, mine cutters, types of ships, etc. You'd think we were in the Navy or something. Oh, and we had a little lecture on sharks. That was enchanting. Soon—the Big Pond. Still waiting for a letter and that photograph. I think of you constantly.

He says, "Love." Then, there's an arrow, pointing to *Love* and a balloon, like in the Funny Papers, and inside the balloon it says, "Convention." Then, there's another arrow, and another balloon, and inside that balloon, it says, "I hope *you're* conventional—a little."
"What does the 'Big Pond' mean?"
"I suppose he was shipping out soon."
"Yeah, he was. Here's a telegram from him."

> NO WORD FROM YOU BUT SHIPPING
> TOMORROW LOTS OF LUCK SKIPPER.

"Were you all broken up when he was killed?"
"Killed!"
"Lissen—"

> If anything happened to him, he wanted me to send you this ID bracelet. He thought you might like it as a memento from someone whose memory he carried into battle. Sorry to be the one who breaks the news, but the official word, of course, goes to his family. He spoke of you often, and died bravely in the service of his country.

Rebecca-Maxine sighs. It is a wistful, dreamy sigh. She is filled with respect, with awe—for me! I am no longer a Wimp. I have lived! Dimly, ever so dimly, I recall that someone whom I dated—once? twice?—died in the War. Yes, I think I recall something like that.

"He carried your memory . . . into battle," she says.

"It didn't mean a thing," I say.

Rebecca-Maxine doesn't listen.

How can I explain. I go over the words in my mind . . . I was not a Glamour Girl. I was not Miss Pinup. I was not the Sweetheart of the Ninety-first. It was all in their heads. Private Schneider was just a lonely kid, facing death. I was . . . Miss Fantasy. A phantom of his imagination. Just a Phantom!

"If it didn't mean a thing, why are you crying?" says Rebecca-Maxine. She answers the question for me. "Probably you blotted out the memory on account of it was basically too painful, right?"

Am I crying? If I am, it's certainly for the wrong reason. Oh, weep for Private Schneider, he is dead. Was he blond? Brunette? Tall? Short? Did he have a sense of humor? Was he a good dancer? A clumsy one? If I'm crying, it's because I *don't* remember him. Aerial Gunner "Skipper" Schneider. Transparent. Casting no shadow. A Phantom, like myself.

I brush my hand across my eyes. My hand is wet. Real tears! Do phantoms weep? This is a puzzling question, worthy of investigation. Something is out of key. An illogical *something*.

"I've decided to change my name to 'Emily' says Rebecca-Maxine. "It sounds neat in the letters."

"You can't do that!" My voice is fierce, almost savage. It startles me as much as it does her.

"Why not?"

"Because it's *my* name, not yours! What's more, they're *my* love letters, too! Listen," I say to her, "you listen to me. Wipe off that corpselike makeup and get up off that couch and go get your own love letters," I say.

The Flood

It had been raining for a week. The rain melted the snowpacks in the mountains, turning the streams into torrents; logging roads were flooded, upland farms inundated; Highway 99 across the Siskiyous was closed by slides. In town, the creek had overflowed, and the merchants on Creek Street put up sandbags. The wind blew in great gusts; the *Norton News Sentinel* said the river, ten miles out of town, was rising a foot an hour.

John Brigham decided he ought to call Hilda Butterwick before the lines went out.

"Look here, Hilda," he would say, firmly, "you better get into town. I'll reserve a room for you at the Hotel, and I'll come out and get you."

That was it. Just a brisk statement, no more. Nothing about The Manse; though a new letter from one of Hilda's daughters, who lived in California, lay upon his desk: "Surely you can persuade her. . . . She would be so much more comfortable and, if anything happened, we could feel assured she'd get the proper care."

John had to chuckle when he read the letter. He felt the

same way Hilda did about The Manse: going there would destroy your integrity as a citizen and human being. He belonged to this town; he had grown up here and practiced law for forty-three years. The Manse was a recent modern monstrosity built upon the hill, just outside of town; it was a colony unto itself; it was even run by a bunch of outsiders—professional Presbyterian social workers. Not that he criticized the project; they provided a useful service, and he even often advised his elderly clients to go there.

"But what about you, John?" Mildred Stone, a recently widowed lady asked him. "You're my age."

"Oh, I've got nothing against The Manse," John said. "It's a fine place, for most folks, but I'm not sure I'd fit in. I might want to pinch one of those pretty nurses they have, and get in trouble."

Milly had pretended to look shocked; then she giggled at his wickedness. They had known each other ever since Emerson Grade School days; he felt certain Milly would feel at home up there.

But Hilda Butterwick! If The Manse were his client, he'd have to advise them not to take her; all she would do would be to stir up trouble; that was her hobby nowadays.

Besides, he was the last person to advise her about anything. He had considered writing back to her daughter and saying, "Appeal to Newman Hunter, not me. I am no longer in her favor." But, of course, you couldn't say a thing like that to children.

Hazel left at five-thirty. At six, John kicked out Olly Ferguson, who made John's office a home away from home. He didn't want anyone to hear, not even Olly, who didn't have all his marbles anymore, for he had publicly vowed never to speak to Hilda Butterwick again.

He put the call through. The Shady Cove operator answered.

"This is John Brigham," he said. "How are all of you doing out there?"

"Well, the lines are still up," she said. "But Benny's Cocktail Lounge had to close last night. It was too wet in there even for the soaks."

"Give me Hilda Butterwick."

"I thought you were never going to speak to her again."

"It's strictly a business matter," said John.

"Half the time she won't talk unless I tell her it's Newman Hunter, and sometimes she won't even talk to him!"

"We'll give it a try," John said.

The rural line buzzed; after a moment Hilda answered. John could hear the operator tell her Mr. Brigham was on the phone.

There was a long pause, then Hilda spoke. Her ordinarily throaty voice had a peculiar high singsong rhythm. "This is a recorded announcement," she said. "Mrs. Butterwick is entertaining guests. At the sound of the gong you may leave a message." There was another silence. Then the Chinese gong, which Hilda had brought back from Hong Kong on one of her crazy trips around the world, echoed stridently in John's ear.

"Oh, for Christ's sake, Hilda, come off your high horse. I'm just calling to see if you need any assistance."

"Mrs. Butterwick asks for no charity, she is able to take care of herself," she replied in the same recorded announcement voice. Then she hung up.

"I told you so," said the Shady Cove operator gleefully.

When John's rage had subsided a little, he decided he was glad he had called, despite the humiliation. Now, if Hilda drowned, he could say, I tried to rescue the old bag. Yes, I swallowed my pride and called her up and offered my assistance ... But then Hilda wouldn't be around to know he had been right all along; as he'd been right about a lot of othe · things, too. Sadly, he realized that she was the only person he'd really want to tell. Goddamn Hilda Butterwick, he thought. She has destroyed the serenity of my old age.

The next evening there was a heavier storm with sixty-mile-an-hour winds. The electricity and the phone service went out, and everyone sat around in Raymond's Bar, huddled up in coats and mittens and stocking caps; they played gin rummy by candlelight and listened to the reports on a transistor radio about the river. Casper's Bridge, below Shady Cove, was out. Schools all over the area were closed.

Army helicopters were attempting to rescue people stranded in isolated mountain communities. The sheriff's men were evacuating people from Sam's Valley on the Left Fork. People with cabins on the river were beginning to come into town. The Red Cross was setting up emergency shelters in the high school gym in town.

"How is Hilda?" Raymond asked John.

"How the hell should I know," he said. He thought he was catching a chill, and he felt morose. "She's not my client anymore, anyway," he added, so it would be on record. "She's going to Newman Hunter."

Newman Hunter was nine years younger than John. He had an office in the old brick Wells Fargo Building, all gussied up with gold scales and bar chairs and an antique safe and a black tufted leather sofa. He dressed in costume, like a movie gambler from the nineties, a red vest and a watch chain, a Stetson hat and boots. Whenever the *News Sentinel* did a feature on the town, they included a photograph of Newman, entitled "colorful local attorney." Since these activities were not properly lawyerish, the local Bar snubbed him. It was just like Hilda to be attracted to a charlatan like that.

Hilda, in her dotage, had discovered the law courts. She had pestered John, continually, to sue the United States government, the county, the Power and Light Company, even personal friends. She had done this, despite the fact that she knew John detested going to court, which meant putting on his hearing aid. Moreover, his experience in the law had taught him that most court cases were unnecessary. If you waited long enough, people either settled out of court or forgot their grievances. Time itself was on your side. But Newman was an actor and enjoyed making court appearances, no matter how outlandish the cases were.

Now Hilda was giving Newman trouble; he wondered if she had used her recorded announcement voice on him. Yes, let Newman persuade Hilda to leave the Chalet, he decided. He could go out there in his movie outfit clothes and no doubt get a story in the *News Sentinel* about how he had endangered his life for his client.

At ten o'clock, John went home. He couldn't drive down Jackson on account of the creek; he had to take a circuitous route down Elm. It was raining buckets, and the street-lamps were out; still, he could have driven the whole town blindfolded after all these years.

His small ordinarily comfortable bachelor home was freezing, and there was a leak in the kitchen roof. He scrambled around in the dark and found a pot to put under it; then he groped his way into his bedroom, undressed quickly, down to his long underwear, threw some extra blankets on the bed and crawled in.

But it was still cold, his arthritis hurt, he couldn't use his heating pad, and there was no hot water for a hot-water bottle. Moreover, he couldn't get Hilda off his mind. Recorded announcement, indeed. Where had she picked that one up? Probably Newman had some new-fangled device like that in his office along with those phony antiques. He could hear the drip, drip, drip in the pot from the kitchen—a loud, lonely, ominous sound. The Manse, he had been told, had an emergency generator.

Well, if he were cold, Hilda would be colder, despite her Spartan ways. The Chalet was really just a big drafty barn. He had not set foot in it now for two years—not since she had thrown that moth-eaten marmot at him, after he had refused to sue Clayton Poole for the bridgework that troubled her. She had missed, and he had kept his poise. In cruel retaliation, he had told her she was growing senile; she should go to The Manse.

Perhaps he shouldn't have said that; perhaps the rupture had been partly his fault. He had let things get off on an unprofessional footing the year before that, when he had asked her to marry him. It certainly had not been her feminine charms; it had been her cooking, which he had to admit was good, and the attractions, though not the comforts, of the Chalet. Right away he had regretted his hasty words; marriage to Hilda Butterwick would have been like punishing himself for all those years of peaceful bachelor life. But his impulsive proposal, made after too many bourbons, had given her the upper hand. He had noted the gleeful look in her blue eyes when she turned him down. The look had implied that he would ask her again; instead he had felt the relief of a reprieved felon.

She had revenged herself, shamelessly.

"John thinks he'd like to move into the Chalet," she said, in his presence, at one of her parties, to Doc Storey. "But can you imagine him living without central heating?"

At other gatherings, she hinted by her manner at attempted intimacies. And one day in his office, right in front of Hazel, she had asked him how his bladder was working after his prostate trouble.

At the same time he was certain she had not wanted to marry him; since her husband's death she had openly cherished her new independence. She was merely disappointed that John had not given her a second chance to demonstrate this.

The next day, after a sleepless night, John put on his old fishing boots and his plaid mackinaw, which he had not worn for years, and drove into town. He could barely see, and the water was almost up to his hubcaps. Main Street was blocked off now.

At the Police Station, the Chief was out helping with the refugees, but Carl Swenson was at his desk. "Well, I see there's no fool like an old fool," he said cheerfully when he saw John.

"I want you to make a check on Hilda Butterwick," said John.

"They're all being evacuated up at Shady Cove," Carl said. "It's a real mess. We've got two pregnant women and four new babies over at the gym."

"I want you to get in touch with the Sheriff and ask about Hilda. She's lived alone so long, she's kind of squirrelly. She probably doesn't even know how serious it is."

"I'll do that if you promise to go to Raymond's," Carl said. "He has a fire going and enough people there to keep warm. I'll drop by and tell you what we've learned."

"Don't just shout it out loud in front of everyone," John said. "You come in and get me aside. It's a kind of, well, a touchy proposition."

"It shall be handled with the utmost delicacy," Carl promised with a wink. "I'm just as scared of Hilda Butterwick as you are."

When the river began to rise, Hilda put on her tarp and waders, took a small stepladder and wrench, and defying wind and rain, marched down to the boathouse. The ground beneath her feet was slippery, treacherous; the fir trees along the path were bent half over; the willows near the water, more supple, swayed back and forth. The river had widened grossly; it was brown and swollen and racked by waves. The small deck of the boathouse already had a half foot of water washing over it. She could hear the flat-bottomed riverboat inside the shed, knocking and straining against the walls like an imprisoned beast. There would be sanding and varnishing to do when spring came.

She waded through the water on the deck and set up the ladder and took down the buffalo horns, which were fastened to the eaves. After this, she returned to the Chalet, hauled the veranda furniture indoors, and stacked it in the Great Hall.

At seventy-five, she was tall, angular, and still strong. Her maiden name had been Christianson; she was of Viking-pioneer blood. Her blonde hair had turned white; she cut it herself in an old-fashioned, practical Dutch bob. She refused to wear glasses, except for reading; her faded blue eyes were like those pale fish that swam in the dark recesses of underground caverns, keeping their dark prehistoric secrets to themselves. The sun had thickened her skin and coated it with liver spots; of this she was proud. How much better it was than the transparent, fragile flesh of her contemporaries.

In her old age her clothes, like Newman's, had become costumes. In the daytime, around the Chalet, or for trips into Shady Cove, she dressed in an old paint-spattered monkey suit that her husband, Eddie, had used for chores; outdoors she wore a pair of Big Mac men's boots, nicely broken in; indoors, a pair of old Indian moccasins. When she entertained company, she blossomed out in a dirndl skirt from

Greece, a Peruvian llama sweater, a red Spanish shawl over her shoulders, long earrings, and silver bangles on her spotted arms. She dotted her leathery cheeks with rouge and mascaraed her eyes, but she did not believe in lipstick. In both costumes she walked with a forthright stride; one foot after the other, a kind of mad purpose blazing in her eyes.

In her youth, before she married Eddie Butterwick, she had taught school up in Bridgeport; she had walked three miles to and from her parents' home to the small country schoolhouse every day. The first lesson in the morning, following this walk, was always calisthenics; deep breathing and proper elocution she considered important. Her ambition had been to become an actress: for years, after her marriage, and while she brought up her two daughters, she had organized and participated in the Norton Little Theater group. Her brightest role had been Portia; she still knew most of the lines. But marriage had dragged her down; younger people gradually took over the Little Theater and she was relegated to minor roles. After having been assigned the part of a shepherdess in *As You Like It*, she wrote a haughty note and resigned.

Eddie had never made much money; he was in insurance, but he had an uncle who had made a fortune in lumber. Just in time to fill the void left by the Little Theater, this uncle died, leaving his money to Eddie and the Chalet to Hilda. He had never liked Hilda, but, as he approached death, he realized that she, alone, would do honor to his house in the woods. His will read, "She will appreciate its character."

Hilda did. The Chalet was modeled on a German hunting lodge; it was adorned with mounted animal heads—moose, elk, buffalo, deer—and the brittle, varnished corpses of steelhead and salmon. Stuffed small animals and birds perched on bookshelves and end tables. An oil painting of a Modoc Indian chieftain in full war regalia hung over the great stone fireplace. The Chalet's drafty, raftered rooms, furnished with Navajo rugs and Indian trinkets, seemed made for a primeval warrior-king. Its site, over the wildest riffle on the Rogue, was spendidly savage.

Hilda made Eddie move into the Chalet, though his insurance business was in Norton, twenty-five miles away. Moreover, she refused to permit him to wire it for electricity; at night, she lit the kerosene lamps herself; stalking from room to room, her shadow against the wall was like a giant priestess performing a magical rite.

For the first time in her life she felt her environment suited her; she was mistress of an establishment, not just a house. Unfortunately, Eddie was not around long enough to enjoy their altered circumstances; he died, leaving Hilda wealthy.

When Hilda was first widowed, her daughters in California suggested she move back into town. By way of an answer, she instituted her famous Chalet Sunday brunches—feasts of kippered salmon, creamed finnan haddie, broiled kidneys, blueberry muffins, and three kinds of homemade jam. John came early and made the gin fizzes. Until this time, she had not believed in strong drink; John weaned her on the gin fizzes, and she went on to become a connoisseur of bourbon, buying Jack Daniel's in cases, which she stored in the attic.

One never knew who might turn up at her brunches. She asked whoever caught her fancy, without regard to their social position or how they would mix with the other guests. The David Hinkses (Hinks Department Store) and the Carter Smiths (Rogue Orchards) and Dr. and Mrs. Storey mingled with Bill Blair, who ran the Shady Cove Gas Station and did odd chores for her on the side, and Muriel Burke, the waitress from Benny's Cocktail Lounge and Riverside Café.

The guests were allowed to fish or merely sunbathe on her deck. But they had to respect the spirit of her gatherings. They had to love the river and appreciate the Chalet. Moreover, the conversations had to be on a high plane, involving either local natural history, of which she was an authority, or reminiscences of her past successes as an actress.

The conversation, however, did not preclude gossip, which she drank in greedily, as if she had been deprived of it at some important stage in her development. This was true; she had always scorned the personal and the trivial. Now, suddenly discovering it, as she had booze, she began to manipulate people in order to create situations. Capriciously, she would drop an acquaintance and add another; her sense of drama gave the brunches a further dimension; people came as they would come to the theater, to be surprised.

But she was not made to enjoy her triumphs; a kind of reaction set up inside of her; she began to sense slights; suspect treacheries. When her guests left, she would stalk the veranda complaining to a contented, well-fed John of their stupidity, their shallow natures. Why did she bother? Why did she slave? They came only to feed their faces; there was nothing inside their brains. Since John came, too, partly for this reason, he remained tactfully silent. But perhaps she suspected treachery here too, for, at this time, she began her jaunts around the world. She traveled alone.

One spring, she visited Europe; another the Far East. She went to Mexico for Christmas and to Lapland in summer. When she returned, she organized slide lectures to which her guests were subjected; the curios she had collected were displayed, for the occasion, on the rustic plank table in the dining room, like wedding gifts. There were amber worry beads from Greece, a pre-Columbian vase from Mexico, an armless, beady-eyed putto from Venice, the gong from Hong Kong.

"There I am on the second camel," she would say. "That is my guide, Domingo, sitting in the boat. I am standing beside the bell tower. If you look closely you will see me next to the Corinthian column. That is our tent—the lioness came within three feet."

She had not traveled now for two years. "It is difficult to get away when you are engaged in litigation," she told people. Litigation was her new hobby. John had dampened her spirit in this pursuit, and she had flung the marmot at him, but with Newman Hunter she blossomed like a young girl. Termite inspectors, repairmen, a distant neighbor with a barking dog, trespassers who ignored her No Hunting, No

Trespassing sign, were all brought to court. It was said, jok-
ingly, that one should take out special Hilda Butterwick insurance before approaching her.

But this, too, was waning. Judges were growing impatient; even Newman had refused to take her last case
against two teenagers who had dumped some rubbish on
her land. She had suddenly felt very much alone.

Now, after bringing in the buffalo horns from the
boathouse, she sat down in the cane peacock chair; it was
her special chair, like a throne. In the glistening wet tarp
and waders she looked like an ancient queen. She was
thinking. Perhaps she had been hasty throwing the marmot
at John. She had not hit him: her aim was not as good as it
once had been. Still, at her age, one perhaps ought to cher-
ish old friends, despite their weaknesses.

This thought gave rise to a new idea. Why not organize a
group of people to go on hikes? Everyone was too sedentary
these days; they only sat around and drank and ate. I know
the trails for thirty miles around, she said to herself. I will
lead. I will wear a whistle in case anyone gets lost. Also the
sun helmet I bought in Calcutta. I'll call John first. When I
present my idea he'll recognize my physical and mental fit-
ness and eat his words about The Manse.

"If you can't hike because of your prostate, you can sit on
the veranda and watch us off," she would tell him.

She would do setting-up exercises, first, to get into top
condition. She got up with new determination. The rain was
beating in gale sheets against the veranda window. The
river made a loud mooing noise, nor entirely unpleasant.

"No weaklings allowed," she would say to John. "You will
be the one exception."

While she was thinking all this, her phone rang. It was
the Shady Cove operator.

"John Brigham is on the line. He's calling to see if you
need any help, Mrs. Butterwick."

Hilda froze. They had not spoken to one another for a
year, and now he was spoiling all her plans by pretending
that it was she, not he, who could not manage alone.

Once, a few weeks ago, she had called the Rialto Theater in town to ask the management if they would be interested in a matinée lecture of her travels abroad. "Around the World with Hilda Butterwick," it would be called. She had been answered by a recorded announcement. This impersonal form of communication, which had infuriated her then, seemed just the way now to respond to John. She said, "Just a moment, please . . ." and took the gong off the wall and dragged it over to the phone.

"Mrs. Butterwick asks for no charity," she said, and hung up. At that same moment there was a mighty crash. The ponderosa pine, next to the house, had fallen across the veranda, crushing the railing in its descent. It lay, a fallen giant, its branches crumpled, its cones scattered around on the decking like ceremonial offerings. Its bulk barred the door and covered the lower half of the large window. The ponderosa had been a favorite; an eagle had nested in its top branches for three summers; Hilda had watched the fledglings with her binoculars, feeling a possessive pride.

Bill Blair, who had offered to help her around the place, had insisted that the pine was dead. "It's no more dead than you or I," Hilda had said. And when he had kept after her about it, she ordered him off her premises forever.

She picked up a lamp and went into the kitchen and poured herself two shots of Jack Daniel's, then returned to the peacock chair and stared gloomily at the great corpse. The water rose higher around it; the little cones drifted off, deserting their matrix. Soon the warm liquor began to cheer her; she commenced to plan the work to be done after the storm. The veranda decking was no doubt badly injured, too. She rose and threw another log upon the smoking fire, then poured herself another slug. Perhaps she would have a wood-sawing party; it would be good for townspeople to use their muscles; afterward, she would serve a hearty wholesome lunch—lentil soup with sour cream, sardines, stuffed eggs, dark rye bread, and several kinds of cheese.

At five o'clock, John listened to the news on Raymond's radio. Sixty miles of highway, twenty miles of railroad track, and three airports were underwater. Five persons were lost, presumed dead in the mountain areas. Three men had been killed on helicopter rescue missions. At least a hundred houses and cabins and forty business establishments in Southern Oregon and Northern California had been swept away by the mighty torrents. Orchards and farms had been turned into lakes. Free surplus grain was being flown in for cattle; the Army Engineers were coming in to put up emergency bridges as soon as the storm abated. Six Air Force C119 cargo planes, carrying twenty-one thousand pounds of telephone-repair equipment would take off as soon as the weather permitted. Flood damage, so far, was estimated in the millions. It would take a year to dry out the redwood from the flooded drying yards. The Red Cross was appealing for blankets and bedding for the evacuees.

And, then, the local news—John listened eagerly. The water impounded behind Paradise Dam, at the headwaters of the Rogue, was due to spill over the top sometime this evening. Residents of Prospect and Shady Cove had all been advised to leave at once.

At five-thirty, Carl came in and took John aside. "They're sending a deputy over to Hilda's," he said. "If she's still there, they'll get her out." At six-thirty, he ordered a sandwich at the bar; at seven o'clock, a wet and cross Hazel strode into Raymond's and humiliated him in front of Olly by ordering him to go to the Hotel.

"They're taking everyone over sixty-five," she said snappishly.

Then she waited, while he put on his mackinaw and boots and followed her out.

Hilda, warmed by drink, had slept well. When she awoke, the fire was out, but she was able to rekindle it. Then she dragged a stool to the window, and peering over the ponderosa pine, surveyed the scene. The river had risen to the porch; the boathouse was gone. It was as if she were on an island in the midst of a brown, raging sea.

Actually, of course, she was on a peninsula; she knew it was possible to wade out the back door where the ground was higher and where she kept her car. But the sense of being on an island pleased her more. She was like Robinson Crusoe, snug, domestic, caring for her needs with no help from anyone.

In her head, she checked her provisions. She had enough firewood for two weeks; her food supply was ample; she bought toilet paper and kerosene and Jack Daniel's and canned goods in wholesale lots, which she stored in the attic. Except for her yogurt, she was not dependent on the accouterments of civilization, as they were in town. With delight, she thought of John's kitchen, whose cupboards were apt to contain no more than a few cans at a time, whose refrigerator was always half empty. He had not been brought up right; his ancestors were not Viking kings.

Then, to occupy herself, she began to rearrange a drawer of slides in the dining room. She was neatly cataloging them, pasting titles on the boxes. "Hilda Butterwick, Africa, 1964." "Hilda Butterwick, Orient, 1960." As she lifted out the box from Scandinavia, she found an unopened letter from her elder daughter; it had been written a month ago.

"Dear Mother," it began, "if you absolutely refuse to go to that nice retirement home, then couldn't you take a little apartment in town and keep the Chalet for weekend visits?"

There was more, but she didn't bother to read it; she tore the letter up in a rage. An apartment! She would die in an apartment. A tiny box, surrounded by other boxes with people in them like dolls in dollhouses. She wouldn't be able to breathe. As for that nice retirement home—what did her daughter know about it? She could imagine the meals. Overdone roasts, soggy vegetables, store-bought rolls. Grace at meals. Organized recreation. A bus to take them into town. A youthful, middle-aged director. Hobby shops. Crafts. Watercolors. Sunday-night movies. Folk dancing. Sweaty palms!

The Chalet was her home, not for "weekend visits." It was her home, and she would never leave it to either of her daughters. Already she could see the For Sale sign up; the

rush of realtors, curious neighbors, tourists, who didn't belong to the community. No, she would change her will. She
knew John wouldn't do it, and now she doubted Newman.
She would find another attorney, maybe leave it to the
county as a historical monument, filled with her artifacts.
Was the county to be trusted, she wondered? Would they
preserve it according to her wishes? This would have to be
looked into as soon as the storm was over.

As soon as the storm was over, she would begin other
projects, too. Perhaps organize a play-reading society. She
would invite only people with fine voices. Well, she might
invite John, who didn't have a fine voice, which was probably the reason he refused to appear in court for her; she
would invite him out of charity.

They would read the classics. Shakespeare. Molière. Ra-
cine. She would be Portia, once again. The role had suited
her.

> The quality of mercy is not strain'd
> It droppeth as the gen-tul rain from heaven.
> Upon the place beneath: it is twice bless'd;
> It blesseth him that gives and him that takes.

Too bad, she thought, that more people did not take those
immortal words to heart.

There was a knock on her back door; then a male voice
shouted, "Anyone at home?"

Hilda quickly ducked into a nearby closet. It contained
Eddie's uncle's guns. The intruder's heavy boots stalked
through her house; in fury she pictured the mud upon her
plank floors.

"Mrs. Butterwick!" the voice called.

Hilda popped out of the closet, holding a carbine; she had
kept it loaded—one never knew what might happen these
days. She held it firmly, its muzzle pointing at Bill Blair,
Sheriff's deputy. "I'll give you exactly two minutes to get
out," she said.

"Hilda, listen, we're evacuating all the cabins on the

river. The dam's going. Everyone's left but you. You've got to get out fast."

"No one's telling me what to do," she said, and marched toward him, the gun aimed at his middle. "I know the river, I've lived here for twenty years; I'll get out in my own good time if necessary."

"Your car won't start, Hilda, and you couldn't drive it if it did. If you won't come with me now, we'll have to get you out by force."

She laughed, haughtily; then she cocked the gun. Bill shrugged his shoulders and stamped out, slamming the back door behind him.

That afternoon, she sat on the high stool at the window, sipping Jack Daniel's, and watched things come down the river. A door, a shed with a rooster on top, pilings, lumber, a cow, a house trailer. Some she recognized. A piece of Casper Bridge, a roof from the Riverside Café, a small boat called *Honey Bun*, which belonged to the Sparks children, who lived a mile upstream. It was like the end of the world, and she, the sole survivor. She found this thought exhilarating. When she finished the glass, she poured herself another.

The sheriff's men came for her at six o'clock. They tramped through the Chalet, calling her name. But she hid cleverly in the attic closet, holding her breath, not stirring a limb.

When they left, she went back downstairs. The water was seeping into the ground floor. She put on her tarp and waders and took the bottle of Jack Daniel's and went back up to the attic. After a while she could hear the water roaring through the house. Still holding the bottle, she climbed the ladder to the roof. It was dark, and the wind and rain howled around her. She crouched behind the chimney, using the fire ladder on the roof as an anchor, and took another big drag of bourbon. Then the house gave a great shudder and slipped off its foundation into the waters. Hilda rode the roof, like a great bird, as far as Peanut Creek, a mile downstream, when she and the Chalet disappeared into the waves.

John executed Hilda's will; she had never written a new one as Newman's client. But long after the private memorial service, after the daughters had left, furnishings from the Chalet were brought into John's office. The Chinese gong, which had been found in a farmer's field; a bloated elk's head, which had floated into Shady Cove; the warped oil painting of the Indian brave, which some children came upon under a temporary Army bridge.

John wrote the daughters; there was no reply. The objects remained in his office, gathering dust. They worried him. One afternoon he gathered them up and took them home and burned the elk's head and the oil painting in his incinerator. He left the gong, which wouldn't burn, for the junkman. Then he went into his empty house and fixed himself a good strong bourbon. He knew he could not live alone much longer, that he would end up at The Manse. He would play cards and go on field trips and tell dirty jokes to the nurses, while, all the time, he would feel the scornful eye of his old friend upon him. She had triumphed over him irrevocably; there would be no redress.